A Diet of Death

A Clara Fitzgerald Mystery
Book 25

By
Evelyn James

Red Raven Publications
2022

A Diet of Death is the twenty-fifth book in the
Clara Fitzgerald series

Other titles in the Series:
Memories of the Dead
Flight of Fancy
Murder in Mink
Carnival of Criminals
Mistletoe and Murder
The Poisoned Pen
Grave Suspicions of Murder
The Woman Died Thrice
Murder and Mascara
The Green Jade Dragon
The Monster at the Window
Murder on the Mary Jane
The Missing Wife
The Traitor's Bones
The Fossil Murder
Mr Lynch's Prophecy
Death at the Pantomime
The Cowboy's Crime
The Trouble with Tortoises
The Valentine Murder
A Body Out of Time
The Dog Show Affair
The Unlucky Wedding Guest
Worse Things Happen at Sea

Chapter One

There was a horde of ladies stood outside the window of the chemist's shop opposite Oliver Bankes' photography studio. He peered at them curiously through his front window.

Oliver Bankes had inherited his business from his father and filled his time with taking family photographs, providing the Brighton Gazette with pictures and, occasionally, serving as the on-call photographer for the police. It was a diverse range of work that kept him busy and amused.

That morning he was preparing for a photography session with Mrs King and her prize-winning Persian cats. He had not decided whether photographing animals was harder or easier than photographing small, defiant children. At least the cats would be brought in a wicker carrier and returned to it once the session was done. Oliver had had far too many experiences of children running amok in his studio while talking to their parents.

Yes, he definitely preferred animals that could be suitably contained when not actually required for a picture.

He had walked through from his studio to his reception space to fetch more powder for his flash and that was when

1

he had spied the commotion across the street. He was sure the gathering of ladies had not been there earlier. He watched them a moment, wondering what they were intently looking at, then Mrs King appeared at his door.

"Mr Bankes, what a morning!" she declared as she stumbled through the doorway with two mewing wicker carriers, one in either hand. "The bus was crowded, and no one would give me a seat! What is the world coming to!"

She set the cats on the floor and noticed that Oliver was not giving her his full and undivided attention. She gazed in the direction he was looking and noted the scrum of ladies.

"A lot of nonsense, if you ask me," she declared. "Standing out there in the late October chill so they can get hold of this new wonder pill."

"Wonder pill?" Oliver asked.

"I should not have expected you to have heard of it, being as you are a man," Mrs King said, only slightly condescendingly. "Miss Pink of Brighton has issued her own diet pill."

"Miss Pink?" Oliver recognised the name. "The same Miss Pink who won the local beauty pageant and then the regionals and finally went to the finals in London?"

"Yes, the same," Mrs King said with a look of disgust for such antics. "She came second and is basking in the glory of being runner-up. Well, it seems she has cast her spell over enough of the foolish women in this town to warrant her keeping up this charade."

"Charade?" Oliver said absently, recalling he had taken pictures of the pageant for the Gazette. He must have seen Miss Pink at the time, but there had been a lot of pretty young ladies present, to the point it had been rather overwhelming. Oliver had spent most of the day trying to avoid looking where he was not supposed to.

"All this stuff she is promoting about her personal diet regime," Mrs King continued. "Have you not seen the notices in the paper?"

"I do not get much time to read the newspaper," Oliver

said, feeling he needed to apologise for his lack of knowledge.

"Since her triumphant return as runner-up in London, Miss Pink has been using her accolade to develop a successful business in all things beauty related. Specifically helping ladies to lose weight and have a figure like her own. She has written a book, if you can call the flimsy thing a book," Mrs King tutted to herself. "Now she has created these diet pills. They are supposed to help you drop weight safely and efficiently."

Oliver's curiosity was even more tickled by this news. He watched as one-by-one the ladies crowding outside the chemist's shop were allowed to enter and purchase their pills.

"Pink's Pills," Mrs King muttered. "Personally, I have never seen a reason to alter my figure."

Mrs King was the sort of woman who had developed a shape best described as 'egg-like'. She had no waist, and her bust was difficult to determine beneath her thick woollen coat. Her ovoid body was in complete contrast to the skinny physiques of the ladies Oliver recalled from the beauty pageant.

"Are we going to take these pictures or not?" Mrs King demanded. "Fluffy hates being in this basket."

Oliver jumped back to the moment and apologised for his daydreaming. He showed Mrs King to his studio which was well lit by several skylights, enabling him to take most photographs with little extra light and no annoying backlighting. He had placed a comfortable leather armchair before his 'Victorian parlour' backdrop, and it was hoped the cats would willingly perch upon the chair to be photographed.

The next hour was a fraught adventure in fur and claws. Mrs King's cats were irate they had been removed from their comfortable home in wicker carriers and had no intention of sitting nicely for a photograph. They protested the way cats do; slinking off to corners and sulking, sinking vicious claws into the leather chair and making fearsome hissing noises when anyone came near them.

Eventually, after Oliver had contemplated both knocking out the pair with ether, or tying them with string in position, they achieved what he hoped would turn out as a reasonable photograph.

The cats were restored to their baskets and arrangements made for Mrs King to return in a week to see the results.

"I apologise for the chair," Mrs King brushed her fingers over the lacerated leather. "Possibly it can be patched?"

Oliver thought it was thoroughly ruined, but he had learned his lesson about what props to put out for cats. Next, time he would use a wooden chair – or better still, one made of cast iron.

They headed back to his reception where his attention was once more drawn to the chemist's shop. A fine drizzle had started outside, but this had not deterred several determined ladies who were queuing up before the door. Mrs King cocked her head at them.

"Have you ever seen bigger fools," she declared. "God gave us the bodies we were meant to have, be they fat or thin. Why should we go about artificially trying to change them?"

"Yes, quite right," Oliver agreed with her in what he hoped sounded a wholehearted fashion.

"Well, I am off to catch the bus," Mrs King peered at the weather with personal affront. "It better not be late or crowded."

She stalked off and Oliver pitied the poor omnibus driver who would find himself facing Mrs King today. After she was gone, he stared across the road for quite some time, his thoughts far away from photography.

Oliver was contemplating his own waistline, which had expanded over the last couple of years. He ate very randomly because of his work, and often consumed things that were not the healthiest of options. He had noticed a slight portliness appearing and, having always had a trim figure, he was mildly alarmed by the sight. Oliver was not vain, as such, but he did care for his appearance, and he had a terrible vision of himself running to fat.

Now, all it would probably take was a few daily walks and being more considerate of his meals and he would regain his normally slim waist, but Oliver was conscious that life had a tendency to get in the way – especially his life. He seemed to always be rushing about and his plans for living a more orderly existence rarely came to anything. Supposing, he thought to himself, there was an easier way?

After a good deal of indecision, Oliver grabbed his coat and headed across the road to take a look at these Pink's Pills. He did not want to look too obvious, and at first stopped by the window and pretended to have developed a deep interest in a razor set, while actually surreptitiously looking at the large advertising display for the diet pills.

There was a photograph of Miss Pink in the centre of a board that was painted in her namesake colour with roses entwining all around. Oliver grimly noted that the photograph was one of his and he had not been asked for permission to use it in an advertisement. There were line drawings of women interspersed among the roses, all slender and with the current fashionable form – meaning no curves of any description. Then came the wording.

Pink's Pills – Safe, Efficient Weight Loss for the Ideal Figure. Tired of Excessive Curves and pinching an inch? We all know that nature can only be improved upon and with Pink's Pills you will be able to achieve the Perfect body almost overnight! No Strict Regimes! No Restrictions on food! Just the delight of a Slender, Fashionable Figure!

Beneath this information were shelves of the pills in neat brown bottles. Each had a label upon it that read Pink's Pills and a smiling portrait of Miss Pink cheering on the purchaser for making the choice to be thin.

Oliver liked the sound of safe and efficient. He also liked the notion of having to put in very little effort to achieve weight loss, other than to take a pill, that is. He wondered if Pink's Pill were suitable for gentlemen as well as ladies?

By now, the queue had ebbed, a combination of the weather and most of the ladies who desired the pills already having made their acquisitions. They were presumably now at home having taken their first dose and feeling the fat just melt away. Oliver had a vision of a plump lady sitting down on her sofa to relax after taking her pill and rising an hour later with considerably less girth. He was excited by the notion. It promised all he wanted, and clearly the ladies who had been buying the pills had felt the same way.

Oliver entered the shop and waited as innocuously as he could for the other customers to depart before he wandered over to the counter. Mr Dyer, the proprietor, smiled at him warmly.

"Mr Bankes, is it about the constipation pills your father ordered?"

Oliver grimaced, having forgotten he was meant to be collecting those at some point for his father. Mr Bankes senior had become a little reclusive these last few years and relied on Oliver to collect the things he needed.

"No, I mean, I suppose I could take them now," Oliver said, keeping one ear open for the bell above the door to ring and announce someone else had entered. He did not want to be overheard. Fortunately, it was close to dinnertime and Mr Dyer would be closing for his lunchbreak soon, so his shop had become quiet. "Actually, it is about those diet pills…"

Oliver tailed off, feeling awkward. Mr Dyer smiled gently.

"You are wondering if they are suitable for gentlemen as well as ladies?"

"It had crossed my mind," Oliver said sheepishly.

"I can assure you that the principle of the pill will work the same for gentlemen as well as ladies. Weight loss is universal, after all," Mr Dyer produced a bottle of the pills from below his counter. "They have proven extremely popular today. I was not expecting quite such a rush, but then I am the only pharmacist stocking them currently and Miss Pink has been doing a good deal of promotion."

Oliver looked at the bottle, but did not reach for it, still wondering if it was proper for a man to take diet pills.

"I assure you, it is quite common for men to take such things," Mr Dyer said, seeming to read his mind. "And they are quite safe. Miss Pink kindly showed me the recipe so I could confirm I was happy to stock them. None of the ingredients are harmful, but in combination will produce a most miraculous effect."

"I do not want to lose too much," Oliver said hastily. "Just a few pounds."

"You take them until you reach your desired weight and then stop," Mr Dyer explained. "It is all rather simple."

He held out the bottle to Oliver, who took it after another moment or two of thoughtfulness. He unscrewed the lid and saw inside a pile of pills.

"They are actually pink," he observed.

"That is purely for marketing purposes," Mr Dyer assured him. "The colour has no bearing on their results."

Oliver screwed back on the lid and placed the bottle on the counter. He had just noticed the price marked on the bottle in white chalk.

"They are not cheap."

"Quality never is," Mr Dyer said solemnly.

Oliver found his hesitation was becoming overwhelming and he had half a mind to walk away from the pills.

"This is my last bottle," Mr Dyer said with the practiced tactics of a skilled salesman. "Once it is gone, I do not expect another batch for, well, possibly months."

"Months?"

"Yes, the demand has been exceptional, and it was not anticipated we would sell so many."

"The last bottle," Oliver said. "But, in the window…"

"Dummy bottles for display purposes only," Mr Dyer informed him. "We could not allow such valuable items to be left in a window."

Oliver took a step back from the counter. It was a lot of money for a bottle of pills when he could just watch what he ate and exercise more. He was paying for convenience, of course. He was about to walk off when another customer walked in the door and some part of him panicked and imagined this last bottle being sold to this new person and him losing out.

He reached out for the bottle while his other hand dived into his pocket and produced money.

"Thank you," he said hastily to Mr Dyer before leaving abruptly and without his father's constipation pills.

Back in his shop he became indecisive again and placed the bottle away in his desk drawer while he got on with his work. He could not decide if he should take one or not – what if he ended up with a feminine figure?

However, once again the thought of the ease with which the pills could lose him weight and Dyer's promises they were safe began to win him over. He took two pills before dinner. It was recommended on the bottle to take the pills three times a day, before meals. Oliver wondered if this was because the pills somehow prevented the body absorbing fat from food.

He put the pills away and gave them no more thought as he tucked into liver and onions.

Later that night, Oliver started to feel unwell. It was nothing specific at first, but when he developed stomach pains he went to his bed and laid down.

He wondered if it was a sign the pills were working.

By midnight, Oliver Bankes was severely ill.

Chapter Two

Clara Fitzgerald, private detective, was sitting at the dining room table finishing her breakfast of toast and jam when the front doorbell rang. Clara rose and headed for the door before Annie appeared from the kitchen.

Her relationship with Annie was complicated on paper – she had started out as a nursemaid to help take care of Clara's brother, Tommy Fitzgerald, who was injured in the war, had then become Clara's housekeeper and was now her sister-in-law – but in reality, it was simple; they were friends.

Annie had only recently married Tommy, Clara's older brother and her partner in the detective business. Clara, herself, was unmarried. She was in her twenties and making her way with her career rather than considering uniting herself with a man. Though she was extremely fond of the dashing Captain O'Harris, former RFC, and there seemed a fair chance he would propose soon. There was an even fairer chance she would accept.

In the meantime, she continued as she had always done, as an independent modern woman.

Clara answered the door and was surprised to see her

old school friend Abigail Sommers stood outside.

Abigail was rather glamorous, had blonde hair (artificially enhanced to make it lighter) and wore make-up, she also had the flattened figure that was considered desirable these days. The only way Clara would have a flattened figure would be with the work of severely torturous devices that would squish and squash her curves and bosom into the desired shape. Clara was sometimes concerned that she was not as waif-like as the fashion magazines informed her, she should be. If she only knew that many a man who met her during the course of a case thought her natural, feminine figure highly attractive she would have been flattered, and then horrified, because she was a professional.

"Abigail!" Clara declared, noting that at Abigail's feet was a suitcase. "This is unexpected."

"I apologise about calling so early. The train was horribly delayed, and I ought to have been here last night. You received my letter I suppose?"

The catch in Abigail's voice indicated she had already guessed the answer was 'no'.

"I don't believe I have," Clara said, feeling apologetic for something that was not her fault. "Is something the matter?"

"I am down on a visit," Abigail said cheerfully. "I finally agreed to take some holiday. You know it is – what – two years since I was last in Brighton."

"I rather fancied after what happened last time you would not care to return to the town ever again."

"Nonsense!" Abigail laughed. "That was unpleasant, certainly, but it is all in the past."

"Where are you staying during this visit?" Clara asked, her eyes suspiciously on the suitcase.

Abigail cleared her throat nervously.

"Well, that is rather what I mentioned in the letter. I had hoped I could stay with you. My experiences with Brighton hotels last time were... unsettling. I would prefer to be in a place I know, with people I trust. But I fully understand if that is inconvenient…"

"Don't be silly," Clara said brightly, because she was placed in a position where manners dictated there was nothing else she could say.

"When I received no response to my letter, I was worried, but I had already made the arrangements for the train."

"You could have rung me," Clara pointed out the telephone behind her.

Abigail shook her head at her own foolishness.

"I utterly forgot you had a telephone," she said.

Clara was not convinced. She rather had the impression Abigail had dashed to Brighton suddenly and had had very little time to make arrangements. She had decided to take a chance that Clara would offer her a place to stay once she was on her doorstep.

"You best come in," Clara said, keeping Abigail outside on the doorstep was becoming awkward. "We do have a spare room."

Clara motioned for her to head into their front parlour where a fire was quietly burning to take off the chill of the day.

"How is everything going?" Clara asked as she took Abigail's coat.

"Oh, very well," Abigail smiled. "The scandal with the Pearl Pink lipstick was difficult and it took time to overcome it, but Albion Industries is back on the up and I am still their top sales representative."

"I am glad of that," Clara replied. "I kept abreast of the Pearl Pink case and Mr Mokano's efforts in court. I was not entirely surprised to see that Albion lost."

"We did not lose," Abigail said firmly. "We agreed on a compromise out of court. We have licensed the recipe for the pearlescent lipstick formula from Mr Mokano and the publicity over the Pearl Pink court case has increased our sales. I should say we rather came out on top, after all."

Clara was not so sure about that, but she allowed Abigail her triumph.

"I am still surprised you chose to spend your first holiday in years in Brighton," she said. "I thought you would have gone to your parents. Where are they living now?"

"South of France," Abigail sniffed. "Father always said he would live there when he retired."

"I did not realise he had retired from his business. Did he not run one of those agencies you can buy arranged holidays from?"

"He did," Abigail said cautiously. "And he did not retire. There were some financial irregularities. He declared the business closed and went to France with mother."

"Ah," Clara said, opting not to press the issue. "Still, Brighton?"

"One has to overcome one's demons at some point," Abigail said firmly. "I cannot spend my life running away from what happened here. I arose from that disaster triumphant, after all."

"I suppose," Clara said uncertainly. "Well, now you are here, we shall have to make some plans. I do not have a case at the moment, so I am happy to be your guide around the town. I don't suppose you saw any of the sights, aside from the Pavilion, the last time you were here."

"Actually, Clara, if you would not mind, I had hoped to spend a little time by myself. I rather want to just rest and enjoy having nothing to do," Abigail gave an awkward smile. "I thought I might do a lot of shopping. I never have the chance to really enjoy buying things normally. I am always in a rush."

"Of course," Clara said, feeling rebuffed and even more suspicious about this sudden visit. "My house is your home for the duration."

"That is so kind of you," Abigail said earnestly. "A hotel would have been simply awful. I shall not get in your way. You will barely know I am here."

"I would like to know you are here, you are my guest," Clara corrected.

"But I am a rather unexpected one," Abigail replied.

"Unexpected or not, you are welcome," Clara promised her.

Abigail dipped her head, acknowledging this comment with abashed gratitude.

"Why don't I show you your room?" Clara said.

Abigail nodded agreeably and followed Clara upstairs to the spare room. Since Annie and Tommy now shared a bedroom, Annie's old room had been left spare. Annie, as always, had taken her housekeeping duties above and beyond and the room was kept spotless and tidy, the bed freshly made up in anticipation of an unexpected guest. Abigail happened to be that guest in this instant, though it was not unheard of for Clara to offer sanctuary to individuals during a case and having a room to put them in was always handy.

"It is a lovely room," Abigail said, glancing around. "I shall, of course, pay for my food, seeing as I have rather dropped myself upon you."

"I could hardly…"

"Do not protest. If I were in a hotel, I would be paying a lot more. I shall put forward some money for the extra provisions it will be necessary for you to buy."

Clara watched her old friend walk about the room and put down her luggage. She was more convinced than ever that there was an ulterior motive to this sudden visit. Perhaps Abigail was in trouble and had needed to get away quickly? If that was the case, Clara was not sure why her friend had not confided in her. Clara would not judge and could be very useful in these things. Something was odd about all this, but Clara decided she could pry at her leisure and sooner or later she would work out this mystery.

"Would it be all right if I hang my clothes in the wardrobe?" Abigail asked, one hand pointing to the item of furniture.

"Naturally," Clara said. "Settle yourself in and then come downstairs for a cup of tea."

Clara left her alone to unpack privately and was almost back in the dining room – where her toast would be stone cold by now – when Tommy entered through the front door with his dogs, Pip and Bramble. Bramble was a small black poodle, who managed to look bedraggled even after he had just been bathed and combed. He had developed the look into an artform. Pip was a black Labrador, still growing into herself and going through a gangly stage when she seemed to have too much leg and not enough body.

They arrived with a blast of autumnal cold and to enhance the effect, the wind blew about some fallen leaves to make its point. The weather was rapidly turning, and soon they would be stacking the fire high to keep the chill from their bones.

Tommy hung up his coat as Pip and Bramble raced to say hello to Clara, despite the fact they had already done so that morning.

"Do you remember Abigail Sommers?" Clara asked her brother after she had been enthusiastically greeted by slightly damp and rather cold dogs.

"Your school friend who was accused of murder last time she was in Brighton," Tommy said lightly.

"That is her," Clara said, thinking she would have preferred to describe her friend in another fashion, though Tommy's version was certainly the most memorable. "She has dropped by this morning and is going to stay a while."

Tommy's smile faded and he gave his sister a look that told her he was thinking the same as she was.

"I know," Clara said, coming closer so she could speak quietly. "She claims she is here on a sudden holiday, but something is amiss."

"She has not confided the matter to you?"

Tommy was puzzled.

"Not so far, perhaps she needs to build up the courage. Anyway, she is a welcome guest."

"And just when I was thinking things were a little boring around here," Tommy grinned. "Life is nothing without a mystery to solve."

Clara was about to say something in response when

there was another knock on the door.

"They must have been right behind me," Tommy chuckled at the sound and spun around to open the door.

Upon the doorstep was Mr Bankes, Oliver's father. He looked worried and that instantly alarmed Clara.

"Mr Bankes, come in out of the cold," she said and hastily ushered him through to the parlour.

"I was not sure where else to go," Mr Bankes shuffled in, hunching up his shoulders and staring morosely at the fire. "Oliver is unwell."

"Does he have the 'flu?" Tommy asked. "It always does the rounds this time of year."

"It is something else," Mr Bankes explained. "I had to summon an ambulance for him."

Clara was truly worried now.

"What has happened Mr Bankes?" she asked urgently.

"Mrs White, who helps at his shop, came to my door today. She had turned up at the front door at nine o'clock as usual, but it was locked and there was no sign of Oliver. She tried to summon him with the bell, but he did not come, and this was very odd. She had had the previous day off and began to wonder if something had happened while she was not there. She could think of nothing to do but come to me," Mr Bankes explained carefully. "I have a spare key for the studio and as soon as she explained, I knew I had to go at once to the shop, even though I rarely leave the house these days. People look at me, you know."

Clara doubted that, but Mr Bankes had developed a deep sense of paranoia over the last few years.

"I hurried to the shop and let myself and Mrs White in. We called for Oliver but had no response. Then we went upstairs and found him groaning in his bedroom. It was a terrible sight, Miss Fitzgerald. He had been dreadfully ill and was in a daze. Mrs White said an ambulance was needed and I quite agreed."

"What is wrong with him?" Clara asked, fearing Oliver had been dabbling with his photographic chemicals again. He liked to experiment and had been known to create some pretty toxic concoctions in his efforts to create the perfect photograph developing solution.

"The ambulancemen could not say, of course, but he is at the hospital now and being seen by doctors. I was not allowed to remain with him, and I could not think what to do with myself, other than to come and see you. Mrs White has kindly remained at the shop to clean up the bedroom. I am worried Oliver is going to die."

Mr Bankes' face fell, and it was apparent he was close to tears.

"He has a weak heart, you know, that was why he did not serve in the war."

Clara reached out for his hand.

"Oliver is stronger than you think, and he is in the best place to be treated."

Mr Bankes nodded his head, but it was plain he was suffering from severe shock. Clara was convincing him to sit down when Annie appeared at the parlour door.

"What is the matter?"

"Oliver is rather unwell and at the hospital," Tommy informed her. "Mr Bankes is rather overcome."

"I can see that," Annie nodded. "Poor Oliver. Is it the 'flu?"

"We do not know as yet," Clara was checking the clock on the mantelpiece. It would be several hours before visiting time, but she might be able to persuade someone at the hospital to talk to her. They knew the work she did for the police and were sometimes amenable. She made up her mind.

"I am going to the hospital. Annie, perhaps Mr Bankes would benefit from some of your tea and a piece of cake?"

Annie had already considered this and nodded.

"Do not fret Clara, he is in my capable hands."

Clara thought the old man had no idea what was about to hit him, but she had other problems to attend to. She hurried into the hall and grabbed her coat. Tommy was a pace behind her.

"It can't be anything really serious, can it Clara?" he

said.

"I don't know," Clara answered honestly. "I hope not."

Chapter Three

When they arrived at the hospital, Clara and Tommy soon discovered they were not the only ones curious about Oliver Bankes' sudden sickness. Inspector Park-Coombs was in the foyer quietly speaking to the receptionist in an undertone that suggested he did not want anyone to overhear his words.

Inspector Park-Coombs was a middle-aged gentleman who had risen steadily through the ranks of the police. He was pretty sound, in Clara's opinion, though sometimes he rushed to conclusions. However, he was always decent about hearing her views on a matter, and that raised him up in her estimation if nothing else.

Park-Coombs glanced up when he heard people approaching and saw that it was Clara and her brother. He made an expression that caused his moustache to go lop-sided for a moment. You could tell a lot about Park-Coombs' mood from his moustache. That morning, he was agitated.

"You have heard about Bankes?" he assumed.

"His father came to my house," Clara nodded. "How is he?"

"A little stronger. They have pumped his stomach,

though I suspect he had already expelled the poison he had consumed. The doctors think he will be fine with time."

"Poison?" Tommy latched onto the word.

"Yes. He was most definitely poisoned, and he was not the only one. The very reason I am here is because the hospital has had a rush of cases just like Bankes' since lunchtime yesterday. A dozen people are currently being treated for the same symptoms, though all the others are women."

Clara could see why the inspector was so worried. Mass poisoning was a scary business.

"Has someone sold bad food?" Clara asked.

"No, I don't think it was that. I have spoken with some of the ladies and asked them what they had consumed through the day. A noticeable trend emerged. They had all taken a type of diet pill yesterday and became unwell shortly afterwards."

"A diet pill?" Clara frowned. "Was this perhaps the intended effect of it, like a purge? And the ladies consumed too much in their eagerness to lose weight?"

"I do not believe so. The ladies insisted they had stuck to the recommended dosage. One had even been overly cautious and only taken half. The severity of the symptoms are far more dramatic than any purge," Park-Coombs explained. "I have sent samples to my lab boys to be analysed."

"How does Oliver fit into this?" Tommy asked.

"Oliver also consumed these pills," Park-Coombs said. "It took me a while to get the information out of him as he was embarrassed to mention he had taken diet pills. In the end, he realised it was more important he reveal his secret than hide it. Whoever made these pills has a lot to answer for. I do not think it is remiss to say they are lucky no one has died from taking them."

"That is a worrying thought," Clara agreed. "Might you get us permission to see Oliver?"

Park-Coombs grinned at her.

"Never one to miss an opportunity."

"You would be disappointed with me if I did," Clara replied.

Park-Coombs conversed with the receptionist again, who in turn telephoned to a doctor to gain permission for Clara to see Oliver outside of visiting hours. The inspector made it plain that Clara was consulting in this particularly strange business and needed to be able to access Oliver whenever she needed to. The doctor reluctantly agreed.

"You are good to go, Clara," Park-Coombs said as he put on his hat and started to walk away. "I have some enquiries to make. Keep me up to date if you learn anything interesting."

They headed upstairs to the ward where Oliver was being kept. A sister started to protest when she saw them arrive out of visiting hours but was quickly informed to summon the doctor who had given permission. Being the sort of woman not to be pushed around – Clara admired her for that – the sister did as they suggested and was instructed brusquely that Clara and her brother were allowed to see Oliver Bankes at any time. The sister was put out by the way the doctor had spoken to her, and Clara sympathised.

"They never appreciate you when you are just doing your duty," she said to the woman, building bridges rather than burning them. "But if you make a mistake, they are quick enough to come down on you."

"Damned if you do, damned if you don't," the sister sighed. "This is about the poisonings?"

"Yes," Clara nodded. "The inspector was telling me you have had twelve patients in so far displaying the same symptoms."

"I am not sure the exact number," the sister admitted. "I am just dealing with the gentleman who has the same symptoms, but obviously I converse with my colleagues and there do seem to be a number of people suffering from the same complaint. It reminds me of the cholera outbreak of 1903."

The sister shuddered at the memory of that terrible

sickness sweeping the town and snatching away whole families.

"It is not cholera," Clara said firmly.

"No. It is something to do with health pills," the sister agreed. "Personally, I think these health pills do more harm than good, and the events of yesterday and today prove it."

With that final declaration she turned around and walked off to get back to her daily chores. Clara and Tommy headed to the bed where they could spy Oliver. He had his eyes shut but opened them when he heard approaching feet. He grinned at the sight of the Fitzgeralds.

"Am I glad to see you!" he said, his throat husky from vomiting and the stomach pump. "It has been the worst night of my life. Well, this morning has not been a good deal better."

He rubbed at his belly mournfully.

"I feel like someone has battered me from the inside with brickbats."

"Tell me what happened," Clara said.

Oliver blushed a little, realising he was going to have to reveal his secret to Clara.

"Old man, the inspector has already told us about the pills," Tommy said to distract him. "Nothing to be ashamed of."

"I was being lazy," Oliver sighed. "I wanted to lose weight without any effort or making any changes to my life. Look where that has got me."

"Oliver, this is not your fault," Clara told him firmly. "Those pills should not have done this to you. They are clearly dangerous."

"Mr Dyer, the chemist who sold them to me, said that all the ingredients were safe and would do me no harm. He said he had personally approved the recipe for the pills before he agreed to sell them," Oliver said miserably.

"Well, it seems either he was mistaken, or the person who made the pills altered the ingredients in the recipe, because you cannot call what those pills did to you safe or harmless," Clara said with a hint of anger to her tone.

She was upset to see a friend suffering so badly, and troubled that the situation could have been a lot worse. What if Oliver had taken a bigger dose? The inspector had mentioned such a possibility occurring when he had said he had asked the other victims if they had taken more of the pills than recommended.

People did things like that, thought they would take more to increase or speed up the effect, not realising how dangerous it could be. People had curious ideas about how medicines worked, she had seen it all when she was a nurse.

"I just think it served me right, in a way," Oliver shrugged his shoulders. "I was looking for a quick fix."

"Oliver, you cannot blame yourself. This should not have happened," Tommy echoed Clara. "The worst that should have occurred is that the pills would have proved useless. Not this."

Oliver was a little mollified by his friend's defence.

"You bought the pills from Mr Dyer?" Clara asked, changing the topic a fraction. "He has the shop opposite your studio."

"Yes," Oliver concurred. "He had this big notice in his window for Pink's Pills. There was a queue of ladies for the bottles all morning. I found myself curious and went over to take a look. The pills promised to help you lose weight safely and efficiently."

Oliver paused for a moment, thinking.

"I will certainly say they are efficient. I imagine I have lost some weight already."

Clara raised an eyebrow at him, and he gave his familiar mischievous smile. It was good to see he felt up to joking around.

"Anyway, I bought a bottle and thought I would give them a try. I did not take them until last night, before I had my dinner. I followed all the instructions to the letter. The inspector asked me about that," Oliver continued. "I read the instructions on the bottle twice to be sure. It said to take two pills three times a day, before meals. I did it exactly like that. Then I had my dinner. About half an hour after I ate, I had this griping feeling in my stomach, it was rather like trapped wind, and I thought little of it. I was going to sit down and read a book, but before long I had stabbing pains in my belly and felt sick. I decided to go to bed and lie down. I had a glass of bicarbonate to try to settle things.

"The pains became worse and worse. It came to a point where I had to throw up. I made it to the bathroom the first few times, but then I started to be overcome too quickly and the pains were making it impossible to move far. Things are a bit hazy after that. I groaned and rolled in my bed. Sometime around dawn, I think I fell into a doze, or maybe I was just so exhausted. I don't recall much until my father arrived and said he was summoning an ambulance."

"Which was a very sensible thing to do," Clara said. "I am very sorry this happened to you Oliver, and I intend to bring the culprit to justice. Selling such products is criminal, both literally and morally."

Oliver smiled at her, glad she was there and on his side, then a thought came to his mind.

"The inspector said other people had been taken ill. Are they all recovering?"

"As far as I am aware," Clara replied.

"I felt so ill I thought I was going to die," Oliver said, his gaze drifting away across the bed as he remembered his awful night. "I rather wanted to die at points, the pain was so bad."

"Mr Dyer is going to have a headache today, with all the complaints that will be coming to him about the pills he endorsed," Tommy remarked. "Who makes Pink's Pills?"

Oliver came back to the present.

"The bottle did not specify the manufacturer, but the lady behind the pills is Miss Pink, the beauty pageant finalist," he said. "She went to London and came second. You know, they are using a picture I took of her as part of the advertising display, and I was not asked permission. It was the photo I took for the newspaper, as well, and I clearly state I retain the copyright on those pictures."

"I rather think you are getting upset about the wrong part of this problem," Tommy said drily. "Though it is good to see you thinking about business and not your mishap."

"Miss Pink?" Clara mused on the name. "I do not recall her."

"There was a local beauty pageant last summer and she won it," Tommy told her. "There was a big spread in the newspaper of all the girls who took part."

Tommy shared a secret smile with Oliver. His sister noticed.

"You paid close attention to this contest then?" Clara said.

Tommy cleared his throat, mildly abashed.

"Anyway, the winner of the local contest went to a regional contest and if they placed highly there, they went to the final in London," he said, trying to sound business-like.

"There was a follow-up piece in the paper about how a local girl had done so well," Oliver picked up the thread. "Since then, Miss Pink has been using her success to launch a career as a… as a…"

Oliver paused to think of the right word.

"I suppose you could call her the queen of dieting. She has written a book on the subject, I am told, and now she has her diet pills. Ladies are obsessed with her," he concluded.

"Certain ladies," Clara made clear. "I personally have never heard of her, and I doubt Annie has either. I do not care for people who make a career out of telling others how to lose weight. There is something so superficial about it."

Clara folded her arms, unwilling to admit that once or twice, while browsing in the book shop, she had paused over one of these 'diet books' and taken a peek. She had concluded most of them involved either abstinence from certain types of food, or some gimmick, such as only eating eggs on a Wednesday. She had been unconvinced by it all.

"Whatever you think, Clara, there are plenty of ladies in the town who are consumed by thoughts of their figure and whether it is what they wish it to be or not," Tommy said. "It is only natural. Look how fashions change and the devices that are created to achieve a certain look. We have barely moved away from corsets that gave an hourglass figure and are now in the age when women are told to wear flatteners to diminish their curves. It is all superficial, all of it."

"But people are so desperate to fit in and look beautiful," Oliver interjected. "Even I am not immune to such pressures, even though men are not as heavily targeted by the advertisers of these things as women. But I was thinking about my waistline when I bought those pills."

"Well, Miss Pink has crossed a line with her products," Clara said staunchly. "She has placed people's health in danger. I am sure Inspector Park-Coombs will be chasing her down and having words. There must be something he can do to make her culpable for her crimes."

Oliver was looking tired and though he valiantly attempted to keep his eyes open, it was plain he needed to rest. Clara patted his hand and promised they would check in on him again. He smiled softly and then sank into his pillow and went to sleep.

"Are we going to leave this in the hands of the inspector?" Tommy asked as they left the ward.

His sister gave him a look.

"No," said Tommy with a smile. "I thought not."

Chapter Four

Their first stop after the hospital was to Mr Dyer's pharmacy. They were following in the footsteps of Inspector Park-Coombs, and he was just leaving the shop as they wandered down the road. He departed in the direction away from them and did not see their approach. For the moment, they were investigating because Clara was angry and not because someone had requested her to, so it seemed best not to let the inspector know what they were doing.

They entered Mr Dyer's shop and the pharmacist glanced up anxiously from his counter. He looked a fraction relieved when he saw they were not the police returning, though he would soon discover his relief was too hasty.

"Clara and Tommy Fitzgerald," Clara introduced them, which instantly raised the shopkeeper's alarm – regular customers did not go around stating their names as they entered a shop.

Mr Dyer found his tongue was tied and did not know the best way forward. Clara did not leave him hanging.

"We have just come from the hospital where Oliver Bankes is quite unwell," Clara stated bluntly, not feeling terribly generous to the purveyor of poison.

"Oliver?" Mr Dyer's eyes flicked to the display of Pink's Pills in the window and then he shut them and gulped. "He is sick?"

"Yes, along with numerous customers you sold those diet pills to yesterday," Tommy interjected, slightly fiercely as he was angry over his friend's sickness.

Mr Dyer grimaced in despair.

"The police have just been to see me on the matter," he said. "You have to understand, I sold the pills in good faith."

"Oliver says you told him there was nothing harmful in the pills," Clara spoke.

"I did, and I truly believed that. Please, just a moment," Mr Dyer hurried to the back of his shop, and they could hear the sound of papers being hastily rummaged through, then he returned. "This is the recipe for the pills that Miss Pink gave me. I insisted I see the recipe before I would sell the pills. There are no ingredients to cause any serious harm."

Clara took the paper from him, which had a handwritten list of ingredients. She noted they were all natural and the sort you could find growing in a comprehensive herb garden. She could also see nothing that would cause a person to lose weight.

"These ingredients prove the pills are nothing more than a con," she said angrily.

Mr Dyer shook his head.

"No, no, they are old remedies, the sort my grandfather would appreciate. There are herbs that promote a feeling of wellbeing, and which improve the digestion, also herbs that are reputed to reduce the appetite and help destroy fat in the body."

"None of which is scientifically proven," Clara remarked. "It is folk medicine."

"What is wrong with folk medicine?" Mr Dyer replied, crossly. "People have been relying on it for centuries. I still make up many remedies that are based on recipes hundreds of years old. If you take a look about my shop, you will find many items that no scientist has bothered to take the time to prove work as they say. Yet, time and time again people buy them and rely on them. And they work. I am, of course, a man of science as my training dictates, but I appreciate that the medical profession has still a lot to learn and home remedies can be just as effective as something concocted in a laboratory."

Mr Dyer had found his temper, feeling his professional integrity was being questioned. He stood a little taller.

"Some medicines work merely by promoting the idea of a change to the body. The mind is very powerful and if you feed a person a pill that you say will make them feel more confident, or sleep better, it could be made of nothing but sugar, but the mind will take up the cause and give a result. I have seen it over and over in my line of work," Mr Dyer was fearsome in the defence of his business. "These pills may have had a helping effect in weight loss, or maybe they would just promote a feeling of wellbeing and healthfulness that would encourage the person to consume less. Either way, the outcome would be the same. The main point is, they are utterly harmless."

"Is that correct Clara?" Tommy asked, glancing at the recipe.

Clara had done some nursing during the war and had a fair knowledge of medicines and poisons. She was not as well-versed on herbs and their effects, but she did not think anything on the list would cause the symptoms Oliver and the others had suffered.

"I do not believe this recipe would result in harm," she said calmly. "But that does not dismiss the fact that several people who consumed those pills yesterday became seriously ill."

"I appreciate that," Dyer said, calming down himself. "I have shown you the recipe, which I accepted as truthful. I was promised that nothing but those ingredients would go into the pills. I am a victim here too. I am the sole stockist of these pills – my reputation could be in jeopardy. Who will buy pills from me if they do not trust me?"

"You should also consider you might be implicated in poisoning people," Tommy warned him. "In which case, you could be arrested by the police."

Dyer looked genuinely shocked by this information. He stared at Tommy, the implication sinking in and filling him with horror.

Clara gave it a moment, then changed direction. They had stirred him up with their accusations but were gaining no real insight into what had happened and why the pills which should have been harmless were harmful.

"Mr Dyer, how many bottles of pills have you sold so far?" Clara asked.

Dyer took a moment to register the question through his horror at being criminally implicated in the matter.

"I was supplied with one hundred bottles, and I have sold all of them," he said. "I did not expect such sales and yesterday was rather overwhelming. My assistant recently left, which means I am running the shop single-handed. I had a queue of ladies out the door. At points, people were getting rather irate."

"One hundred bottles sold, but only a dozen poisoning victims in the hospital," Tommy performed the simple calculation. "That would suggest the recipe is not at fault."

"It would mean that a dozen of those bottles were tampered with, changing the contents to make them poisonous," Clara concurred. "That causes us to ask, why? Before, we supposed that someone had been careless with their pill ingredients and had concocted a drug that would induce these symptoms either through ignorance or perhaps to cause a purging effect, which would, over time induce weight loss. Now we seem to have another motive at work."

Mr Dyer was trying to decide if this new information would get him off the hook and out of trouble.

"Who supplied you with the bottles?" Clara asked him.

"Miss Pink personally delivered them," Dyer explained.

"Did she make the pills herself too?" Tommy asked.

"That I am not clear on," Dyer admitted. "They appeared very professionally made, by someone experienced at producing pills. I still make many of the pills in this shop up myself, such as my cough drops and breath mints. I know what a pill should look like, these looked correct and proper. All the same size and consistent colour. Perhaps Miss Pink has previously worked in a pharmacy shop?"

"Perhaps," Tommy said, feeling that somewhat unlikely. "You were certain they were not made in a factory?"

"Aside from the fact asking a manufacturer to produce such a small run of pills would be costly and few would be interested, you can tell a factory pill from a handmade one. No, these had been made individually by someone, but they were professionally crafted."

"What of the recipe? Did Miss Pink indicate who had devised it?" Clara asked.

"She explained it was a remedy her own grandmother had used. Miss Pink said it had enabled her to lose weight before the beauty pageant," Dyer answered. "The nature of the ingredients suggested a home remedy. The ingredients she listed are harmless, even in substantial quantities."

"Then something else was added to the suspect pills," Tommy said the obvious. "Why would anyone do such a thing? Someone could have died."

"The attacks are random, too," Clara nodded. "The poisoner could not have known who would purchase the doctored pills."

"Miss Pink did not seem the sort to want to poison strangers. That is surely the work of a madman?" Mr Dyer said.

It was certainly peculiar.

"Of course, the pills would have been made in batches," Clara said thoughtfully. "Perhaps all the contaminated bottles came from one batch that somehow ended up containing a poisonous substance."

"An accident?" Tommy mused. "Pretty careless."

"A good chemist would never be so negligent in his work," Mr Dyer said firmly, wary he might find the accusations turning against him again.

"People are not always as thorough or careful as they should be," Clara replied. "However, the immediate concern is that we prevent anyone else from becoming sick. We cannot be sure all the contaminated bottles have been discovered. Someone might not have taken the pills they bought yesterday."

"I have placed a notice in the window recalling the pills," Dyer said, pulling his lips back at the distaste of having to do such a thing. "I have had several ladies come in and request their money back. No doubt there will be more to come."

He looked morose, considering the sizeable sum he had raked in yesterday, which he was now forced to return.

"We need to spread the word more efficiently than that," Clara said. "We should ask the Gazette to run a notice on their front page. They have an evening edition today."

Dyer's expression worsened as he thought of the undue publicity he was about to receive. He looked fit to crumple up in a corner in despair.

"I thought I saw an opportunity," he mumbled miserably. "It seemed such a good idea. Miss Pink is such a celebrity locally and her products would surely improve business. And when she said I would be the exclusive seller of her pills, I was honoured. Now I fear she chose me because no other pharmacist would permit those pills in his shop."

Dyer gazed at the window display of Pink's Pills.

"I need to take that blasted thing down!"

As he spoke, a woman entered the shop. She was in her fifties with a portly appearance. She had a face like thunder and wagged a bottle of Pink's Pills at Dyer.

"I want a refund on this poison!"

"Yes, madam, of course," Dyer said with a weary smile. "I am most sorry for the inconvenience."

"Inconvenience!" the woman blustered. "I could have died. Thank goodness I only took a single pill last night."

"Were you at all unwell?" Clara asked the woman, assuming she had had a mild scare.

"I had a dream about my late husband," the woman told her. "It was most disagreeable. I much prefer him now he is dead. I blame the pills!"

Clara masked her smile as she stepped away from the counter and allowed Dyer to deal with his irate customer.

Clara and Tommy left Dyer alone after that. He had a long day ahead of him, facing angry customers and their accusations. He did not seem likely to have brought this upon himself deliberately and Clara fancied he was an innocent dupe in the whole affair. But just why had Miss Pink handed over products that contained poison? Had she really just been grossly negligent in their manufacture?

As Clara stepped outside the door, she nearly stumbled into Abigail, who was studying the Pink's Pills display intently.

"You hardly need to lose weight," Clara said to her friend.

Abigail had been so absorbed in the display, she started at the sound of Clara's voice. She turned to her, losing the curious frown that had been etched into her forehead.

"I have never taken a diet pill," she said with a hint of pride.

"Glad to hear it, especially as these ones are making people ill," Tommy said.

Abigail raised an eyebrow.

"How ill?"

"A dozen people are in hospital," Clara explained. "Including a friend of ours."

"Oh dear," Abigail's face softened. "That is truly awful, and it demonstrates plainly why it is always best to buy from proper manufacturers. Albion Industries has protocols in place to prevent their products being hazardous to anyone. I look forward to the day when these dreadful hack remedies, made up in people's kitchens, are no longer allowed to be sold to the unwitting."

Abigail sounded quite vehement.

"Well, this situation has certainly tarred Pink's Pills," Clara said. "I don't think they will ever be sold again."

"Good," Abigail said darkly.

Clara waited for her to say something else, her intense stare at the display of diet pills was rather unsettling. Then Abigail relaxed.

"I was on my way to fetch a cake from the bakery," she said. "I wanted to treat you all for allowing me to stay with you. I asked Annie first. I did not want to offend her. She advised me of the singular bakery that she approves of."

That sounded about right. Annie baked all her own cakes and much of her own bread, but she had clearly felt amenable to Abigail and had agreed to allow her to purchase one.

"From diet pills, to cake," Tommy chuckled. "Quite the turn around."

"I am not against cake," Abigail smiled at him. "I am fortunate to have a naturally slight figure and it remains that way with little effort."

Clara's good will towards her friend almost evaporated at that comment. She cleared her throat to change subject swiftly.

"We have a lot to get on with," she said. "We best be going."

"You are investigating this matter?" Abigail asked sharply.

"Our friend has been affected," Tommy pointed out. "We cannot ignore that."

Abigail had a strange look on her face.

"If you need any advice from someone in the beauty industry about these things," she waved a hand at the pill display, "you can always ask me."

"Of course," Clara said brightly, though she was still annoyed by Abigail's previous comments. "In any case..."

"Oh yes, you must get on. This is a terrible situation that must be put to rights at once," Abigail wished them well and headed on her way.

Tommy, who had missed the tension concerning Abigail's blunt comment about never having to worry about her weight, assumed the look on Clara's face was because she was thinking about the case.

"Time to speak to Miss Pink?" he asked.

"After we put that notice in the paper," Clara said firmly. "No one else is to get sick."

Chapter Five

Gilbert McMillan was taking a quick cigarette break outside of the newspaper office when Clara and Tommy arrived to speak to him. He had been banished from smoking indoors after he had carelessly dropped a cigarette onto the cluttered mess of papers that constituted his desk. He had started a small fire that had threatened to consume the entire news floor and had destroyed all of Gilbert's copy for that week's issue. He had meekly agreed to smoking outside after that.

He pulled up his collar against a biting October breeze as Clara came before him.

"Good morning," Gilbert said cheerfully. "What case are you on at the moment?"

Gilbert rightly assumed that the only reason Clara would pause to speak to the slightly slimy reporter was when she was investigating a case and hoped he could assist her.

"Have you heard of Pink's Pills?" she asked him.

Gilbert raised an eyebrow.

"You have no need for those, Miss Fitzgerald, you are a fine figure of a woman."

Tommy coughed behind his sister, to remind Gilbert of

his presence and to mind his manners. Gilbert merely grinned at him, baring nicotine-stained teeth. Clara was immune to his dubious charms.

"Pink's Pills have caused a number of people to wind up in hospital today with symptoms of poisoning. I wish to see an announcement placed in the paper to prevent others from taking them," she said.

Gilbert was intrigued, his journalistic instincts for a story fully kicking in.

"That is quite an accusation," he said. "Do you have proof to back it up?"

"A dozen people are in the hospital after consuming Pink's Pills, including your newspaper photographer Oliver Bankes. The only circumstance they have in common is that they all took Pink's Pills yesterday. The police have already taken the pills to test them for something poisonous."

Gilbert's grin had grown, making his ears rise in his glee.

"Oliver took diet pills?"

Clara realised her mistake at saying Oliver's name. She had meant to prove her point and get Gilbert's full attention. She did not want to leave her friend in a position to be mocked by Gilbert over something so personal. Thankfully, Clara was good at thinking on her feet.

"Yes, he did," Clara declared. "At my behest. I thought these pills a fraud and my purpose was to have Oliver consume them and then demonstrate they had no visible effect. It seemed best to ask someone who was removed from the matter, rather than take them myself as I could be claimed to be biased. Had I at all supposed they would make him sick, I should never have asked. I feel just awful I placed him in this position."

Clara gave a deep sigh to reinforce her sorrow over the matter.

"I only meant to demonstrate you cannot take a pill to make you lose weight," Clara pressed on. "Miss Pink is playing on the desperation of so many women and taking their money while supplying them with a pointless product. I should add, I have seen the recipe for the pills, or at least what she claims is the recipe, and none of the ingredients are capable of making a person lose weight."

The recipe was in fact stowed in Clara's handbag. She had slipped it away while Mr Dyer was distracted.

Gilbert was further intrigued.

"Can any of the ingredients in the recipe cause the sickness these people have suffered?" he asked.

"No, that is the most curious part," Clara admitted. "And not all the bottles of pills appear to be affected. It would seem one batch has been tampered with, either on purpose or by carelessness."

"Now that is interesting," Gilbert said, seeing the full potential of the story.

"I need a warning run in this evening's issue, to ensure no one else takes these pills. We cannot know how many of the poisoned ones are out there," Clara reminded him.

"I can arrange it," Gilbert nodded, his eyes lighting up. "I shall ask the editor to run a front-page article on the matter, it will catch everyone's attention."

That was certainly better than a small notice at the back of the paper.

"Thank you, Gilbert," Clara said.

"It is better than the prettiest duck contest results which we are currently running on the front page," Gilbert said merrily. "And we can use that picture of Miss Pink, Oliver took at the beauty pageant."

"Please be tactful, Gilbert," Clara groaned. "Whatever has occurred, Miss Pink may be wholly blameless, and this could destroy her. As much as I am angered about the pills, I do not want to see a witch hunt. Not until we have the full facts."

Gilbert was too lost in his vision of a significant story and the attention it would bring him to hear her.

"To think, Miss Pink a poisoner!" he said, lost in his thoughts. "I interviewed her just a few weeks ago in regard to the launch of her diet pills."

"You did?" Clara said. "What is she like?"

Gilbert shrugged.

"Pretty, but a little artificial. You know the sort of girl who without the make-up and smart hairdo would be rather a dog."

"Mind your tongue, old man," Tommy grumbled. "You should not speak of any woman like that."

Gilbert was untouched by his criticism.

"She had that arrogance of a woman who knows men find her attractive. I didn't take to her. She was not professional like you Miss Fitzgerald."

Clara refrained from rolling her eyes at his blatant flattery.

"I take it Miss Pink did not seem like someone who was planning on poisoning people?" she asked instead.

Gilbert laughed.

"Not really. She is a tough businesswoman if you ask me. Got her head screwed on. The beauty pageant was a means to an end for her. She has this diet book. It has sold really well. The pills were to be the next step. I should say she will be devastated by all this."

Clara found herself having a pang of sympathy for the woman, even if she had been marketing a pointless product, she had not intended to make people sick.

"I always thought the beauty industry was cutthroat," Gilbert continued musing. "Like that episode at the Brighton Pavilion a couple of years back with someone trying to sabotage Albion Industries' trade fair, and that scandal over the Pearl Pink lipstick."

Gilbert considered what he had just said.

"Do you suppose it is when you put the word 'pink' in a beauty product it takes on a sinister edge and attracts all sorts of madness?"

"I think it is a coincidence," Clara said drily. "Miss Pink, after all, is using her own name. It is her own name, I take it?"

"Oh yes," Gilbert nodded. "You were only allowed to use real names for the pageant. We traced the families for the main contenders to do interviews. If someone were using a fake name, they would have been disqualified."

"With a name like Pink, you rather fancy it was natural to go into beauty products," Tommy said.

"Her full name is Rose Pink," Gilbert beamed. "I like parents with a sense of humour."

"Could you supply us with her address, at some point we shall need to speak to her," Clara asked.

"I'll have to look it up. It will take a while. I could pop it through your letterbox later tonight. In the meantime, I have a story to write," Gilbert clapped his hands together, dropped his cigarette to the pavement and ground it out with his heel, and then headed back inside without a word of farewell.

"I don't like him," Tommy said.

"Gilbert does not intend to be liked," Clara shrugged. "He specialises in irritating people into saying more than they should."

"In that regard he is doing a fine job. Where to now?"

Clara glanced at her wristwatch.

"I suppose we ought to take this recipe sheet to Inspector Park-Coombs and if it just happens he has the results of the laboratory's inspection of the pills, well, he might mention it."

"Oh yes, because we are not meant to be investigating as no one has employed us yet," Tommy winked at her.

"We shall tell him about the newspaper too. That was doing our public duty," Clara said firmly and completely unabashed.

They headed to the police station to report to Inspector Park-Coombs. He happened to be by the front desk collecting some paperwork before he went out to investigate another case – chicken rustling in Hove. The local county councillor had been targeted and was demanding Park-Coombs came to him in person.

"Clara," Park-Coombs said without looking up, as an afterthought he added. "Tommy."

He was still not used to Clara's brother being her

partner in the detective business.

"I wanted to let you know we went to the Gazette and asked them to run a notice about the Pink's Pills and warn others not to take them," Clara said.

"That is a dreadful business," the desk sergeant spoke, always ready for gossip. "My wife bought some. Actually, she shared the price of a bottle with a friend. She took some last night before we knew all this. Thankfully she is fine, but I brought all the pills she had left into the station."

"My wife would not allow such things in the house," Park-Coombs remarked. "Her opinion on diets is that they make you maudlin and unhealthy. When the doctor suggested she lose a bit of weight, she accused him of trying to kill her off. She is convinced it was the diet her best friend went on that cost her, her life, you see."

"Oh dear, did she become ill?" Clara asked.

"She was knocked down by an omnibus," Park-Coombs answered. "My wife contends if her friend had been still of the robust nature she had been before the diet, the driver would have seen her sooner and stopped."

There was no appropriate response to such a statement.

"Anyway," Clara said, clearing her throat. "The newspaper is going to run something on the front page, so hopefully no one else will take contaminated pills."

"That was good thinking, Clara," Park-Coombs smiled at her.

"We would hate to think of others suffering like poor Oliver," Tommy said. "Someone who was of a weaker constitution could die. I am surprised diet pills are not illegal."

"Poisonous ones are," Park-Coombs said wryly.

"That brings me to something else," Clara reached into her handbag. "I went to Mr Dyer to tell him what had occurred to poor Oliver. He was rather upset and gave me the recipe for the pills. Or rather, the recipe he was supplied with to approve them, because none of these ingredients would cause the symptoms people are suffering."

Clara showed Park-Coombs the recipe, he scanned

through it quickly.

"Herbs," he said. "Nothing fatal there."

"Precisely," Clara said. "Either Miss Pink lied about the recipe, or someone doctored some of the pills. For what purpose we can only speculate upon."

"Whoever did this, they are bloody callous," Park-Coombs shook his head. "Making innocent people sick. It beggar's belief."

"It is frightening," Tommy nodded. "We trust the pills we buy at the chemist. We assume they are safe. To suppose we could be buying poison is shocking."

"It is the sort of thing that might have happened a hundred years ago, but not today," Park-Coombs agreed, he was about to say more when the telephone rang, and they all politely fell quiet so the desk-sergeant could answer it.

"I have chickens to hunt for," Park-Coombs whispered to Clara and Tommy, pulling a face to show his thoughts on the matter.

He was heading for the door when the desk-sergeant called to him.

"Inspector, that was the hospital," he said, having finished his telephone conversation. "One of the poisoning victims has passed away."

Park-Coombs' shoulders sagged. His despondency was mirrored by Clara and Tommy.

"Not Oliver?" Clara asked quickly.

The desk-sergeant shook his head.

"A woman. Mrs Wood. She had a weak heart, and the doctors say the strain was too much for her body."

Park-Coombs walked back to the desk.

"Now we are looking at murder," he said bitterly. "And I have to run after missing chickens."

"I had hoped it would not come to this," Clara groaned. "I knew there was a chance, however, I hoped with the newspaper announcement and everything, that no harm would come, but it was already too late."

"We did our best," Tommy reminded her. "Mrs Wood

was ill before we even knew about the pills."

"The boys in the lab are still running tests on the pills we collected from the victims' homes and are comparing them with other samples which people have consumed and were unharmed by," Park-Coombs explained. "They have not confirmed anything yet, but the doctors at the hospital felt the symptoms were consistent with arsenic poisoning."

"Arsenic," Clara sighed. "Far too common a substance for people to get their hands on and easy to mix into things."

The desk-sergeant was looking sick, thinking how close his wife had come to being poisoned. Just the randomness of chance had spared her.

"I need to get to Hove," Park-Coombs muttered. "Thank you for your help, Clara, give my best to Oliver when you next see him and do not worry. He seemed on the mend."

He gave them a nod and departed. There was not much else to be done at the station. The desk-sergeant needed a few words of consoling about his wife nearly being poisoned and swore he would make sure she knew he loved her just the way she was. Then Clara and Tommy headed off again. Matters were becoming urgent, and they needed to get to the root of the problem.

"Miss Pink is going to be facing a great deal of backlash over this," Clara said to her brother as they left the station. "We ought to forewarn her of how much trouble she is in and see what her take on the story is."

"Except, we do not know her address," Tommy pointed out. "Gilbert said he would get it to us tonight."

"We cannot wait that long," Clara said firmly. "We shall have to discover it another way. Perhaps Mr Dyer has it?"

"Worth a shot," Tommy said, and they started back the way they had come. "Have you wondered about Abigail Sommers appearing in Brighton just at the time of all this trouble?"

"I have," Clara smiled at him.

"And?"

"Oh, I have not come to any conclusions yet, but I rather fancy Abigail's arrival is far from a coincidence."

Chapter Six

They arrived at Mr Dyer's shop in time to hear a commotion break out. They had not yet opened the door, when an older man with a stick scurried out in haste and nearly collided with them.

"You don't want to go in," he told them with a worried look on his face. "She is a banshee!"

He hastened away as fast as he could.

"Who is a banshee?" Tommy asked.

"Well, I am curious to find out," Clara said, as a raised woman's voice could be heard screeching from within. "Only way we shall know is to go in. Brace yourself."

"You ought to blow a whistle, like when we went over the top," Tommy winced.

"Now, now, I doubt whoever is in there is quite as terrible as all that the Germans threw at you."

"Yes, but she is present and dangerous now, whereas the war is comfortably in the past. Danger in the present is always far more alarming than danger you survived."

Tommy said this authoritatively. Clara tsked at him and then hurried into the shop to determine what new drama was unfolding. There was no one on the actual shop floor, an abandoned set of scales with some sort of remedial powder partly measured out on them indicated that whatever had occurred had happened suddenly. Clara guessed the powders were what the older gentleman with the stick had been waiting for. He had clearly decided they were not urgent enough to warrant remaining while trouble erupted.

Raised voices were coming from the back of the shop. Mainly one raised voice. A female voice that shrieked like a siren – the older gentleman's description of the woman as a banshee was not so farfetched. The voice had reached such a pique that it was hard to make out words. They ran into one another and were being yelled at a pitch only suitable for the hearing of dogs and cats.

Mr Dyer was silent, taking the outrage of whoever was present with quiet grace. Clara wondered if the person was a relative of someone who had consumed the diet pills – could they even be a relative of the unfortunate Mrs Wood who had just succumbed at the hospital?

She edged around the counter to try to get a view to the back room. No one had responded to the ringing of the shop bell, though she suspected they had not even heard it.

"Mr Dyer?" she called out firmly. "Is everything all right?"

Her first shout failed to rouse anyone. She called again, louder, and slower, cutting across the banshee's wail. Her words must have reached to the back of the shop because everything went suddenly quiet. It was like a wireless radio had been on and someone had abruptly turned it off. After a long moment, a curtain that did a half-hearted job of masking the back room from prying eyes was hauled back and, in the doorway, stood a woman. She looked at Clara with venom in her eyes.

She was a tall woman, made taller by the shoes she wore. She had bleached blonde hair that was savagely cut into a bob and had rather overdone her make-up. Clara surmised she was looking at Miss Rose Pink herself, and she saw that Gilbert had had a point about the woman using artificial means to mask over a lot of what might be considered flaws. It was safe to say that without all her make-up she would have been rather plain in appearance, though Clara was the sort who believed beauty came from within and there was no such thing as a plain face, only ugly personalities.

What was very noticeable about Miss Pink was the presence she exuded. It was like electricity flickering from her and it clearly had the effect of binding people, men especially, under her spell. It was a combination of self-confidence and ambition that merged into this remarkable aura around the woman. You could not capture that 'beauty' in a photograph, nor a painting, it was something that had to be felt.

However, right in that moment the look Miss Pink was giving Clara was like knives thrown at her and was clearly intended as intimidation. Clara, who had not been a detective this long without getting used to such fearsome looks, smiled politely.

"You must be Miss Pink," she held out a hand for the woman to shake, one female professional to another.

"Have you murdered Mr Dyer?" Tommy asked bluntly from behind his sister.

Miss Pink turned her glower on him and refused Clara's hand.

"We are having a private conversation," she declared.

"Firstly, a conversation requires two to participate and all we could hear was you yelling, secondly, if you wished for your talk to be private you might have spoken a little quieter," Clara told her, smiling sweetly.

"You are rude!" Miss Pink told her.

"No, I am merely observant," Clara replied. "I would suggest your balling at Mr Dyer because your pills have poisoned people the only rudeness on display here."

Miss Pink was appalled at this remark and started to bluster. The accusation had taken the wind out of her sails for an instant and she had to work her way back up to knowing what to say. Before she could, Clara carried on.

"I am Clara Fitzgerald. This is my brother Tommy. We

are private detectives, but more importantly, we are friends of someone who is currently in hospital after taking your pills," Clara's tone which had been light until then, hardened over her final statement and her own fire made a brief appearance.

Clara did not need to shout and scream to demonstrate her anger, or to cow people. Her outrage was more controlled, steadier, and far more deadly.

Miss Pink hesitated. Tommy suspected this was a surprise for her, as much as for them. She was not a person who normally met her match.

"I am sorry," she said, the words coming out torturously. "But it cannot have been my pills. They are perfectly safe."

Mr Dyer had emerged from the back room and was hovering before the curtain. He appeared unscathed, at least physically, from his encounter with Miss Pink.

"The recipe contains nothing harmful," Miss Pink continued. "I told Mr Dyer he should not have even suggested there was anything wrong with them."

"It was not Mr Dyer who did so," Clara responded. "It was the police who made the connection. A dozen people are sick in the hospital and the only thing that connects them is your pills."

Clara paused.

"Actually, I suppose it is now eleven people. Mrs Wood passed away a short time ago."

Mr Dyer stepped onto the shop floor.

"Not Mrs Wood!" he was mortified. "She is such a dear woman. She has been a customer for years."

"She had a weak heart, and it could not take the strain of the poisoning," Tommy explained. "We heard the news from the police ourselves."

"That is awful!" Mr Dyer pulled his lips back in a wild grimace. "And just yesterday she was here buying those wretched pills. I never should have stocked them!"

Miss Pink had fallen silent at the news of Mrs Wood. She did not even react to Dyer's statement. She seemed to not know what to say. Mr Dyer did, however.

"It is murder now!" he snapped at Miss Pink. "Your wretched diet pills have killed someone!"

"They are harmless!" Miss Pink rallied, when in doubt, her anger could get her through most things. "I showed you the recipe!"

"Clearly, you did not list all the ingredients!" Dyer snapped.

"Arsenic," Clara said, cutting through the brewing argument. Dyer and Miss Pink went mute. "The hospital suspects arsenic is the culprit."

"Arsenic?" Miss Pink whispered the deadly word. "But I would never…"

She clasped a hand to her forehead and looked ashen all of a sudden.

"I never, ever intended this," she said, reaching out for a stool behind Mr Dyer's counter so she could sit down. "The recipe is an old family one. I was honest when I said I had used the pills when getting into shape for the pageant. I made them up myself. I would never have sold something that could make people unwell."

"Did you also make up the batches of pills you sold through Mr Dyer yourself?" Clara asked.

Miss Pink shook her head.

"I was not skilled enough. I had someone make them for me. My intention, once they became a big seller, was to have them factory made, but that was too expensive for the small quantity I wanted for the time being."

Miss Pink was thinking how things might have been different if she had been prepared to use a factory instead. Her gaze fell forlornly on the display of Pink's Pills.

"It is all over now, anyway," she groaned. "My enterprise is destroyed before it had a chance to flourish."

"We shall need to meet the person who prepared the pills," Clara said, ignoring the maudlin statement. She was not feeling terribly sympathetic towards Miss Pink at this moment in time. First the woman had created pointless pills to sell to people at extortionate prices, then her wares had ended up poisoning people, and finally she had tried to drop all the blame on Mr Dyer.

"I will want to see where he made the pills, too," Clara added.

Miss Pink nodded her head.

"You think something happened when they were being made? Accidental contamination," she said.

"No pharmacist in his right mind would have arsenic anywhere near where he was making up pills," Mr Dyer said stoutly. "At best it is carelessness."

"But I am not responsible," Miss Pink hammered a finger into her chest to emphasise those words. "I did not deliberately sell poison."

"You may find you have to prove that," Tommy said to her. "Ultimately, the final blame for these things tends to lie with the person behind the pill. If it is found you used a pharmacist who was careless around poisons, you could be considered culpable along with him. I believe it is called something like failing to do your duty of care."

"That is preposterous!" Miss Pink said in horror. "It would finish me!"

"I assume the pharmacist you used is registered with the Royal Pharmaceutical Society?" Mr Dyer said with a sniff. He was looking rather self-righteous for someone who had sold poisonous pills.

Miss Pink hesitated, clearly not sure. Dyer pounced.

"An unregistered person acting as a pharmacist! This is scandalous!"

"Do not forget who sold the pills without doing a thorough check of their process of manufacture," Tommy warned him before he could get carried away.

Dyer shut up.

"I don't understand how this happened," Miss Pink had lost her bluster. She had burned out her anger and had reached a place of exhausted calm. There was simply no fury left. "I was trying to help people."

"You were trying to make money," Clara told her bluntly. "If you truly wanted to help people, you would not have been charging so much."

Miss Pink gave her a sharp look, but Clara was not to be swayed from her accusation. Miss Pink found herself backing down, an unusual situation for her.

"How is Oliver doing, Miss Fitzgerald?" Dyer asked in the silence that followed.

"He was comfortable, the last we saw of him," Clara replied.

"I was thinking I would pop over to the hospital at the evening visiting hour and speak to my customers," Dyer continued. "Or do you think that would be ghoulish and I best stay away?"

Clara was not sure what was the appropriate way to behave in such a situation. If she were a patient at the hospital, would she want to be visited by the man who had sold her the drugs that had poisoned her?

"Maybe stay at home," Tommy advised. "I think people might not be in the best mood to receive you."

Mr Dyer nodded his head, understanding.

"I see you point. I just feel truly awful. I should have never agreed to selling these pills."

"You were quick enough to take them on when I told you how much commission I was willing to let you have," Miss Pink mustered enough defiance to growl at him.

"My reputation is ruined because of my greed," Mr Dyer bemoaned.

"What of my reputation?" Miss Pink said. "I was only just beginning my enterprise. I was trying to make a future for myself. Now... now there is nothing."

Miss Pink became glum, and the sombreness of her mood touched them all. She might have been thinking of profit and she might have been careless in her choice of pharmacist, but the price she was paying was still harsh.

"You should know," Clara said carefully, "the Gazette has heard of the story and will be running an article in the evening edition to warn people not to take the pills."

Miss Pink winced but did not seem to twig that Clara had been responsible for the newspaper picking up the story.

"I should have stuck to diet books. No one dies from reading," Miss Pink groaned.

Clara thought that debatable, considering some of the notions poured forth in diet manuals, but Miss Pink had been punished enough for the time being and she made no comment.

"We need to track down your pharmacist," Clara said. "See how this contamination all came about. People will need to know exactly who is responsible."

Miss Pink made a small movement that indicated she concurred. Then she rose from the stool.

"Will I be charged with murder?" she said in a small voice.

"I would not like to say," Clara admitted. "I think, as it was not your intention to harm anyone, manslaughter more likely, but these sorts of cases become complicated."

"The Royal Pharmaceutical Society are cracking down on rogue pharmacists," Mr Dyer could not resist prodding Miss Pink. "They might want to make an example."

Miss Pink sagged at this new information.

"You might wish to think about that too, Mr Dyer," Tommy told the pharmacist who was becoming too quick to make out he was whiter than white in this scenario. "What does the Royal Pharmaceutical Society do to registered pharmacists who sell pills made by unregistered ones?"

Mr Dyer opened his mouth and found there was nothing he could say.

"Come along Miss Pink. The more helpful you are to us, the better it shall look for you," Clara said, encouraging the woman to come around from behind the counter.

They were nearly at the door when two women came in. They had been talking merrily to each other but fell into horrified quiet at the sight of Miss Pink.

"It's her Mavis!" one declared.

"The lady behind the pills!" Mavis responded.

Their faces quickly took on expressions of anger. Clara

grabbed Miss Pink's arm.

"I think we best go out the back," she said.

Chapter Seven

They managed to get Miss Pink away from the pharmacy without anyone else seeing her, mainly by diving down a back street and through a neighbourhood where the ladies had no need of a diet pill to keep them thin, they managed quite well with simply lacking sufficient food.

Miss Pink had made her way to the shop via the bus but returning that way as she was seemed foolhardy – too many people liable to recognise her. They had to disguise her and swiftly. The distance to Clara's home was too far and would require either a lengthy walk or taking the bus. Too much opportunity for the unfortunate Miss Pink to be recognised. It was obvious she was now a social pariah and would be launched upon by irate women if they were not careful.

Things would only worsen after the evening paper came out and the news of Mrs Wood's passing became public knowledge. They needed a plan. It was Tommy who came up with the suggestion.

"Oliver's studio is just across the road," he said, pointing back in the direction they had just come in their flight from the pharmacy. "Why don't we duck in there? He has props and things for his photographs, we could muster up a disguise for Miss Pink."

"I am not wearing ghastly cast-offs that dozens of other people have worn before me!" Miss Pink declared vehemently.

"Would you prefer to risk being accosted by some of those women you have upset?" Clara asked her. "I doubt they would resort to violence, but they will certainly give you a verbal lashing you will not forget in a hurry."

Miss Pink let this option sink in and reluctantly conceded it would be better to change her appearance. Clara gave her own hat to her as a temporary disguise. Tommy wrapped his scarf around her neck and covered up the lower portion of her face. Miss Pink started to protest at being treated like a doll to dress up.

"Trust us," Tommy informed her. "Much better this way."

They ushered the beauty queen back towards Oliver's studio and made it across the road without being spotted. Tommy knew where Oliver kept his spare key – in a narrow gap along the edge of his front window – he retrieved it and opened the door. They were all relieved to get inside and away from public eyes.

Clara glanced around the reception area of the studio. It felt empty and hollow without Oliver's presence. A wave of sorrow came over her as she thought about him in the hospital. He would be fine, she told herself firmly, no need to mope or became maudlin.

Miss Pink had gladly stripped off the scarf and hat and was taking stock of her surroundings.

"Who owns this studio again?" she asked, noting the many photographs displayed on the walls as examples of Oliver's work.

"Oliver Bankes," Clara said. "He works occasionally for the newspaper, taking pictures on their behalf."

"Oh, there is my picture!" Miss Pink pointed to a black and white image on the wall. In it she was stood side-on to the camera, posed with one hand elegantly lifted above her head and a smile like that of the Cheshire Cat on her face.

"He took the photos of the beauty pageant?"

"Yes," Tommy said. "He also tried out your pills. He was one of the unfortunates who bought the dodgy batch."

There was no mistaking the hard edge to his voice. Miss Pink had the good grace to hesitate and glance away.

"That should not have happened," she said bitterly. "I would never have knowingly sold pills that were hazardous."

"Well, somehow they became hazardous," Clara stated. "And we need to find out just how that occurred. As soon as we have you disguised, we shall get on the bus and seek out the person who made those pills. Who are they, anyway? You were coy about giving us a name when we were stood before Mr Dyer."

Miss Pink pulled a face.

"That was for a very good reason," she said. "The pharmacist who made my pills, who, in fact, helped me come up with the idea and even looked through the recipe for me to make sure it was safe, happens to be Mr Dyer's former assistant."

Tommy frowned.

"His assistant resigned a couple of months ago. It was quite sudden. Mr Dyer has been short-handed ever since."

Miss Pink nodded meekly.

"It was not meant to be awkward," she sighed. "Sigmund did not mean to hurt Mr Dyer, but he realised his situation with him was never going to progress his ambitions. He wanted more than just to be a pharmacist in a shop. He saw no future as Dyer's assistant."

"Wait a moment, take us back and tell us about this man properly," Clara said. "How did you come to know him?"

Miss Pink looked heavenwards, frustrated at being forced to reveal her private life to the detectives.

"His full name is Sigmund Coppleburg," she said at last. "We met at a dance. Nothing dramatic about that. It is how a lot of people meet. We rather took to one another and began walking out. Sigmund rather saw through my beauty queen façade. He found the real person beneath, and it was… nice."

"He was a logical person to tell about your diet pill idea," Tommy guessed.

"Yes. He knew I hoped to make something of myself. In that regard we had much in common. We both wanted to do more with our lives. I told him about the pills and asked his opinion. He saw potential, saw it as a start of my own line of beauty products. He had the experience and knowledge to make the pills, and I was able to deal with the marketing. It was perfect."

"Why did he leave Mr Dyer's employment?" Clara asked.

"It was purely for practical reasons. He worked long hours for Dyer, many more than just when he was serving in the shop. He had to make up pills and other things, sweep the shop, dust the shelves. He rarely had a moment for himself. If he were to make my pills and help me, he simply had to give up his job. We thought the pills would be such a success, he could afford to give up his employment for just a short time."

"Makes sense," Tommy agreed. "He had a lot of pills to make, after all."

"Thousands," Miss Pink murmured. "And those were just the start. We knew once the pills took off, we would need many more. There was going to be a point where we needed more than we could make swiftly, but not so many to be worthwhile have a factory make them. So, Sigmund has been working hard to create a stockpile for us."

She paused, biting on her lower lip, and leaving an impression from her teeth.

"Sigmund would never deliberately poisoned those pills, and he is far from careless. I could not say more before Mr Dyer, but I know this is not his fault."

Tears formed in Miss Pink's eyes. Her words had an edge, as if she was starting to doubt her own convictions and was beginning to consider the possibility of betrayal.

"Whose idea was it to have Mr Dyer as the sole supplier of the pills?" Tommy asked her.

"Sigmund's," she said glumly. "He said it felt like compensation for up and leaving him. He would make a tidy sum from selling the pills. Sigmund always felt awkward about resigning and leaving him without help. He also knew Mr Dyer was more willing to sell homemade remedies than most of the pharmacists in town."

"Sigmund holds no grudge against his former employer?" Tommy asked carefully.

Miss Pink gave him a sharp look.

"No!"

Her voice wobbled and once again she was questioning her certainty.

"No, he would not do such a thing," she mumbled.

"It leaves us with something of a conundrum as to how poison came to be in your pills," Clara told her. "Opportunity is the key to this, and so far, we do not have many people with that."

Miss Pink shook her head.

"Why would anyone do this on purpose?" she said, close to sobbing.

"Revenge, upon you or upon Dyer, or both," Clara said bluntly.

Miss Pink's face fell.

"Not Sigmund. He wouldn't," she said.

"We need to talk to him as soon as possible," Clara said. "We best get a disguise arranged for you. This way to the studio proper."

She led Miss Pink through to the area where Oliver took his studio pictures. The heavy armchair he had used for Mrs King's cats was still sitting in the centre, ornamented with white hairs and scratch marks. There was a wardrobe in one corner and a clothes chest beside it. Clara opened the wardrobe and started searching for something to disguise Miss Pink with.

"You should take your make-up off," Tommy told the beauty queen, perhaps not as diplomatically as he could have. "Your make-up is distinctive."

"What does that mean?" Miss Pink bridled.

"He means that most women around Brighton wear little make-up," Clara interjected, bringing over a green shawl and a fur stole that had seen better days. "You look noticeably glamorous wearing it."

Clara had smoothed the water and Miss Pink was soothed.

"I take your point. Most women rush about with little concern for their appearance. I stand out because I take care to make myself beautiful. Is there a bathroom I can wash my face in?"

Clara indicated there was one down the hall. It contained little more than a toilet and a sink, but it would serve the purpose. Miss Pink departed to remove her gilding.

Tommy gave a derisive snort as soon as she was out of earshot.

"Glamorous?" he said to his sister. "She looks like a dog's dinner with all that powder and eyeliner. I can't tell what is real and what is not. I am not sure there is an inch of visible skin she has not ornamented garishly."

"Shush," Clara scolded him lightly. "She moves in a different world to us, one where that sort of elaborate paint job is necessary, expected, even. Remember the trade fair for Albion Industries we held at the Pavilion? All the girls who worked for Albion were just the same."

Tommy cast back his mind and did recall.

"I thought then it was awful," he said. "Why do women do it?"

"The same reason as certain exotic birds grow elaborate tail feathers and create their own unique song to sing. To attract others to them."

"Miss Pink does not seem the sort to be desperate for a husband," Tommy said. "And she has Sigmund, who she admits is not swayed by the make-up."

"The exotic birds are attracting a mate," Clara corrected him. "With humans, it is a little more complex. We use our appearance to attract people to us for a variety of reasons. Including, to improve our business prospects."

Tommy understood at long last.

"You mean, the make-up is a way of getting other women to notice Miss Pink?"

"Her false glamour makes her stand out and draws their attention," Clara nodded. "The way beauty products sell is because you are creating this idea in a person's mind of what they ought to look like and are selling them the promise that if they use your product, they shall achieve that desired effect. You don't have a housewife with tired eyes and sore knees on your advertisements because people do not want to look like that. They want to look like someone who appears glamourous, dramatic, and somewhat out of the ordinary. It is all about allure."

Tommy considered this for a while.

"Makes the adverts for men's safety razors seem rather dull in comparison," he said. "All we get is promises for no more razor burn and a blade that does not need sharpening quite so often. I don't recall any advert that made shaving seem glamorous."

"That is the difference between men and women," Clara patted his shoulder. "You want what is practical, what is achievable. Women want the impossible."

"You rather denigrate your own sex there," Tommy said.

"I am speaking the truth. Women are sadly conditioned to feel their worth depends largely upon their appearance. They are taught that only the pretty girls get good husbands and so must do all they can to enhance what nature has given them. It is the way of the world."

"That is depressing," Tommy's brows sunk down as he listened. "Do you feel that way?"

"Sometimes I fret about my appearance," Clara admitted. "But not often. I hope I am more than just my outward features."

"I think O'Harris would gladly agree you are," Tommy promised her.

They were distracted from their heart-to-heart by the return of Miss Pink. It had taken a considerable effort, much scrubbing, and the relentless application of soap to remove her heavy mask. Now she walked in through the door and for a second neither recognised her.

Without her make-up, Miss Pink was decidedly plain. She had small lips that framed a narrow mouth. Her eyes were rather sunken and her cheekbones undefined. She was utterly unremarkable and would not have been cast a second look if she walked down the street as she was. It was hard to suppose this was the runner-up beauty queen of Britain.

"I know," she said, seeing the looks on their faces. "I am not exactly an oil painting."

"Looks are fleeting," Clara reminded her. "Beauty fades. It is what lies beneath that matters."

"If you are a private detective, maybe," Miss Pink snorted. "Or a secretary, or a schoolteacher, or some other job where it is more about your mind than your looks. But a beauty queen? There is only one thing the judges are looking for. Presence. A beautiful, ethereal presence. Girls would kill for that."

"Spoken in rather poor taste, under the circumstances," Tommy reminded her.

Miss Pink merely shrugged. She headed over to where Clara had been piling suitable items of clothing for her to choose from. She selected a dark black shawl to go over her red coat and wrap around her neck. Then she picked up a cloche hat that completely smothered her head when she donned it. Her bleached blonde hair vanished, and she started to look very ordinary.

"Well?" she demanded of them angrily. "Do I look dowdy enough yet?"

Clara would have said that just removing her make-up had changed her so dramatically it was unlikely anyone would recognise her, but she thought that might be pushing her luck under the circumstances.

"It will do," she said instead. "Now we need to find Sigmund and see what he has to say about all this."

Chapter Eight

No one gave Miss Pink a second glance as they made their way by bus to the home of Sigmund Coppleburg. This clearly irked Miss Pink, who was rather more used to people giving her their undivided attention. It suited their purpose but reinforced to her delicate ego that without her intense make-up regime she was rather ordinary – worse than ordinary, not worth even the look that an ordinary person might receive. She sat in sullen silence, pretending the lack of attention did not sting, nor enhance her deep fear that she was ugly.

Her mood was not assisted by the snippets of conversation they heard as they travelled. The Pink's Pills scandal was spreading, and it was the most exciting thing that a lot of people had to talk about.

"Brenda bought some of those pills, you know."

"Ooh, did she!"

"Always worrying about her weight, is Brenda. I told her, 'Love, you have nothing to fret about, it is natural to be a little plump after four kiddies'. But it makes no difference."

"Did she take them?"

"She did. They didn't make her sick like the others,

though. She reckoned they made her sleepy, that's all."

"Well, I heard from Gloria, that her neighbour's daughter bought some and being a cautious sort, fed one to the cat first before taking it herself, and the cat died!"

"Since when did you believe a word Gloria said? She was claiming she met the king at the train station last summer!"

"Did you hear about poor Mrs Wood? Dead she is, because of those pills."

"That's murder that is! Plain murder!"

"Poor Mrs Wood, such a frail thing at the best of times. Don't know why she got it into her head to take them."

"That will be her Alf's influence. He is a scoundrel and hounds her about her appearance."

"Well, he can't hound her now."

"Someone ought to be hung for it!"

Miss Pink closed her eyes and tried not to let the pain she was feeling show on her face. It seemed every other person had their opinion on the pills, and few were kindly. Clara patted her hand in a friendly fashion, not sure if it would be appreciated, but deciding it was worth the effort.

Miss Pink turned her gaze to her slowly.

"I am finished," she said, softly.

"Now, now, that is never the case," Clara reassured her.

Miss Pink gave a cynical snort.

"I might as well give myself up now. Throw myself on the mercy of the courts. I might at least get some media attention and I would be able to smarten myself up."

Clara sighed.

"It is all about people looking at you, isn't it? You cannot abide being out of the limelight for just a moment."

"I am not you," Miss Pink said snidely. "I could not be happy as someone dull and ordinary."

"Thanks," Clara removed her consoling hand, her sympathy used up. "Maybe you ought to think less about yourself and more about the people who are lying in hospital right now. They are truly suffering."

Miss Pink did not want to hear such talk; she was not

about to feel remorse for something she deemed not her fault. She turned her head and scowled out the window at the world beyond.

They were all relieved when they could leave the bus at the stop nearest Sigmund's house. He lived in the countryside, down a rutted lane that was hellish for car springs. He had a little cottage he rented, that was heading towards a dilapidated condition, which was why he was able to afford it. The thatch was several years past its best, the walls grey instead of white, and with green patches that suggested a growth of some description infesting the plasterwork. The windows were fast going rotten, and the door was not far behind. It must have stuck at some point and an overly enthusiastic homeowner had attempted to fix the problem by sawing a chunk off the bottom. The result was a distinct gap all along the lower edge of the door. As they approached the door, Tommy noted a snail working its way through the gap with ease.

Miss Pink knocked on the peeling wood.

"Sigmund has been working all hours on our next batch of pills. Which will be pointless now."

It was not long before a gentleman in his mid-twenties opened the door. He was what you would expect from a pharmacist's assistant. Tall and gangly, with very neat brown hair and very clean hands with long, dextrous fingers. He looked younger than his age; you could have described him as boyish in appearance. His shirt and trousers were covered by a long apron, which made him look even more like a shopkeeper.

"Rose?"

"We need to come in Sigmund," Rose said gruffly. "It is urgent."

"You are not dressed up?" Sigmund said, though his voice sounded pleased rather than disappointed.

"We need to come in," Rose repeated and then she rudely pushed past him and entered the cottage.

Sigmund stepped back to let her through, apparently more curious about her lack of make-up than troubled by her attitude. Clara and Tommy paused on the doorstep before him.

"Clara Fitzgerald, and Tommy Fitzgerald," Clara introduced them.

"Sigmund Coppleburg," Sigmund responded. "Something has occurred?"

"Rather," Tommy winced. "Can we come in?"

Sigmund seemed to have assumed they would just barge past him like Miss Pink had. He blinked and was startled to be asked, then he stepped back to let them in.

They found Miss Pink in the front room of the cottage, which was best described as quaint, though more realistically it should be described as cramped, damp and a potential hazard to health. The chimney was pouring smoke into the room and the fire in the grate was failing to remove the 'moist' feeling in the air of the room.

"I told you to get that chimney swept," Miss Pink complained to Sigmund the second he appeared. She had opened a window to let out some of the choking smoke.

"I was getting around to it," Sigmund replied. "I wasn't expecting you today."

Sigmund was not a quick-thinking chap in some regards, and it took him time to work out when a situation was serious. It was now slowly getting through to him that his lover had turned up without her usual decadent flamboyance and at a time of day he had not expected. Not to mention the extra people who had turned up with her. Sigmund was beginning to feel the first pangs of anxiety.

"Something has happened?" he asked.

Miss Pink had been bottling her anger, trying not to blame him for this disaster, but now she stood before him, it was as if someone had flicked a switch in her brain and all she really wanted to do was put her hands around Sigmund's throat and squeeze until he went blue. Words would not work their way from her mouth, at least not the words that were appropriate to say, and silence, for the moment, was preferable.

Clara interceded.

"Some of the Pink's Pills sold yesterday have made people seriously sick."

"What?" Sigmund seemed genuinely surprised. "It must be a coincidence."

"No, old man, the pills are the culprits. A dozen people are in hospital after taking them and one woman has sadly died," Tommy said.

Sigmund sat down suddenly in the nearest armchair, which groaned alarmingly under his weight.

"Nothing in those pills is harmful," he said, repeating a refrain they had heard plenty of times already.

"Some of the pills have arsenic in them," Miss Pink said, her voice a hiss, her words thrust through her teeth and shot at Sigmund like daggers. "Or so the doctors think."

"Arsenic!" Sigmund was aghast.

"The contaminated pills may have been accidental," Clara said, sensing things were going to get nasty between the lovers and business partners fast if they were not careful.

"You were careless, Sigmund!" Miss Pink barked at him. "You mixed arsenic with some of the pills!"

"No!" Sigmund said fiercely. He had previously seemed content to take Miss Pink's sharp words with an affable and forgiving manner. Now he was angry, and it was something to see. "I take pride in my work, Rose. I would never be so negligent! For that matter, you won't even find a pinch of arsenic in this house!"

"You must have mice," Clara glanced up at the bulging ceiling and aging beams. "An old cottage like this would attract them. How do you deal with them?"

"Snap traps," Sigmund growled. "Far more humane than arsenic. Even mice deserve a little consideration. If I am honest, the mice don't bother me. Live and let live."

Miss Pink gave a theatrical shudder at this statement.

"On that front, I can confirm it is true. Sigmund has a rather soft nature for animals. I once went into the pantry and discovered two mice sitting bold as brass on a shelf eating some bread."

"I left it out for them," Sigmund added. "I work upon the theory that if I supply them with food I do not require, they shall leave alone that which I do want."

"I think that might be overly optimistic about the thinking power of a mouse," Tommy said.

Sigmund merely shrugged.

"If you have no arsenic in this cottage, you will not be troubled by us taking a look around?" Clara asked him.

Sigmund's placid nature was being pushed to the limit. "Who are you?"

"They are private detectives," Miss Pink stated. "They helped me get out of town when things became a little hairy. People were marching up to me and accusing me of all sorts of things."

"Hence your change of appearance," Sigmund nodded. "How bad is it?"

"Terrible Sigmund," Miss Pink was too proud to cry, but if she had been otherwise inclined now would have been the moment for tears to prick her eyes. "I am ruined."

Sigmund picked up the use of the singular but refrained from mentioning it.

"How do private detectives help us?" he said.

"We are here on behalf of a friend who was poisoned by the pills," Clara explained. "We wish to determine what happened."

"And who is to blame," Sigmund said quickly, indicating he was not so mild-mannered and oblivious as they might have supposed.

"That too," Clara agreed.

"I am going to ask them to work for me," Miss Pink suddenly interrupted, her voice firm. "I need someone independent to find out who is responsible for this. If there is some way I can salvage my reputation from this wreckage, I must at least try."

Miss Pink was looking directly at Clara, defying her to refuse to assist her. Clara merely smiled. She would continue investigating this case whether she was working for Miss Pink or not but having her cooperation would be extremely useful.

"Can we search the house?" she repeated.

"You can," Sigmund said, though his tone was hard. "You will find nothing, though. Certainly, no arsenic."

Clara gave him a polite smile and left the room with Tommy. The cottage was not vast, which was just as well, for it was filled with places that arsenic could either be stored or hidden. There seemed innumerable hidden cupboards, built into the walls, tucked beneath the stairs. The moment you thought you had searched the last one, you spied another.

Behind the front room there was a kitchen, the cosiest area of the cottage with an ancient range and a sink vast enough to wash a whole family in at once. There was a pantry leading off the room and this Clara entered cautiously, not wanting to be taken by surprise by mice. She found the shelves were rather bare of supplies and surmised Sigmund was feeling the pinch of his current financial circumstances.

He had a lot to lose with these pills, much like Miss Pink and it made no sense that he would have deliberately poisoned a batch. That left them with a careless mishap, which he denied.

The pantry was arsenic-free, so was the kitchen and the cupboard under the stairs. They headed to the top floor which only contained a bedroom. The room was loosely furnished and clearly was a functional place which did not warrant much attention from Sigmund. Having searched all the places feasible to hide arsenic in, they concluded there was nothing there and returned downstairs.

"Where do you make your pills?" Clara asked the pharmacist's assistant.

"I have a workshop adjoining the house," Sigmund said. "I shall show you."

He rose and led them back to the kitchen. Opening a door into a paved area, he turned right to a long, low building that had been attached to the cottage at some later date in its history. It looked to be in slightly better condition than the rest of the property.

"Outhouse, washroom and workshop," Sigmund indicated three doors along the wall of the extension. "The outhouse is actually rather smart and not at all ghastly when you consider it is an outside convenience. Rose finds it distasteful, but I think it is rather hygienic having it separate from the house."

"We shall need to search these places too," Clara told him, ignoring his ramblings on outside plumbing.

They started with the outhouse. The room housing the toilet and a sink (which surprised them by having running water) must have once served another purpose as it was far larger than such places normally were and had a window in one side. There was no arsenic to be found and the washroom - which seemed rather under used – told a similar story. They chased away spiders in their hunt into old forgotten corners and upon dusty shelves, but they found no sinister white powder.

At last, they entered the workshop. It was a well-lit space, with not only a large window in one wall but a skylight in the roof. A table in the middle was carefully arranged with all the tools required for pill making. A dresser against the wall was stocked with herbs, jars, bowls, and spoons. Against the opposite wall was a small oil stove, used by Sigmund occasionally to heat his mixture.

They performed another thorough search and once again failed to find any arsenic.

"Now do you believe me?" Sigmund said, an edge to his voice.

Clara was carefully examining one of the bowls on the worktable, looking for any suspect traces of white powder. There were none.

"There is certainly no sign of arsenic here," she said.

Miss Pink visibly relaxed. Sigmund shot a glance at her, shocked by her lack of faith in him.

"Your workshop does not have a lock," Tommy said, lifting the latch on the door thoughtfully.

"No," Sigmund shrugged. "Why would it?"

Tommy exchanged a look with his sister. A new possibility had sprung to mind.

Chapter Nine

They stood outside the workshop and stared at the door, which was closed simply on its latch.

"You mean, just about anyone could have slipped into my workshop and poisoned a batch of pills?" Sigmund had repeated this statement twice so far, seemingly aghast anyone would be so underhand.

"If you did not poison the pills, then that has to be the solution," Clara informed him.

"I didn't poison the pills," Sigmund said firmly. "I had everything to lose doing that. As it is, I am not sure I shall make next month's rent. I suppose I shall have to grovel to Mr Dyer and ask for my old job back."

Miss Pink placed a hand on his arm in stoic support. After her initial anger and blame, she had realised her error and was now attempting to create a unified front with her business partner and lover.

"The next question would be – who would want to do this?" Tommy said. "Quite obviously it is someone wishing to do serious harm to either Miss Pink or Mr Coppleburg. A rival, perhaps?"

Miss Pink pulled a face.

"You hardly have to look far to find someone who hates

me. Every girl at every beauty pageant I have attended and beaten would be glad to stick a dagger in my back."

"Nasty business," Tommy winced. "Who would have thought something that was all about beauty would be so ugly underneath."

"It's an ugly business in general," Sigmund said. "The rivalry is appalling. It is why I want Rose to get out of it and settle into a life where people are not constantly criticising and belittling your appearance. Personally, I think beauty pageants are a disgrace."

"Says the man making diet pills," Clara said to him with an arched eyebrow.

"That is different," Sigmund said hastily. "Diet pills are not just about beauty. They are about health. Some people need to lose weight for medical reasons and if we can assist them, then we are doing them a service. We are not judging people."

Clara was sceptical on that but opted to say no more. They had other things to concern themselves with.

"Out of your rivals, Miss Pink, who might have gotten wind of your diet pill endeavour?" she said instead.

Rose Pink gave a sigh as she tried to conjure an answer for this question.

"I am not sure. I have not mentioned this to anyone, unless you count the printer who made up my labels and advertisement materials."

"Someone might have been watching you," Tommy said. "People do crazy things when they are jealous of others and your diet book was already in circulation and doing well. Someone might have thought to begin following you to determine what you would do next."

"That is possible," Sigmund interjected. "Remember, Rose, the other night you said you thought someone had been following you from the bus stop?"

"That happens all the time," Miss Pink waved away his suggestion. "People recognise me, and they want to talk to me, but they do not have the courage."

"Which bus stop?" Tommy asked.

71

"The one near the Tram Inn," Miss Pink replied. "I was heading home, and I thought someone was behind me, but they had disappeared by the time I reached my front door."

"Has anyone been lurking around your cottage, Sigmund?" Clara asked the pharmacist.

Sigmund scratched his head.

"I spend a lot of time in my workshop and so I don't really see people in the lane or so forth. There is a footpath that runs along the bottom of my garden and during the summer it can get quite busy with walkers. If someone was walking along there, I would not give them a second glance."

They seemed at a dead end.

"Do you have any enemies, Sigmund?" Clara persisted.

Sigmund scratched his head again, making a rustling sound like the bristles of a broom being swept on stone.

"I am not the sort to collect enemies. I live a quiet life."

"Someone could be jealous of your relationship with Miss Pink?" Tommy suggested.

"Not that I know of," Sigmund shrugged. "The only person who could potentially be angry with me, would be Mr Dyer if he knew why I left his employ. But I don't think he does know and, anyway, poisoning the pills has harmed him too."

There was truth in that statement, and they all knew it.

"What now?" Miss Pink asked them.

Clara was not really sure. Without a suspect to pursue it was hard to say which direction to take next. It seemed obvious that whoever had contaminated the pills had done so by slipping into Sigmund's workshop. It would have been the easiest opportunity for them, but it was also a solution that offered no real clues as to the identity of the culprit.

"I think you should stay with me until this matter is resolved," Sigmund said to Miss Pink. "I don't think your house will be safe. People will go there to try to find you."

"He has a point," Clara concurred. "Your address is in

your diet book, informing people to write to you."

Tommy glanced at his sister, wondering when she had perused Miss Pink's diet book. Clara avoided his eyes.

Miss Pink pulled her mouth into a waspish pout, angered to be forced to leave behind her home and find sanctuary in the crumbling cottage. Had she not had the encounter in the pharmacy, or heard the talk on the bus, she might have been unmovable on the matter. As it was, she realised there was a real danger to her going home.

"Very well," she said at last. "Seeing as it is for the best."

"Why don't we all go in and have a cup of tea?" Sigmund suggested. "Maybe we can think up another idea or two?"

Clara was more inclined to head back to Brighton in time for visiting hour at the hospital. She might have been given the freedom to come and go as she pleased to see Oliver by the inspector's influence, but she felt it was best not to push her luck.

"Another time," she told them. "If you see anyone about the cottage, get a message to me. In the meantime, perhaps Miss Pink you could come up with a list of people who truly resented you and might go to such lengths as this."

Miss Pink nodded her head, then she and Sigmund headed into the cottage, leaving Clara and Tommy to find their way back to the bus stop.

"A thank you would have been nice," Tommy huffed.

"I am not sure Miss Pink knows the words," Clara replied. "She is hard to the core. She takes what she can get from this world and assumes people will do things for her because of who she is."

"She is arrogant."

"She is a narcissist," Clara elaborated. "A complicated one because her ego is fragile, and her beauty comes from artificial devices. She is easily knocked of her confidence. I feel sorry for her rather than annoyed or offended. I cannot see a happy future for Miss Pink, not while she is so focused on a false façade to give herself worth."

"She has Sigmund," Tommy said. "He seems a sensible

sort."

"How long will he survive her ego?" Clara responded.

"That makes me sad," Tommy said, glancing back at the cottage they had left behind. "For all it seems that Miss Pink has a lot, has everything in fact and women are jealous of that, your words make me think she really has nothing that truly matters."

"Not quite, she has Sigmund for the time being," Clara held up a finger as she made her point. "If she realises he is a true blessing in her life, she might just get lucky. If she does not, well, yes, she will likely end up with nothing truly worthwhile in her life. Still, that is not our problem. We have a poisoner to find."

They waited for the bus, each lost in their thoughts and travelled nearly all the way home before Tommy had an idea.

"You know how you said Abigail's arrival in Brighton just as the Pink's Pills were launched seemed a little suspicious?"

"Yes," Clara said.

"Supposing it was intended and supposing the tampering with the pills was… what do you call it? Oh, yes, industrial sabotage!"

"I cannot imagine Abigail or Albion Industries would stoop to poisoning a rival's products."

"Really? They stole a lipstick formula quite blatantly and were pretty callous about how they treated its creator after he was no longer of use to them."

"That is different," Clara said, though she had to admit she could not quite explain why it was different.

They hopped buses until they found themselves at the hospital in time for visiting hour. They headed inside with the other visitors and upstairs to Oliver's ward. Oliver was looking much brighter as he sat up in bed. He had his grin back and beamed it at Clara.

"Good to see you again," he said happily.

"We have quite a tale to tell you!" Tommy chuckled at

him.

Then he settled down to regale Oliver with the events of the morning, including how they had used his studio props to disguise Miss Pink. Oliver was less than impressed with this information.

"I cannot feel gracious towards that woman after what I have been through," he grumbled. "I confess it was my own stupidity and vanity that caused me to buy the pills, but I should not have been harmed by them for that."

"No, you should not have been harmed," Clara sympathised with him. "However, it does seem very unlikely that Miss Pink caused this debacle either on purpose or by carelessness. It has cost her tremendously too."

Oliver was not mollified by that information.

"Well, whether she is a victim or not, I would not mind an apology."

It was a good point and something Clara would bring up with Miss Pink the next time she saw her. They talked with Oliver about other things after that, trying to distract him from his misfortune. He had been told by the doctors that he could return home possibly as soon as the following day.

"I am out of danger and there is not much more they can do for me," he explained. "I have been able to eat some soup today and they might let me have some sandwiches later. All being well, as long as my stomach holds up, I can go home to my father's house tomorrow. They won't let me go home alone, not just yet, so I shall be inflicting myself upon the old man."

"I am sure he will be glad to have you there," Clara said. "He was very worried about you."

"He is a funny old coot," Oliver chuckled. "Got a heart of gold, really."

They used up every minute of the visiting hour and did not leave until the matron appeared and started to kick out any visitors who were hanging around after the bell had gone. Oliver thanked them for coming and was still grinning as they departed.

"He seems to have survived all right," Tommy said with relief once they were back in the corridor.

They were just heading for the stairs when they spied Inspector Park-Coombs stood in the doorway of a room. He gave them a nod.

"Collecting some details about Mrs Wood," he informed them before they could ask what he was up to. "Were you visiting Mr Bankes?"

"Yes, he is doing well," Clara replied. "I am sorry to hear about Mrs Wood."

"She has been taken to Dr Deáth," Park-Coombs said, referring to the police coroner. "But the doctors are fairly confident her heart gave out from the strain of the poisoning."

"It just makes the blood boil," Tommy shook his head.

"You are not alone in feeling like that," Park-Coombs said with a raised eyebrow. "Mr Dyer's shop window was splattered with eggs and flour when he was closed for lunch. No witnesses, of course, but we can guess the reason behind it. I have suggested he stay closed for a few days."

"People are angry, but they are lashing out in the wrong direction," Clara said. "I was angry with Dyer too, but when I calmed down, I realised he had done everything expected of him and possibly more besides. He was only selling a product after all, and he had been assured it was safe and had seen the recipe to confirm that. The only other step he could have taken was to try a pill himself, but even then, he might have taken a pill from one of the uncontaminated batches and so we would be no further forward."

"I have had my constables out all-day confiscating Pink's Pills from people. Most were glad to give them up, though one or two protested even after they were told what had happened. Some people have no sense," Park-Coombs waggled his moustache in annoyance at the thought. "So far, we have not encountered any other bottles with contaminated pills. It seems it was those dozen bottles that had been tampered with."

"A dozen bottles out of a hundred," Tommy sighed. "Quite the lottery."

"Have your lab boys come up with anything?" Clara asked.

Park-Coombs nodded.

"The poison was definitely arsenic, but it was not in the pills themselves, rather it was added to the bottles. On the whole it was not a lot, either. You see, the pills are powdery, and the powder collects in the base of the bottle, as well as coating the pills. The arsenic mixed with the powder and when someone took a contaminated pill, they consumed arsenic without realising it."

"Then we can exclude the pills being accidentally mixed with arsenic in them," Clara nodded. "By the way, we had to rescue Miss Pink from an ugly scene, and we helped her to escape to the cottage where her lover and business partner makes the pills for her. We searched the place and there was not a hint of arsenic, but the workshop where he makes the pills would be easy for someone to enter and lace the bottles with poison."

"Great, then we have a lot more suspects to start considering," Park-Coombs groaned. "Care to give me the address of this cottage?"

Clara was happy to do so.

"There is one last thing, and it may be unimportant, but it would be remiss of me not to mention it," Clara continued. "Abigail Sommers appeared on my doorstep yesterday."

"Abigail Sommers?" Park-Coombs did not recall her for a moment, then his memory clicked in. "Albion Industries! Now, that is curious."

"I know, Inspector, but leave her to me," Clara smiled at him. "I shall winkle out the truth from her."

Chapter Ten

It was early evening as they arrived home after a long day. Annie had dinner waiting on the table, a brown teapot steaming gently and promising dark, restorative tea. Clara felt a weight lifting off her shoulders.

"How is Oliver?" Annie asked at once, she had a soft spot for the slightly bumbling photographer.

"He is much improved and shall hopefully go home tomorrow. He shall be living with his father for the time being while he makes a full recovery," Clara explained.

"Then I shall make sure he has plenty of meals to keep him going. I dread to think the sort of food Mr Bankes prepares for himself. Men are thoughtless with their meals. It shall be bacon and fried potatoes every night, or worse. No, I shall make him stews and pies and all sorts of things to restore him," Annie said firmly.

Considering Oliver had ended up in this situation because he had been agonising over his waistline, Clara fancied being faced by Annie's cooking talents while recovering would only compound Oliver's original problem. Still, she was not going to argue about it. She quite agreed that Mr Bankes senior did not seem the sort to be much of a cook.

"Where is Abigail?" Tommy asked, noting that only three place settings had been arranged at the table.

"She went out and informed me she would not be back for dinner," Annie said, a hint of hurt in her voice.

Annie felt someone missing a meal she had prepared was rather an affront.

"Now where could she have gone?" Clara mused. "She is supposed to be down here on holiday."

"She could have gone to the picture house," Tommy suggested. "Though, they do not usually have a showing at this time of day."

"You ask me, she was not off for a leisurely evening," Annie said darkly. "She was not dressed up for a dance and she was wearing a very nondescript coat. I would almost say she was dressed to avoid being noticed."

"She is up to something," Clara declared. "I am convinced it is to do with Pink's Pills. I really wanted to talk to her."

She sighed, but Abigail could wait, and her stomach could not. She had not eaten since that morning, and she had an unwelcome hollow feeling in her belly. All thoughts of poisonings and suspicious pills were pushed to one side as she focused on dinner.

Abigail did not return home until later that night. Clara was still up, compiling notes on her case and responding to correspondence she had been putting off for a couple of days. She had received two messages while she was out from people who were anxious about the Pink's Pills fiasco and suggested she investigate it, though neither intimated they were prepared to pay her for the effort. She wondered if people supposed she was rather like a policeman and was paid by some government fund, and so she would investigate something whether she was hired to do so or not. Now, sometimes Clara did investigate things without being hired to do so, usually when someone unfortunate was placed in an impossible position and there was no one else to help them, but these were exceptions and had to be worthwhile. She did not place the Pink's Pills scandal in the same category.

Of course, she was investigating the matter on her own initiative, because of Oliver. But that was different, besides, Miss Pink had made the suggestion she would be prepared to hire her to find the solution to the mystery – she ought to have clarified that matter further.

She pushed the messages to one side, feeling they were rather pointed and imposing, implying she was neglecting her civic duty if she did not investigate the pill affair for nothing.

She was mulling over all this confused thinking when Abigail came in the front door. The woman entered quietly, and pushed the door closed softly before locking it. Presumably Annie had given her the spare key.

Abigail seemed to think no one would still be up. Clara moved to the doorway of the parlour to disabuse her of that idea. Abigail managed her surprise with dignity.

"Oh, I thought you would be abed. I did not see a light in the parlour."

"I am working by the fire, it gives enough light for what I am about," Clara replied. "Did you have a nice evening?"

"Yes," Abigail said quickly and in a manner that seemed overly bright and somewhat insincere. "It was very pleasant."

Clara wondered what it had entailed, noting that wet leaves were stuck to Abigail's usually spotless shoes and there was a thin tendril of ivy laced through the belt of her coat. It suggested she had been hanging around in bushes.

Abigail did not strike her as the sort of girl to meet a lover in such a clandestine fashion. She was too keen on her home comforts for a start. It raised the question of what she had really been up to.

"You look a little cold," Clara said. "The nights are really turning bitter. Come sit by the fire and warm through."

Abigail accepted the invitation without a murmur and followed Clara to the aging armchairs by the parlour fire. She sat down and held out her hands to warm them. She had discarded her coat in the hallway. Clara had half a mind to search it for further clues but told herself that was an intrusion too far on her guest's privacy. She settled down instead to some gentle interrogation.

"I met Miss Pink today," she began.

"Miss Pink?" Abigail asked, her feigned ignorance not convincing.

"Pink's Pills," Clara picked up a newspaper from the floor. It was the evening edition and contained the front-page piece on the pill panic. Gilbert had dropped a copy to her when he delivered Miss Pink's address. She had not informed him that she already knew where Miss Pink was.

Abigail took the paper and glanced at the news article. She was too tired to act surprised or shocked, indicating she already knew what it contained.

"Oh yes, the pills," she said quietly. "Miss Pink has really made a fist of things."

"She claims sabotage and I have a mind to believe her," Clara responded. "It rather reminds me of the affair with Albion Industries' trade fair a couple of years ago."

She wanted to remind Abigail of the position she had been placed in during that ordeal. Abigail had been under suspicion as the saboteur, (among other things), she ought to have sympathy for someone else wrongly accused.

"It is not really the same," Abigail shrugged. "This woman should never have been dabbling with diet pills."

Abigail said this very firmly. Clara sensed something behind her words.

"Does Albion Industries make diet pills?" she asked.

"Not at this moment in time," Abigail said, though her eyes did not quite meet Clara's.

"Perhaps they are considering it?"

"I doubt it," Abigail gave the newspaper a last glance and then yawned dramatically. "Gosh! I am exhausted."

"You should not go to bed without a warm cup of tea inside you," Clara said swiftly, determined not to lose her so soon. "It will take the chill from you and prevent a cold. Annie tells me so and she would never forgive me if I failed to make you a cup before you went to bed."

"That is not necessary Clara," Abigail assured her.

"Oh, it is," Clara said brightly. "I insist. I am making myself one, anyway."

Abigail protested a little more, but Clara would not hear a word and made her way pointedly to the kitchen, where she set the big copper kettle on the stove to boil.

"What are your plans for tomorrow?" Clara asked her as casually as she could.

"I haven't made any as yet," Abigail replied.

Clara wanted to call her a liar to her face but doubted that would achieve much.

"I must say, I never thought to see you with leaves caked to your shoes!" she said laughingly.

Abigail seemed to notice the state of her footwear for the first time. She had not removed her shoes upon entering the house. She now glanced down at them in horror.

"I am so sorry Clara! Have I traipsed leaves into the parlour?"

"No, no, that is not what I meant," Clara said lightly. "It was an honest assessment. You have quite ruined those shoes, you know. Where on earth did you go walking?"

Abigail sat down in a kitchen chair and pulled off one of her shoes, looking at the soft leather now marred by the wet leaves. She realised, belated, that her stockings were wet also.

"Oh, bother!" she declared.

"Abigail, did you encounter some trouble while you were out?" Clara asked, her tone now gently (and genuinely) concerned.

"Don't be ridiculous Clara, what trouble could I find here?"

"I just cannot fathom how you ended up with wet leaves all over your shoes," Clara said. "It is not like you at all. You skirt puddles and stick to pavements. The thought of you walking down a country lane or across grass doesn't make sense to me. Yet clearly you have done something of the sort."

Abigail was trying to pry the leaves from her shoe, caking her fingers in dirt in the process.

"They are ruined, aren't they?" she said plaintively and without answering Clara's implied question. "They are my favourites. Is there no hope for them?"

She looked so bereft in that moment Clara went to her aid.

"Let me look," she took the shoe and noted that it was sodden inside. Abigail had stomped through somewhere very wet. The sole and sides of the shoe were caked in mud as well as leaves. Clara surveyed the mess thoughtfully.

"Maybe if we let them dry by the fire, then the mud will be easier to remove with a brush? Annie might be able to salvage them."

Abigail looked relieved.

"I know it sounds absurd. I can afford to buy a dozen pairs of shoes, but these ones have always been so comfortable," she laughed at herself. "Listen to me, mourning a pair of shoes!"

"Where were you tonight, Abigail?" Clara persisted. "You were gone so long."

"I met with an old friend," Abigail answered without hesitation. "We took a walk, and I was not as careful with my shoes as I should have been."

"Not like you at all," Clara muttered.

Abigail did not seem to hear her, so she added.

"I did not know you had further friends in Brighton, aside from myself."

"It is nothing scandalous," Abigail laughed at her. "I met them quite by chance, in fact. I was going to the Lyons teahouse for a light supper – Annie must forgive me for not being present for dinner, but I am on a strict diet, and I knew I could not dissuade her from feeding me up."

"Strict diet?" Clara asked.

"Not for my weight," Abigail said with a smile. "Oh, I might as well tell you. I have become a vegetarian."

Abigail was quite proud of this.

"I knew Annie would not understand and would try to feed me roast beef or something."

Clara had to admit this was the most likely reaction from Annie who could not understand how a person could survive without meat in their diet.

"Anyway, as I was entering Lyons, I spied someone I had not seen in years and went over to speak to them. They were alone also, so we ended up having supper together and then we took a walk."

It was a perfectly reasonable explanation, but Clara did not believe it. It was not just the shoes, but the length of time Abigail had been supposedly walking around with her friend.

"I am glad you had a nice evening," she said, now pouring hot water into a teapot. "Look, I have to work on this case with the pills…"

"You have been hired?"

"Not precisely, but I have been tentatively asked to investigate," Clara hedged around her concerns over Oliver. "What I was going to say was, I shall make some time for us to do something together."

"That is not necessary, Clara. I am already imposing upon you. I never expected you to keep me company as well."

"Nonsense, it will be nice," Clara said firmly. "First thing tomorrow, we shall go into town and do some shopping."

"I cannot," Abigail said awkwardly. "I have to be somewhere."

"You said a moment ago you had no plans for tomorrow," Clara pointed out.

Abigail pulled a face at being caught out.

"I had forgotten, for just a moment, that I made some plans. Another time Clara if that is ok?"

Clara had not really been interested in a shopping trip anyway. She had mentioned it to see what response she received.

Abigail was now serving herself tea and making haste

to consume it so she could get away from Clara.

"Gosh, Brighton is different in autumn, is it not?" she said brightly, making the effort to switch subject. "It seems like a completely different place!"

"Abigail, if you were in any trouble, you know you could come to me and speak freely," Clara said seriously.

"Trouble?" Abigail laughed off the word. "I have kept very clear of mischief since that awful encounter at the trade fair. You have nothing to fret about in that regard."

She gulped down her tea. It must have been far too hot and would have burned her mouth.

"Thank you, Clara, but I must change my stockings before my feet freeze. I shall see you in the morning, I expect."

With a cheery smile she departed, her stockinged feet making a slap-slap noise on the floor tiles. Clara watched her leave, a frown slowly forming on her brow. Abigail was involved in something, something she was determined to keep secret. Perhaps it had nothing to do with the Pink's Pills matter. Maybe she was reading more into the situation than was necessary. But something was afoot, and Clara was not a great believer in coincidences. Abigail's sudden arrival was too nicely timed.

It slowly occurred to Clara that if someone wanted to walk along the footpath near to Sigmund's cottage at this time of year, they would be best advised to wear stout walking boots, for the path would be strewn with wet, fallen tree leaves and surely muddy in places. Just the sort of path to ruin a nice pair of shoes walking along it.

Clara glanced at the shoes drying by the fire. Could it be Abigail had gone out to spy on the cottage? Or was Clara seeing connections where there were none? Speculating on such a thing because of wet shoes was surely a stretch.

Clara decided to leave the matter for the moment. Something would turn up and show her what Abigail had truly been doing.

Chapter Eleven

The following morning, Clara was disturbed from her first cup of tea by the arrival of Gilbert McMillan on her doorstep. The journalist was bubbling over with excitement and talking so fast he was largely indecipherable. Clara suggested he come through to the morning room at the back of the house, where autumnal sunlight was making everything glow, and have a cup of tea to calm him down.

"I hope no one else has died?" she asked anxiously as he settled into a chair and was offered a teacup by Annie.

Tommy had been summoned to hear the news also, and naturally Pip and Bramble were alongside him. There was no sign of Abigail and it seemed she had departed the house early on another of her mysterious errands.

Gilbert calmed down after a couple of sips of tea, though he managed to spill quite a lot into the saucer in the process, which earned a fierce glare from Annie.

"The newspaper article we printed yesterday evening really stirred up a commotion," Gilbert began. "We have had people hammering on the doors of the newspaper office from six this morning, wanting to speak to someone and tell their story. Honestly, the things I have heard today already."

Gilbert whistled in amazement to himself.

"Has anyone else been severely ill?" Tommy asked.

"Not that we have been told," Gilbert answered. "We have had people claiming the pills made their hair fall out, or that they developed pimples, and one lady insists they made her ankles swell, but that is the worst of it. Interestingly we have had several people come to us claiming the pills work for weight loss and they think our article was scurrilous."

"There are always some," Clara sighed. "The evidence is before them, and they refuse to see it."

Gilbert nodded.

"But it is all grist to my mill, if you see my point," he smirked. "Anyway, that is not what I am here about, though it is all very entertaining."

"Please recall that some people have been made severely ill by this entertainment," Clara reminded him. "Mrs Wood has died."

Gilbert made the effort to become more sober in his mood, but it was clearly not anything he felt sincerely.

"That is not why I am here. I came to see you because among those who were at our door today was Miss Pink herself. She was dressed incognito when she arrived, but it was her all right. Once I heard her voice and the way she talked, oh yes, it was her," Gilbert made a backwards snorting sound through his teeth. "I said she would look like a dog without the make-up."

"That is very rude Mr McMillan," Annie told him sharply.

McMillan shrugged his shoulders.

"I can't say she is pretty when she is not. Perhaps I could have used different words, but she has not exactly endeared herself to me. Shall I go on?"

"I think you should," Clara said, not playing up to the hurt tone in his voice.

McMillan was not one to hold on to offence, anyway. He had already shrugged off and forgotten Annie's scolding.

"Miss Pink came to place an announcement of her own in the paper," he said. "Of course, our next issue is not out until Friday, but she insisted we make a special exception and publish an early supplement."

"That does not sound like something the newspaper would do without good reason," Tommy remarked.

"Oh, she gave us good reason," Gilbert grinned. "She even offered to pay for the extra issues, though on that front we refused. It might compromise our integrity as an unbiased newspaper if people started to pay us to have their own stories published."

"You have integrity?" Tommy asked, raising an eyebrow.

"Underneath it all," Gilbert retorted.

"Deep underneath it," Clara said in a whisper that was not precisely quiet.

Gilbert merely chuckled.

"Well, we would not take her money, anyway, but after she told us what she wanted, we agreed to print a special supplemental edition. It won't be much, just a page or two, but it will get her the attention she wants."

"She is printing a denial of being responsible for the poisoning?" Clara asked.

"More strategic than that, though of course, she will be stating that her pills are perfectly safe."

"How can she when the evidence is before us all?" Annie gasped in exasperation.

Gilbert was now grinning his familiar ear-to-ear leer.

"Miss Pink is claiming her pills were maliciously sabotaged by a rival and that they are inherently unharmful. She intends to prove that by taking one of her own pills at a public meeting where everyone can see her consuming it direct from the bottle. I think it will be quite dramatic, all told."

"It sounds like the sort of huckster display travelling medicine men perform. Getting a stooge to consume a bottle of medicine and claim it makes them feel better in an instant," Tommy said cynically.

"She is doing it to demonstrate the pills are safe," Gilbert said. "That they were poisoned after they were made and not due to carelessness on the part of Miss Pink or her pharmacist."

"I am not sure it is a wise move," Clara said, feeling the performance was just as Tommy had remarked – a act that would have some intrigued and others jeering at the falsity of it all. "People are not so gullible."

"People bought those diet pills in the first place," Gilbert countered, amused she would say something like that. "Look, whatever your feelings on the performance itself, you have to admit it will be very interesting."

"You mean it will make good material for the newspaper and sell more copies," Annie interjected.

"Madame, you truly have a low opinion of me," Gilbert said, acting deeply hurt. "I am merely a purveyor of information."

"Hmph!" Annie huffed.

"Why are you telling us all this?" Clara asked the reporter. "Though I appreciate the advanced warning, I fancy you are not giving it to us merely as a gesture of good will."

Gilbert thought about acting hurt again, but he was tired of that charade and gladly smiled at Clara's insight.

"Miss Pink said she felt it would be prudent to have security at her little display. My editor thought that wise and after some debate, we felt the most logical person to ask would be you, as you are already involved, and people respect you, Clara."

"And also, the newspaper is hoping I shall do as you ask free of charge, saving you the task of hiring some burly men to act as security," Clara said, knowing how the minds of the newspapermen worked.

Gilbert smiled pleasantly, refusing to comment.

"I want to be paid for my time," Clara informed him. "Either by you or Miss Pink."

"But, as you are already investigating the mystery of the

poisoned pills, I thought you might consider this another opportunity to gather information," Gilbert said wistfully. "Someone at the event may prove the very suspect you are looking for."

"I doubt it," Clara said. "In any case, if you wish for me and Tommy to be there to guard Miss Pink's wellbeing, you shall have to pay us to do so. I could, after all, just turn up as an observer to look for suspects. You want me to take further responsibility and be potentially placed in danger."

"Danger?" Annie spluttered in alarm.

"I doubt it will amount to much, Annie," Clara said to her swiftly. "But Miss Pink has upset people and those people may wish to accost her. If I have to be between her and them, I think I deserve some compensation."

Gilbert worked over the idea, muttering under his breath, and clearly annoyed it had come to this, though also acutely aware that Clara could do exactly as she said and refuse to help. He sighed at last.

"Fine, Miss Fitzgerald, we shall compensate you for your services."

"Financial compensation," Clara made plain. "Not some subscription to the newspaper or free coupons to enter the monthly raffle you run, understood?"

Caught out again, Gilbert grumbled to himself and then nodded.

"Agreed."

Clara was satisfied.

"When is this event occurring?" she asked.

"Tonight, at seven o'clock. At the Methodist Hall," Gilbert explained. "We shall have the supplement out by lunchtime, so everyone knows. I am anticipating quite a crowd."

"I fear you are right," Clara said, thinking Miss Pink had no idea what she was doing and fearing this whole performance would be a disaster.

"We are arranging transport for Miss Pink," Gilbert added. "We felt it was best she arrives safe and sound."

"Public omnibuses are not a good place for Miss Pink at

the moment," Clara concurred.

"If you could arrive, say, at six-thirty, that will give plenty of time before the event to be sure all is well. Miss Pink will be very glad to know you are watching over her," Gilbert rose from his chair and handed back his teacup to Annie. "I have to go. Typing to be done! This is really turning into the story of the year."

"You mean, instead of the murder at the dog show, or the dramatic confessions of a certain local dentist?" Tommy asked wryly.

Gilbert cast him a grin.

"But those stories have already been written about, this is something new, and new is always better for newspapers. Anyway, see you later."

He was off down the hall and letting himself out before they had a chance to follow him. Clara folded her arms and stared at the closed front door a while after he was gone.

"She is a fool," Annie said, referring to Miss Pink. "What will taking one of her own pills prove?"

"She thinks it will demonstrate her innocence," Tommy remarked. "The problem is we are no closer to explaining how the pills were poisoned, so whether she proves her innocence or not, we are still left with sizeable questions."

"Where did Abigail go?" Clara suddenly asked, a thought that had been annoying her for a while returning to her mind.

"I could not tell you. She appears to be sneaking around worse than a scullery maid with a crush on the butler," Annie stated.

Clara frowned as she tried to work out this analogy. Annie came out with these phrases every once in a while, and it was best not to question them.

"The state of her shoes!" Annie added. "I spotted them by the kitchen range early this morning, when I went to see the chickens were all right."

Annie fretted over her chickens.

"There were leaves and mud stuck to them. I honestly thought for a moment they were your shoes, Clara."

"Should I be offended?" Clara asked.

"You are always ruining your shoes," Annie explained. "You walk about in the strangest of places."

"A muddy lane is hardly strange," Clara said, feeling her eyes wandering to the shoes she had been wearing the day before. They were sat innocuously by the coat stand and berated her silently by their marred appearance.

"Anyway, I could hardly believe they belonged to Abigail. I did not think she was the type," Annie concluded.

"She certainly has been skulking around in a most extraordinary manner," Tommy agreed. "She has to be up to something."

"I tried to get some information out of her last night, but to no avail," Clara said. "I am more worried than ever that this is connected to the Pink's Pills fiasco."

They were all thrown into silence by that idea. Annie was the one to intrude on their solemn thoughts.

"You will have to follow her, the next chance you get," she said firmly.

"You make it sound so easy, Annie," Tommy remarked.

"Isn't it?" Annie said stoutly. "I would do it if I were not so busy. Anyway, what other choice do you have?"

Clara was thinking a discreet telephone call to Albion Industries would not go amiss. For the moment, however, they had other things on their minds.

"I wonder if Abigail will come to this performance tonight," she said.

"I wonder how much trouble can be caused at such a thing," Tommy said, pulling a face. "Miss Pink has some nerve."

"She is desperate, it makes people brave in unexpected ways," Clara replied.

"I call it reckless," Annie declared. "What does she intend to achieve? She can't start selling her pills again with all this poisoning business hanging over them."

"She is trying to salvage her reputation," Clara said. "In the hopes that she will then be able to bring back Pink's Pills from the ashes of disaster at some point. She has to do something to mitigate the damage caused to her. Otherwise, her business plans are truly at an end."

Annie, though not inclined towards being a businesswoman, saw her point.

"That would be sad," she concurred. "Especially as this does seem to be the work of a jealous rival against her. That isn't fair."

Having said her piece, Annie departed for her kitchen. Tommy turned to his sister.

"What is the plan for today? We have quite some time to waste before our security duties tonight."

Clara tutted to herself, wondering why she had agreed to any of it and then reminding herself if she had refused and something occurred to Miss Pink, she would feel terrible about it.

"I was considering returning to Mr Dyer and seeing if there was any way the bottles could have been contaminated at the pharmacy."

"By Mr Dyer?"

"No, I fear by someone slipping in and deliberately tampering with bottles. I also thought Dyer might appreciate a little moral support. He is being targeted in all this too and while he might have sold the pills, he does not deserve to have his shop egged."

"That is true," Tommy agreed. "He might also recall someone paying undue attention to the pills?"

"Or he may remember someone who was overly interested in the pills. Someone who might have developed the idea of tampering with them."

Tommy's eyes widened at this suggestion. It was a good one.

"We ought to get going then," he said, shuffling the dogs away to the kitchen.

"Walkies later," he promised them.

"Yes, along a country footpath that runs beside a certain cottage," Clara added. "If only Pip were trained to pick up certain scents, like a bloodhound."

"You mean tell us if Abigail has been on the footpath,"

Tommy elaborated.

"I do mean that. Bramble has proven remarkable at tracking animals, but we have yet to develop that talent for tracking people. It could be quite the asset."

Tommy was contemplating how one went about teaching a small poodle to track people as he fetched his coat and left the house with his sister.

Chapter Twelve

Mr Dyer's shop door bore a notice that explained his premises were shut for the duration. He did not state the duration of what, but it was easy enough for anyone to guess if they had read the paper. The window display of Pink's Pills had been hastily removed and there was a gaping space where the bottles and advertisements had stood. This was largely obscured by the dried egg and flour that had been flung at his shop window and had formed gloopy puddles with great drips running down the glass. It would take some cleaning to remove it, but Mr Dyer was not in the mood for such a task at that moment in time.

Clara was unimpressed by the petty vandalism. She could understand people's anger and outrage, but to resort to such tactics was childish, especially when they were vented only at the man who was selling the pills in good faith. Now she had investigated the case further, she could see that Dyer had acted appropriately. He had not been duped by a reckless charlatan. In fact, everything she had seen suggested care and thoroughness had been taken over the pills from manufacture to delivery.

There were mistakes made, such as the failure of Coppleburg to have a lock on his workshop door, but then who would have imagined someone would go in and poison the pills? Few even knew about them until they were launched.

Clara turned her attention to the notice stuck to the door with thick, yellow tape. There was a note at the bottom that stated if someone urgently needed a prescription filled, or repeats of a certain medicine, they should go next door to the butcher's and ask after Mr Dyer.

Curious about this instruction, Clara and Tommy went next door and spoke to the butcher. He informed them he was acting as a doorman for Mr Dyer and only allowing people through to see the pharmacist who seemed genuine and not about to throw eggs at him.

"I just knock on our adjoining wall when I have someone to see him," he said cheerfully, moving to the wall behind his counter and thumping hard on the white tiles, so that various items rattled and clattered at the vibration. "He won't be long."

Mr Dyer appeared at the back of the butcher's shop a few minutes later. He had gone through his yard rather than use the front door and entered the butcher's shop from the back. He was still obviously anxious at who might be waiting for him but relaxed at the sight of Clara and Tommy.

"I am glad it is you two," he said. "I have had a rough couple of days. I could not have faced more irate customers."

"We thought you might need some moral support," Tommy told him, reflecting that not so long ago they were the irate customers, angered over Oliver's incapacitation.

"Thank you," Mr Dyer said gratefully. "Did you get Miss Pink home safely?"

"Yes, and we have a better idea of what happened to those pills that were poisoned. Might we come to your shop and talk?" asked Clara.

The butcher's shop was busy and some of the customers were looking over at Dyer. He was keen to get away.

"This way," he said and led them on his secret,

circuitous route back to his shop.

He let them into his parlour and asked if they wanted tea, which they declined.

"Mr Dyer, someone laced the pills with poison after they were in the bottles. Or rather they laced the bottles, not the pills, but because the pills were powdery, they picked up the poison and no one would have noticed the difference."

"Oh my," Mr Dyer said. "Yes, that would make sense. The pills were all coated in this fine powder. They broke up very easily, you see. I was going to mention it to Miss Pink as something to correct in the next batch. No one likes a crumbly pill."

"What we are yet to determine is how the poison was slipped into the bottles," Tommy added.

"What was the poison?" Mr Dyer asked nervously.

"Arsenic," Clara shrugged.

Mr Dyer shut his eyes and winced.

"Yes, that would make sense," he sighed. "The symptoms were consistent with arsenic poison."

"Do you sell arsenic in your shop?" Clara asked him.

Mr Dyer shook his head.

"I decided to stop selling rat and mouse poison some time ago."

"What about fly paper? Those contain arsenic," Tommy pointed out.

"I do not stock those either. Though my neighbour next door has quite the quantity of them hanging from his ceiling. The business of butchery rather attracts flies."

Mr Dyer had said this all without giving it much thought, now he realised what they were saying and stiffened.

"Are you implying I poisoned those bottles?" he said in fury.

"No," Clara said quickly. "I am just considering if it would be possible for someone with malicious intent to have come into this shop and tampered with some bottles. It has been known to happen."

Dyer's eyes wandered in the direction of his shopfloor, though he could not actually see it through the parlour wall. He considered for a moment.

"You raise a troubling possibility, but I would be a fool to ignore it. Over the years of my career, I have heard some strange tales of how poison has become mixed up with medicine. One of the reasons I stopped selling arsenic is I heard of a case where a shop boy accidentally knocked packets of rat poison from a shelf. They were unlabelled and they mixed with some packets of sleeping powders on a lower shelf. He endeavoured to sort out the packets, but they all looked identical. A wiser lad would have reported the mishap to his employer, but this boy did not want to be punished for the error, or lose his role, so he just pretended it didn't happen. I still shudder at the thought," Dyer shook his head. "You know how many people died because of that mishap? Six, in total. I swore to myself I should never allow something like that to occur in my shop, and now it has. Despite my best intentions."

He became morose again, lost in his thoughts.

"Mr Dyer," Clara roused him. "Perhaps we could go through all the places the pills were kept in your shop to determine if at any point they could have been tampered with?"

The pharmacist lifted his head and focused.

"Oh, of course," he stood and showed them through to his storage room. "I received the pills the day before they were to go on sale. They were delivered by Miss Pink in cardboard boxes with all the pictures and posters to accompany them. I placed them directly in this storage room."

The storage room was long and narrow, with only a very small window high up in a wall. Clara glanced around the shelves, looking for any products that could contain arsenic and which Mr Dyer might have forgotten about. It was not that she doubted his word, but sometimes people overlooked things. She had to admit that all the raw ingredients for his homemade pills were innocuous, and the manufactured products were equally innocent and well-labelled.

"Do you keep this storage room locked?" Tommy asked, having noticed the door had a lock.

"I do," Mr Dyer said. "It is not unusual for attempts to be made to steal medicines. Most of the boxes on my shop floor are for display only and are empty. All the real pills I keep locked in the big cabinets behind my counter, and the extra is kept locked in here."

"It was not locked just now," Tommy pointed out.

"Because the shop is closed and I have been using the opportunity to conduct a stock take," Mr Dyer had a ready excuse. "But I can assure you that normally it is kept locked."

"If the boxes were not tampered with in here, then perhaps they were tampered with once they made it onto your shop floor," Clara suggested.

"I spent the evening before the pills went on sale creating the display," Dyer explained. "I had to put up extra shelves, and all the advertising material, not to mention arranging all the dummy bottles."

"That's right, the bottles in the window did not contain pills," Clara said, suddenly recalling something she had been told earlier. "And there I was wondering if someone could have laced some of the bottles in the window while you were busy with customers."

"They could do so if they wished, but it would have achieved nothing. Those bottles were not for sale and did not contain pills," Mr Dyer was pleased to think he could have thwarted the poisoner in this regard. "It would have been foolish to stack the actual pills in the window. Someone might have stolen them. I told Miss Pink all that and insisted she supply dummy bottles for the window display."

"Then, we seem to have reached an impasse in regard to the shop being the place the bottles were poisoned. The opportunities were just not there," Clara said. "You are certain this storage room was locked overnight?"

"Miss Fitzgerald, I never forget to lock this room up when I go to bed. It would be unthinkable to fail to do so. Besides, I sleep above this room, and I do not sleep deeply. The chances of someone coming in here and tampering with bottles without awakening me are... are..."

Dyer groped for the right word to finish his statement.

"Slim?" Tommy suggested.

"I felt that was a rather inappropriate word, under the circumstances," Dyer said, pretending he had thought of that word. "I was thinking more along the lines of miniscule."

As he finished speaking, they heard a thudding, cracking noise outside the shop. The sound of further eggs being sent towards his window. Mr Dyer pulled a face.

"I have never known such hate from the people I have spent so many years trying to help," he slumped back against a shelf, causing several bottles of milk of magnesium to wobble perilously. "I have done all in my power to avoid a crisis such as this. I have tried to protect my customers. I have failed."

"Please, try not to be so hard on yourself," Tommy told him. "You could not foresee someone acting maliciously against Miss Pink like this. That was out of your control."

"An accidental poisoning, I would be angry over, but I could also understand it," Dyer said. "After all, we have all heard the stories. But, to suppose someone deliberately set out to tamper with the pills and make people so ill. To kill someone who was wholly innocent to this whole affair, it just sounds so utterly hideous and evil."

"I know," Clara said. "It is callous and shameful. The complete randomness of the victims. The culprit had no qualms about letting innocent people suffer for the sake of their revenge."

"Do you have any idea who did this, or why?" Dyer asked.

It was a question Clara had pondered a lot without coming up with many answers.

"It is a conundrum, as it seems few knew about the pills

until they were mentioned in the newspaper, and that was only shortly before they went on sale. That does not leave a lot of time for someone to consider sabotage," she said. "Aside from yourself, can you think of anyone else who knew about the pills?"

Dyer considered the question for a moment.

"I am afraid I cannot help you. My discussions with Miss Pink were always conducted in private and I had no reason to mention the pills to anyone."

"Everyone at the newspaper knew about them, once the article was arranged," Tommy pointed out.

"I cannot imagine anyone at the newspaper office being upset about diet pills or vengeful over them," Clara replied, finding an image of Gilbert McMillan springing to mind. "The logical assumption would be one of Miss Pink's former beauty contest rivals who wished to ensure she failed to profit from her success."

"I cannot help you there," Mr Dyer said. "I was not involved."

"It rather failed to reach my attention too," Clara admitted. "Though I suppose it was a big event for the town."

"Miss Pink was rather keen to inform me that it was quite the pageant. A lot of influential sponsors were involved," Dyer added, trying to be helpful. "She wanted to impress on me just what an honour it was to come runner-up in the contest."

"The contest certainly launched Miss Pink," Clara agreed.

Tommy was glancing around the storage room, and his distraction caught his sister's attention.

"What have you done with all the Pink's Pills stuff?" Tommy asked Mr Dyer.

"It is in that corner," Dyer pointed to a couple of boxes shoved beneath a shelf and with a mop and bucket placed in front. "The police told me I must not get rid of anything, because they may have to take it as evidence, or something like that."

"What are you after, Tommy?" Clara asked her brother.

"This idea sprang to mind while you were talking. I have this notion I saw something that could be important."

Tommy removed the mop and bucket and dragged out the boxes. He started to rummage in them, looking for whatever had caught his attention earlier. There was a rattle of pill bottles.

"Shame about those bottles," My Dyer remarked. "They would be handy to reuse. Glass bottles for pills are expensive and I try to reuse them as much as possible. I give my customers a discount on their next order if they return their pill bottles to me."

Clara thought it was funny how even in a dire situation, people could become distracted by something quite mundane. Tommy emerged from the box with one of the bigger advertisements in his hands. This one was printed on card and was a picture of Miss Pink at the beauty pageant – the very photograph Oliver had taken and had not been asked for permission to use it in such a way.

"What have you seen?" Clara asked, certain her brother had not dragged out the picture just to get another look at Miss Pink in her glamorous outfit.

"There," Tommy pointed to the top right corner. "I remembered glimpsing something when we first looked at the display. It was just something that wedged in my mind."

He showed the picture to Clara.

"It might be meaningless, and I might be mistaken, but in the background of this picture is a partial word. I would say it was an advertisement for one of the pageant sponsors."

Clara looked at where he pointed, and she saw the letters he meant. A-L-B-I-O. She stared and stared. Could it be?

"Albion Industries," she whispered to herself.

Chapter Thirteen

The obvious person to ask about the possible involvement of Albion Industries was Abigail but, yet again, when they returned home, she was nowhere to be found.

"I feel like she is treating our home as if it was no better than a boarding house," Annie huffed when she explained Abigail's absence to Clara and Tommy. "She doesn't even stop for meals."

"She is not on holiday," Clara said firmly. "No one goes on holiday and rises at the crack of dawn and stays out until late at night. Not every day, at least."

"She does not exactly seem to be taking the chance to relax and rest," Tommy concurred. "Well, what now?"

Clara thought for a moment.

"That photograph was one Oliver took for the newspaper. Perhaps, they have more information about the involvement of Albion Industries in the pageant?"

It was as good a plan as any. Annie reminded them to be back for supper as they left. She was busy with a big pot of hearty Irish stew she was about to deliver to Oliver.

"Oliver will be eating well for a while," Tommy chuckled as they left home again. "He may get too used to it."

Clara smiled back at him. She was just relieved Oliver was on the mend. They had had quite a scare with him. They caught the bus and headed back to the Brighton Gazette.

Gilbert was all grins when they arrived. He was already in the process of starting an article about Miss Pink's pill demonstration, filling in all the general elements and leaving room to add actual facts and quotes when he had them. The editor of the paper, Mr Pontefract, believed the event would up his sales. The pill fiasco had already increased their distribution because everyone wanted to read the warning they had published – written by Gilbert and full of dramatic prose and less than subtle insinuations about how the pills were poisoned. He had walked close to the line with the article, keeping just one step away from libel. He was very pleased with himself.

"Have you more news?" he asked with glee as they entered.

"Actually, we have more questions," Clara replied. "You were involved in reporting on the pageant?"

"I was," Gilbert said cheerfully. "It was a very pleasant few days."

Tommy frowned at him, feeling he was being rather uncouth.

"Do you recall if Albion Industries were involved in the pageant also?" Clara asked, ignoring his comment. She always felt Gilbert threw in these remarks to get a reaction and it was quicker to ignore them in the long run.

"Albion Industries?" Gilbert looked at her aghast. "They were the main sponsor!"

Clara glanced at Tommy, a silent exchange happening between them.

"Oh, you have found something out!" Gilbert said in delight. "What is it?"

"It is not so much I have found something out," Clara said. "As that I have this idea that might – just might –

turn into a theory."

"I am all ears!" Gilbert said, which was a rather unfortunate use of words, for he did have decidedly large ears.

Clara knew she could not avoid explaining further, not if she wanted Gilbert's assistance.

"It is all rather vague, nothing you could print just yet."

"I understand," Gilbert said, aiming to appear serious. "I might seem a loud-mouthed, irresponsible and uncouth journalist," he nodded at Tommy, indicating he had heard his silent rebuke, "but I do take my work seriously and I cannot afford to get this paper into trouble."

Clara felt he was being honest with her. She also knew Mr Pontefract had final say on everything and had no intention of placing the newspaper in a position where he was being sued for publishing falsehoods.

"We are now aware that the pills themselves were not tampered with, but that the bottles they were in were laced with arsenic," Clara began.

"Ruling out the pharmacist as the culprit, because whether it was by accident or design, he would have mixed the poison into the pills. It would have simply been more convenient," Gilbert agreed.

"Honestly, the pharmacist was an unlikely suspect for a deliberate poisoning attempt. It would have been utterly foolish for him. I have also assured myself there was no arsenic anywhere near where the pills were being made," Clara carried on. "Now I fancy that someone sprinkled arsenic into a handful of bottles at some point between the pills being produced and them ending up at Mr Dyer's shop."

"The bottles in the window display!" Gilbert said excitedly. "Easy to target! Just wait until the shop was busy and open a few lids, drop in a pinch or two of arsenic and no one would be the wiser."

"The bottles in the window display were dummies," Tommy burst his bubble. "The most likely place for the bottles to have been contaminated remains at the workshop where they were produced. The door had no lock, and someone could easily have gained entry at night."

"Which brings us back to the puzzle about who would have done this," Clara said. "Someone who wanted to destroy Miss Pink, obviously, and someone who knew about her pills. Well, the answer to one of those questions rather answers the other, seeing as the pills were largely a secret."

"We published the article about them the week before the launch," Gilbert pointed out. "I could imagine a few of the girls I met at the pageant being bitter and angry enough to want to do something about the pills. Have you ever been to such a thing? You would not believe the hate circulating beneath the smiles."

"A week certainly is time to come up with this idea, but it would be harder to determine who was making the pills and where," Tommy pointed out. "It would require effort and cunning. How many of the girls you met would go to such lengths."

Gilbert's gaze lost focus as he went back in his memory to the strange and exciting couple of days he had spent at the beauty pageant.

"In my opinion, all of them," he said. "I was somewhat surprised no one ended up with a knife in their back as it was."

"Well, we have no evidence for a rival beauty contestant being behind this, but there is something odd about the link between the pageant and Albion Industries," Clara explained. "Tell me more about their sponsorship of the pageant."

"What is there to tell?" Gilbert shrugged. "They supplied gifts for all the girls, samples of their make-up and so forth. They were sponsoring not just the regional events either, but the final in London. The winning girl was to become the new face of Albion Industries. She would be part of all their advertising materials and would go to product launches to handle things like speeches and so forth. Albion, quite rightly, realised a pretty girl launching their products was more interesting than having one of their stuffy directors or executives mumbling about face cream or eye shadow."

"That is some prize," Clara said, realising why the competition was so fierce and cutthroat. "But the pageant was in the summer, and I have not seen any Albion posters with this new girl on them."

Gilbert shrugged.

"That is not something I have cared to follow up, though it is starting to look interesting now."

"In any case, now we know there is a strong link between Albion and Miss Pink, which makes the arrival of Abigail Sommers in Brighton just before the launch of Miss Pink's diet pills all the more suspicious," Clara added.

"Abigail Sommers?" Gilbert's smile was back, and it made his ears waggle. "I remember her from the scandal at the Brighton Pavilion."

"She arrived on my doorstep rather unexpectedly," Clara explained. "She told me she had been allowed a sudden holiday and had decided to come to Brighton, then made a strange excuse for why she did not want to stay in a hotel. I believe she is here to spy on the launch of Pink's Pills."

"And it has crossed your mind that maybe it is more than simply spying, that maybe sabotage is afoot?" Gilbert filled in the blank Clara had deliberately left.

She took in a deep inhale, because she was thinking exactly that, but admitting it to Gilbert rather than just thinking about it was harder than she had thought. Abigail was her friend after all. Admittedly, they had drifted apart since their days at school, and she had not heard a word from Abigail after Albion hosted the trade fair at the pavilion, not until she had appeared on her doorstep. But she still felt she had a duty towards her.

"As I said before I began, there appears to be a link, but I cannot say precisely what is going on. It may be that Abigail has been sent to gather information for Albion."

She was thinking about the mud and leaves on Abigail's

shoes and trying not to imagine her old classmate slipping into an unlocked workshop and sprinkling arsenic into bottles, knowing full well she would be poisoning innocent people.

"Albion Industries does not make diet pills," Gilbert was musing over the matter, rubbing his chin thoughtfully. "That is one area they seem to have stayed away from. They concentrate on beauty aids rather than dieting products."

"Which makes my theory seem incomplete," Clara agreed with him. "You see why I said I was cautious about all this, and why you cannot publish anything about it."

"Not about this, no," Gilbert nodded. "But there is a link between Miss Pink and Albion. Just think, she was one step away from being the face of Albion Industries! The fortune she would have made and the opportunities that lay in store would have been endless."

"The runner-up must have received a prize too?" Tommy said.

"Nothing as dramatic as being the face of Albion," Gilbert said. "I believe the second prize was a lifetime supply of Albion products and a cash sum."

"Enough to fund the publishing of Miss Pink's diet book?" Clara suggested.

"I should say so," Gilbert nodded. "Now, let me think. We published the article about the pills last week and I believe Mr Pontefract said the article was picked up by a London paper. They do that quite often, take a snippet from an article we have written as a bit of 'news from the nation', remind Londoners they don't live in isolation and there are other places with people living their lives outside the city. Someone from Albion could have spotted the notice and warned their superiors."

"It still does not explain the panic this seems to have caused," Tommy said. "Why would Albion Industries be so agitated?"

"Just because they have not launched a diet pill yet, does not mean they are never going to," Gilbert said with that same twinkle in his eye. "Or, for that matter, that they might not be interested in stealing Miss Pink's idea. We all know that Albion Industries has no qualms about stealing from others if they think a product will be a huge success."

"I am saddened Abigail is involved in this," Clara groaned, wondering what had happened to her friend to make her so nefarious these days.

"The coincidences all stack up," Gilbert was enjoying himself. "Starting with Abigail's abrupt arrival. She must have been sent by Albion the minute they saw the news snippet. They would have told her to keep a low profile. Rather than risk being recognised in a hotel, she came to you. We have the connection between Miss Pink and Albion Industries, and boy, would I like to delve into that deeper and discover just how connected they are! And then there is the sabotage. It is all looking like another of Albion's games."

"Last time, Albion Industries merely lured away the man who had the idea for Pearl Pink lipstick and used him. No one was harmed in the process, at least no one indirectly involved," Tommy spoke. "But this is different. Innocent people were poisoned, and one has died. Would Albion stoop so low?"

"I find once someone starts to stoop, the limits they will go to changes considerably," Gilbert grinned. "Once you step upon the path... and all that."

Clara was frowning. She was not sure if she believed Albion Industries would take such a risk, even with their might and greed they would surely draw the line at harming people, if not out of principle, out of fear of the legal repercussions. But would Abigail think the same? Or might she be under pressure to do all she could to ruin the launch of Pink's Pills, and in her desperation had done something dreadful?

"This is all very interesting," Gilbert said, turning back to his typewriter and using the end of a pencil to flick away some dried ink that had gathered in a lump on his paper. "When you have something other than speculation, come straight to me. In the meantime, I shall see if I can dig anything up about the connection between Miss Pink and Albion. Is that fair?"

"It's fair," Clara concurred. "Now, we best go get ready for Miss Pink's presentation this evening, seeing as we are now security for it."

Clara gave Gilbert a look, but he was not ashamed of what he had done in cajoling them into assisting the paper.

"It will be an interesting evening," he promised. "I am looking forward to it."

Clara was not. She thought Miss Pink was being rash and she was worried about the possible outcomes.

"One thing, I would like a moment on the podium to address the audience," Clara said. "I would like to make a few things plain, in particular that Mr Dyer is not at fault in this matter and that a terrible travesty has been committed against both Miss Pink and the public."

"You best run that past Miss Pink," Gilbert said darkly. "My understanding is that she intends to claim there is nothing wrong with her pills."

"What?" Tommy said, stunned. "She cannot. The evidence is before us all."

"I can only tell you what she said to me," Gilbert shrugged. "Miss Pink intends to claim her pills are utterly safe and the poisoning had nothing to do with her."

Chapter Fourteen

Abigail had still not returned home by the evening and Clara was starting to worry about her. Perhaps her lengthy absence was not from choice and some misfortune had befallen her? Even if that were the case, Clara had limited options with what she could do. She had no real idea where Abigail had gone (though she suspected she had spent time lurking near Coppleburg's cottage) and it was too early for the police to consider her a missing person. Clara stared out her parlour window as she brushed her hair (longer than fashionable, and with a natural wave, she tended to keep it pulled back in a braid when working) and hoped for Abigail to suddenly appear.

"Still no sign of her?" Annie asked, wandering into the parlour to see what was occurring.

"No," Clara replied. "If she has still not returned when we come home from this ordeal, I shall set out to look for her."

"You would have to search the whole town," Annie told her. "You simply cannot."

Clara knew she had a point.

"She will turn up soon," she said, trying to sound confident. "Anyway, Tommy and I have to go."

"I shall send word to you if Abigail returns before you do," Annie promised her. "And I shall be having words with her too. She is not behaving like a thoughtful guest, and I am tired of these games."

"Me too, Annie," Clara sighed.

She headed off with Tommy. They were wrapped up warm against the autumnal air, which was sharp and crisp, and stung the back of the throat if you breathed in too deep. There was a frost already forming in the gardens and along the grass verges.

The Methodist Hall was brightly lit and a welcoming beacon of glowing orange as they drew closer. It was too early for the event, but that had not prevented people from queuing up outside, determined to be the first in and to get the best seats. Clara noted that nearly all those waiting were women. She wondered how many had bought Pink's Pills and were now seeking an explanation.

"I suppose we go around to the back," Tommy said to his sister, the main doors being firmly closed and no sign of anyone manning them.

They headed down an alley that ran between the hall and a florists' shop, finding their way to the backyard where there was a door stood open. To one side of the door, Gilbert was stood in the yard smoking. He grinned at them as they arrived.

"No smoking allowed inside, would you believe!" he puttered. "What is the world coming to? If it carries on this way, they will ban smoking in all public places!"

"I think that unlikely," Tommy chuckled. "Too many people smoke for it to be even considered. It is not as though it does any harm."

"I imagine the Methodists prefer not to have their hall filled with the smell," Clara added. She was not a smoker and never had been. "And the nicotine does yellow walls and furnishings something dreadful."

Gilbert shrugged, clearly thinking this a minor inconvenience for the sake of being indoors in the warm smoking.

"Glad you are here," he said, dropping the remains of his cigarette to the ground and grinding it out with his toe. "Did you see the hoards waiting outside?"

"We did," Tommy said, his expression revealing how remarkable the scene had appeared to him.

"They have been arriving since just after six," Gilbert's grin was getting broader. "I knew this would attract them all, but never thought they would be so eager."

"I hope this does not mean they intend to cause trouble," Tommy said uncertainly.

"That is why you are here," Gilbert responded brightly.

Tommy's dark expression told him what he thought of that.

"Well, I am going inside out of the cold," Clara informed them and marched through the open door.

Tommy and Gilbert were just a few paces behind. The hall was not vast and was arranged to accommodate a large meeting area, a couple of smaller rooms for use as offices and a substantial kitchen. The local Methodists were keen on holding charitable functions, to raise funds for good causes and the church. These typically revolved around a nice meal, with entertainment or a raffle.

Miss Pink was in the main hall, stood upon some staging that had been hastily put in place. There was nothing on the stage apart from a podium where she would stand and speak. She glanced up as Clara and Tommy arrived.

"I was told you were coming," she said to them, it was not clear if she was happy or unhappy to see them, her voice was gruff. "This has to go well."

"I will gladly stand upon this stage and inform everyone that I believe the pills were tampered with maliciously, by someone wishing you ill," Clara said.

"That will not be necessary," Miss Pink said swiftly.

Too swiftly and Clara recalled what Gilbert had said about her determination to deny the pills had caused this problem. Clara did not have the energy to object. She thought it was foolish to make such a staunch denial when it was only going to be proven wrong. The police had evidence the arsenic came from the pill bottles, whether it was actually in the pills or not was somewhat irrelevant in the scheme of things, the outcome had been the same.

"Are you sure about this?" Clara asked Miss Pink, an uneasy feeling creeping over her.

Miss Pink gave her a condescending smile.

"This is business," she said. "This is how it works."

Clara was annoyed and only her better judgement kept her from suggesting that from where she stood it seemed this 'business' of Miss Pink's was all about bare-faced lies and duping the general public. She simply smiled.

"I was not aware that Albion Industries sponsored the beauty pageant," she said to change the topic.

"They were the main sponsor," Miss Pink agreed. "They wanted a girl to be the face of Albion products. In a way, it was more a job interview than a beauty contest. They were looking for the full package, a girl with looks, manners, common sense and intelligence. Someone they could rely on."

"You must have been angry to have been overlooked," Tommy remarked.

"I was not precisely overlooked," Miss Pink said, glaring at him. "I came second, the competition was fierce and to get as far as I did was a huge achievement."

"But it did not make you the face of Albion," Tommy persisted.

"No, but it presented me with other opportunities," Miss Pink said calmly, refusing to rise to his bait. "In a way, I am better off, as I am able to be my own woman. I shall not be beholden to a company, only valuable to them while I am young. I shall make my own path and my fortune along with it. At least, once this inconvenience is past."

Clara admired a woman with such determination and fire. She could respect that about Miss Pink.

"Have Albion Industries had any contact with you since the contest?" Clara asked her.

Miss Pink gave her a sharp look.

"Why?"

"Certain circumstances have made me consider the slender possibility – and it is slender – of Albion being somehow involved in this..." Clara floundered for the right word. "In these troubles."

Miss Pink frowned.

"That would be... Albion Industries are professionals."

"They stole the Pearl Pink lipstick from Mr Mokano of House of Jasmine," Tommy remarked. "No one has forgotten that."

Miss Pink was silent a moment considering that situation and the outcome.

"It is one thing to steal an idea and another to poison people," she said at last.

"I agree," Clara said. "But it just seems odd there is a connection here, right now, with Albion."

She did not elaborate on the connection, not wishing to bring Abigail into trouble until she had had the chance to learn the truth from her.

"I am shocked," Miss Pink said. "Albion Industries would not stoop so low, surely."

"Then, they had no way to know about the pills other than through the newspaper article?" Clara hinted.

Miss Pink was starting to feel alarmed by everything, feeling that the world had slipped from under her feet.

"Before I launched the pills myself," she said. "I thought it might not be possible. I thought perhaps I would be best to have a company backing me. I suggested the idea of the pills to Albion Industries, using my connection as the runner-up in the contest they had heavily sponsored. They never responded to my letter. I have not given it another thought since."

"Was that a while ago?" Clara asked.

Miss Pink frowned.

"It was before Sigmund became involved with my idea. Perhaps the end of summer. Not long after the contest, at least. I was about to launch my diet book and I was hoping Albion might help with publicising it, maybe give me a recommendation or something. As I said, they never wrote back to me."

Miss Pink did not mention the hurt that had caused, or how she had felt disregarded. She had aimed to put the matter behind her.

"Everyone ready?"

They were distracted by Mr Pontefract appearing.

"It is dead on seven and I am going to open the doors," he added.

"I am ready," Miss Pink said, sounding as if she was bracing herself for battle. Perhaps, in a way, she was.

Clara glanced at her brother.

"You take that side of the stage. I shall take this side."

"Right-o," Tommy said cheerfully. "Nothing will happen of course."

"Do not underestimate a group of irate women who feel they have been hoaxed along with having their lives placed at threat," Clara warned him.

Tommy chuckled and wandered to his position. He would have to learn the hard way, Clara supposed.

Mr Pontefract had opened the doors and people were filing in. The hall filled up fast and there was pushing and shoving from the back as people tried to get a good view. As Clara had observed earlier, the majority of the crowd were female, though she spied an odd man here and there in the throng. She wondered if any of the audience were connected to someone who had been made sick by the pills. She particularly wondered if Mrs Wood's friends or relatives had opted to come.

Her eyes were scanning the crowd for anyone who looked primed to make trouble, when she spied Abigail. Abigail was doing a good job of avoiding looking in Clara's direction. Clara was cross; had she not got a job to do, she would have marched over to Abigail and had words. She was feeling used and betrayed. For the time being, however, she could do nothing about it.

Mr Pontefract was upon the stage, kicking off the evening and setting up the crowd.

"Good evening, everyone," he declared. "I am delighted to see so many of you here tonight. Now, we have arranged this evening so that Miss Pink, the creator of Pink's Pills could speak to you concerning recent accusations that her pills are dangerous."

There were mutterings among the audience.

"Miss Pink wishes to explain that such a thing is simply not the case and intends to demonstrate the safety of her pills to you, herself. But I shall not hog the limelight, because you have come to see Miss Pink."

He smiled at the audience, while avoiding meeting any gazes directly, then he departed the staging. Miss Pink took his place, to quiet murmurs and vengeful looks. Someone began to boo but was shoved hard by the person next to them and choked on their words. Miss Pink had faced worse at beauty pageants and did not let the ire of the crowd touch her.

"Thank you for coming," she said in a crystal-clear voice. "I am very grateful to the Brighton Gazette for enabling me to have this chance to speak to you all. Terrible accusations have been thrown at me and at my health products. I am here before you to speak the truth."

Clara managed not to cringe at this blatant lie.

"Pink's Pills are developed from an old family recipe," Miss Pink carried on. "All the ingredients are harmless and non-poisonous. I have had it confirmed by the police themselves that none of my pills contained poison."

That was a good example of spinning the truth to suit.

"This terrible situation is purely coincidental. Why, I am sure there are people in this room who have taken my pills and suffered none of the ill effects of those in the hospital," Miss Pink looked around keenly for someone to react. A hand drifted up. "Yes, you. You took my pills?"

The person, a middle-aged woman with sizeable hips clearly wished she had not put up her hand. All eyes had swung to her and not all were friendly.

"I did," she squeaked.

"Were you made unwell?" Miss Pink demanded.

"No," the woman replied. "But I didn't lose any weight, either."

"How many did you take?" Miss Pink said, unfazed.

The woman looked sheepish.

"Two doses."

"Not sufficient to have the desired effect," Miss Pink said confidently. "It quite clearly states on the label results will not be seen until at least a week's worth of pills have been consumed. However, my point was not about weight, but about how the pills are harmless. This lady took them and was fine. The majority of people who took my pills are fine. Therefore, why should we suppose those who were made ill did so because they took my pills? The evidence we have indicates the pills are safe, which is quite the opposite of what has been otherwise suggested, is it not?"

People started to talk among themselves, a lot of them probably remarking on how they had taken the pills without any harm befalling them. Clara guessed most of the people present had bought Pink's Pills and were here because they were worried about the consequences of taking them.

"Even if my word is not enough," Miss Pink pressed on. "I have another way to demonstrate my faith in my pills."

She lifted a bottle up from the podium.

"Here I have some of my very pills, in the same familiar bottle. I shall take a double dose of them before you, to show that not only are they safe when taken properly, but even when taken at double-strength."

Abigail poured some of the tablets into her palm and consumed four before the audience.

"Do you see? I am fine. In fact, I shall take all these pills in this bottle to prove to you they cause no harm!"

Miss Pink then swallowed pill after pill. Clara lost count of how many she consumed.

"You see?" Miss Pink repeated. "They are harmless!"

Chapter Fifteen

Silence filled the hall. It seemed that people were waiting for something to happen, and when it did not, they were slightly unsure what to do.

"That is all I have to say on the matter," Miss Pink concluded, casting a firm look across the audience to impress upon them she had said all she intended, and they best accept it for what it was. "Thank you for coming. I hope to have this nonsense resolved shortly and then there will be no more trouble with Pink's Pills."

She marched off the stage, past Clara and into the corridor that led to the kitchen. The audience was unsure what to do and started to look to one another and mutter. Mr Pontefract stepped up to the podium.

"Now you have heard Miss Pink's statement and seen her demonstration," he said. "I hope you all felt it was valuable coming tonight and will have a safe journey home."

"I thought we would be able to ask questions," someone called out from the audience.

"I do not recall stating anything in the announcement that suggested that," Mr Pontefract said politely. "In any case, this meeting is at an end."

The audience were clearly stunned that the demonstration had been so short. In truth, Clara was surprised Miss Pink had kept things so simple. She had expected a longer speech, but she supposed the brief nature of the display had in essence demonstrated all that was needed.

The crowd did not want to leave so suddenly, and they lurked hesitantly about until Pontefract waved at Gilbert and he very pointedly opened the main doors. A cold draught swirled in, and it was obvious what was meant. With reluctance, the onlookers slowly departed, talking in low voices about their disappointment at the haste of the talk. They had only been in the hall for twenty minutes and most had waited outside for much longer than that.

Clara glanced around for Abigail, not wanting to miss this opportunity to speak to her. She was proving elusive. Abigail was close to the door, threading herself deep into the crush of people. It could have been innocent, but Clara suspected she was trying to avoid her. She hurried forward and lunged through the crowd to grasp at Abigail's arm. She startled a woman who scowled at her as she barged past, but Clara was not caring about that for the moment.

Abigail tried to resist her pull, not looking back. Now it was clear she was avoiding Clara. Clara yanked her arm harder, ignoring the woman she had pushed past and angered, who was now berating her about her actions.

"Abigail!" Clara said sternly, finally getting her friend to look at her. "We have to talk. At once."

She refused to let her arm go, and the irate woman behind her was getting herself in a dither that Clara was blocking her way. Clara was doing her best to pretend she could not hear her.

"Abigail," she hissed.

Abigail frowned, looking at the hand on her arm. She clearly hoped to pull away, but also knew Clara was rather like a terrier in her determination. Reluctantly, she stepped out of the crowd towards Clara, allowing the unfortunate woman who had been detained by their antics to finally go past, though not without taking the time to give them both a sharp rebuke.

"Clara, I was hoping to have an early night…" Abigail said, noting that Clara had not let go of her arm, as if she supposed she would bolt.

That was exactly what Clara was thinking.

"We need to have words about what you are up to," Clara said.

Tommy was wandering over to join them.

"Up to?" Abigail asked, feigning surprise at the statement.

"You have been skulking around, leaving the house at all hours and behaving in a manner that does not suggest you are here on holiday. I was quite concerned this evening that you had not returned home, and I feared some mishap had befallen you," Clara continued.

"Mishap?" Abigail chuckled. "Really Clara."

"Then where have you been," Clara demanded.

"Oh, just around," Abigail said. "I have been indulging myself shopping."

"I have not seen a single shopping bag about the house," Tommy remarked. "And you do not go to the shops at six o'clock in the morning."

"And since when did you have to walk through mud and dried leaves to get to the shops?" Clara added. "You are up to something, Abigail. I know there is a connection between Miss Pink's pills and Albion Industries. Albion sponsored the beauty pageant that Abigail came runner-up in, and she mentioned the idea of the pills to them, which they apparently ignored. Now you are here, and I do not think it is just a coincidence."

"Clara!" Abigail said, acting hurt. "You really doubt me so?"

"Under the circumstances, yes," Clara sighed. "Your behaviour makes no sense, nor your sudden dramatic arrival."

"I explained that," Abigail waved off her comment.

"Yes, you mentioned a missing letter. The problem is, I do not believe you sent any letter. I think you had to hurry down to Brighton in secret on behalf of Albion and your decision to stay with me was because you did not want to attract attention to yourself."

"You really do have wild ideas, Clara! It is all this time you have spent being a detective. You start to see conspiracy everywhere."

"No, Abigail, it is because as a detective I am sharp enough to note when things are amiss and unusual," Clara said firmly. "Please stop denying it."

Abigail gave a false laugh. She was convincing no one.

"Those leaves on your shoes," Clara persisted. "You got them walking along the footpath near the cottage where Sigmund Coppleburg has been making the pills."

"Who?" Abigail asked.

"I assume you followed Miss Pink to learn the location. You must have acted fast. You only arrived at my house the day the pills went on sale. At least, that is what you claimed. You could have been here sooner, tracking Miss Pink. Once you knew where she was based you could tamper with the pills and then come to me and act as if you had just arrived to cover your tracks."

"Clara, what are you saying?" Abigail said in horror at the accusations. "Tamper with the pills? Are you accusing me of poisoning people?"

"It does seem rash and preposterous," Clara concurred. "But your behaviour is far too suspicious, and someone added arsenic to those bottles."

"Miss Pink just stated her pills were perfectly safe," Abigail retorted.

"We both know she is adjusting the truth to suit her," Clara said in a low voice, though they were now the only ones present in the hall. "Someone tampered with those bottles, and you have been behaving very oddly."

"I do not like your tone, Clara," Abigail said haughtily. "I thought, as friends, we owed each other a little more faith and trust. I see your line of work has corrupted you and made you cynical of everyone. I shall not suffer your accusations any longer. I shall go back to the house, collect my luggage and depart for a hotel. I am sorry things have come to this and we must part on such poor terms."

"Abigail," Clara did not want her to leave just like that. "You do not need to leave my home."

"But I do," Abigail said. "Clearly my activities disturb you too much and I do not care to think my comings and goings are being constantly monitored."

Abigail swept away; her head held up in a self-righteous fashion. There was nothing Clara could do. She could not keep clasping the woman's arm and preventing her from leaving. She was saddened things had come to this and feared she had not handled the situation as well as she could have. She sighed.

"You tried, old thing," Tommy squeezed her shoulder. "Whatever Abigail is up to, she is determined to keep it a secret."

"You're right," Clara nodded. "This just adds to my suspicion she is hiding things from me. She is playing a good game, but she will make a misstep sooner or later."

"Can we go home now?" Tommy asked.

Clara was going to say she did not see why not, no one had asked them to escort Miss Pink home, and Clara fancied getting back to her warm parlour, but just then Gilbert hurried up behind them.

"Miss Fitzgerald, you need to come quick!"

There was alarm on his face. Genuine, stark concern. It was novel to see such a look on the usually belligerently cheerful reporter's features. He never seemed to be unduly concerned about anything.

"What is wrong?" Clara asked.

Gilbert screwed up his face.

"Miss Pink is unwell. I think her own pills poisoned her."

"Heavens, no!" Clara said in alarm, rushing towards the corridor that led to the kitchen.

They found Miss Pink collapsed in the bathroom near

the kitchen. She was sitting on the tiled floor, propped up against the wall. Her face deathly pale and Mr Pontefract crouched before her, patting her hand.

"Has Gilbert gone for a doctor?" he asked as Clara approached. "I told him to summon you and then go find someone."

Gilbert had vanished, so it seemed he had done as instructed.

"I think so. What has happened?" Clara crouched next to the editor and gently reached out for Miss Pink's pulse.

The woman's eyes fluttered open.

"It was ghastly," she said, seeing Clara. "The moment I took the pills I tasted something gritty in my mouth. I knew that was not how the pills should taste. They are rather pleasant to consume, like sweets."

"Why, on earth, did you take more?" Tommy asked, astonished by her statement.

"I had to prove my products were safe," Miss Pink said softly. "I could not stop and make things worse. As soon as I had consumed them, I rushed into the bathroom and made myself sick. I fear, it has not been sufficient."

She groaned then and placed a hand on her stomach.

"Did you bring pills from the batches that were returned to Mr Dyer?" Clara asked, thinking that there must have been one other poisoned bottle among them, and Miss Pink had been unlucky.

"No," Miss Pink grimaced as her stomach spasmed. "Sigmund made me a fresh batch yesterday."

"They should have been fine," Tommy said, his puzzled expression matching Clara's.

"Someone must have tampered with them, too," Miss Pink said, breathless. "They saw the announcement and decided to do this to me."

Clara rather felt that all this business was throwing suspicion back upon Sigmund. He had seemed innocent and innocuous, but perhaps that was not quite the case. She could not see his purpose yet, but it now seemed more likely he had poisoned the pills than someone had snuck in again to sabotage them.

Except, Abigail had been absent until late yesterday, and had also gone early this morning. If she had been lurking around the cottage, might she have done this? Clearly, she had learned about the demonstration. Had she stood in this hall to watch her handiwork take effect?

Clara felt a little sick at the thought of her old school friend being so callous and calculating, but that would explain why she was here, when she had previously been trying to keep any connection between Albion and Miss Pink secret.

"Where is the bottle?" Clara asked Miss Pink.

"In my handbag," Miss Pink said weakly.

Clara glanced at her brother, and he sped away to find it.

"Proving a point was not worth all this," Clara told Miss Pink. "It is not worth your life."

"You do not understand," Miss Pink said wearily. "This is my life. If I fail with Pink's Pills, what else can I do? I invested all the money I won into them and my diet book. I have to make this succeed."

"No wonder you bolted off the stage," Mr Pontefract added. "Don't you think this is all rather dangerous? Making these claims when there could still be bottles of poisoned pills out there?"

"Now you think of that," Clara sighed at the editor. "If we had acted as I said, and given an honest explanation of the situation, we would not be having this drama now."

"I could not be honest," Miss Pink arched her back as the stomach pain returned. "Telling people someone had been trying to sabotage me would look like I was making excuses. Besides, it would not make people want to buy my pills. They would still not trust them or me. I had to say the pills were safe and harmless. It was the only way."

"Well, I think you are a fool," Clara told her. "I just hope this action does not cost you your life."

Miss Pink gave her a weak smile.

Gilbert and the doctor had arrived. Clara and Mr

Pontefract moved out of the way as the doctor knelt by his patient.

"What has occurred?" he asked.

"She has consumed arsenic," Clara said bluntly.

"Arsenic?" the doctor was aware of recent events. "Did she take some of those terrible diet pills everyone is talking about?"

"A lot of them," Clara replied, before Miss Pink could speak. "She was trying to prove they were harmless."

"Women!" the doctor said in despair.

Clara was offended.

"Will she be all right?" Mr Pontefract asked nervously, thinking that he had helped organise this evening, had promoted it and now its star attraction was collapsed before him.

"Has she been sick?" the doctor asked without answering the question.

"Repeatedly," Miss Pink answered him.

"That is something," the doctor nodded. "We need to get her to the hospital to have her stomach pumped. If we can get enough of the poison out and she has a strong constitution, then there is a good chance of recovery."

Clara did not think this was the sort of thing you should say right in front of the patient being discussed. She intervened.

"You will be fine, Miss Pink. You have to be so we can solve this affair and bring the culprit to justice."

Miss Pink gave her the slightest of indications she had heard and understood.

"Miss Pink?" if the doctor now realised he was before the creator of Pink's Pills and had denigrated her products bluntly, he opted not to show it.

He repeated his instruction that an ambulance must be summoned, and Gilbert was once more dispatched on an errand. The doctor stepped back from his patient and said he would wait until the ambulance came, then asked if someone would make him a cup of tea.

Mr Pontefract agreed to the task, for which Clara was

glad. The doctor was infuriating her. She crouched by Miss Pink again and took her hand. It was icy cold.

"You have to survive this, Miss Pink," she said.

Miss Pink stared at her with silent determination in her eyes.

"I will," she said.

Chapter Sixteen

The evening had not shaped up like anyone had expected. An ambulance arrived at the Methodist hall, pulling up to the street entrance. It seemed highly unlikely anyone would fail to notice its presence and wonder who it had been called for. Before the night was out, more rumours would abound.

Gilbert stood with Clara and Tommy as Miss Pink was removed from the hall on a stretcher. She had passed out, which in some regards was a relief for her, but it made everyone else nervous.

"She took those pills even after she knew the first ones were poisoned," Gilbert said, not sure whether to admire such reckless determination or to consider it utter idiocy. "She didn't have to do that."

"She thought she did," Clara replied quietly.

Tommy had the pill bottle in his hand, having retrieved it from Miss Pink's handbag. He now tipped it up, noticing the fine film of powder that swirled in the bottom. Some of that powder was debris from the crumbly pills, the rest was poison.

"If these pills were a fresh batch," he said, airing his thoughts aloud. "Then we must wonder if Sigmund did this."

"He would have to be some sort of madman," Gilbert said, pulling out a cigarette from his pocket. "He has to know the blame will come straight back to him."

"How else could the bottle be laced with arsenic," Tommy pointed out. "The other pills we could assume someone had tampered with them before they were sent to Mr Dyer, but these pills were made specially for tonight. Who would know about them?"

"Someone who was watching Sigmund's cottage," Clara suggested.

She did not say aloud who she was thinking of, she could hardly comprehend the thought herself. If Abigail had lurked by the cottage and done this terrible thing, it must be under Albion orders, but it was so despicable that she hardly dared to consider it of her old friend. Had Abigail changed so much? Yet she was keeping plenty of secrets and her continual lies were making her seem more and more suspect.

Clara rubbed at her temples, feeling the familiar pangs of a tension headache.

"We ought to go to Sigmund and tell him what has occurred," she said.

"It is too late for the buses," Tommy pointed out. "How are we going to get there?"

Clara did not have time to answer because just then Inspector Park-Coombs arrived with a constable. She was surprised to see him.

"I had a telephone message from a doctor who said he had attended another poisoning victim here," the inspector said, his eyes switching to the ambulance as it began to move off. "I take it they were correct."

"Miss Pink has been poisoned by her own pills," Clara said in a low whisper. "She is in the ambulance."

Inspector Park-Coombs raised his eyebrows in surprise.

"That was not what I was expecting."

"She was meant to be demonstrating her pills were safe by taking them at a public performance," Gilbert interjected. He had already finished his first cigarette and was onto the next.

"Miss Pink says the pills she took tonight were a fresh batch made by Sigmund for her," Clara added. "Very limited time for them to be tampered with."

Tommy held up the bottle.

"Looks like the same process. Arsenic added to the bottle and mixed with the powder from the pills."

Park-Coombs frowned at the bottle.

"You realise, since all this, I haven't been able to take so much as an aspirin out of concern for its contents," he grumbled. "Is Miss Pink capable of talking."

"She was unconscious when she was placed in the ambulance," Clara replied. "I imagine the hospital will pump her stomach as soon as she arrives, and she will need to recover before questioning. Personally, I would like to have some words with the person who made these pills."

Park-Coombs smiled at her.

"You know who that is?"

"I can direct you to him, except I have no transport."

Park-Coombs took the hint.

"I shall have the police car summoned. In the meantime, tell me everything that happened tonight while we wait for it to arrive."

The station was not far from the hall, and the car did not take long to arrive. Clara had to continue her explanation of the night's events while they rode in the car out of the town and towards the quieter rural lanes where Sigmund resided. Gilbert had tried to hitch a lift in the car, claiming a journalist's prerogative. Park-Coombs had given him short-shrift and sent him packing. He already had enough for the next edition, anyway.

They arrived at the muddy track that led to Sigmund's cottage and bumped along it with the police constable in charge of driving looking a tad worried they might get stuck. There was a light on in a downstairs window of the cottage, which implied Sigmund was at home.

"If he did this," Park-Coombs said, "he must be a

simpleton. He could not have made his guilt more obvious if he had stood in that hall with a gun pointed at Miss Pink."

"People's minds work in peculiar ways," Clara sighed. "Perhaps he wants everyone to know he did this?"

Park-Coombs contemplated such a possibility, his expression growing more and more troubled as he worked through it.

"That isn't possible," he said at last.

Clara felt like saying that anything was possible, and people were not always logical, but the car had managed to bring them to the cottage gate, and it was time to clamber out.

They were faced with frost-crusted mud beneath their shoes – a treacherous combination. Clara felt a heel slip into a slight rut and the crunch of the crisp ice beneath her sole. Tommy nearly skidded over as he reached the gate and had to make a grab for the gatepost. Park-Coombs was having similar problems behind him.

Sigmund emerged from the front door of his cottage, having heard the car engine and assuming Miss Pink had returned. He had insisted she stay with him while the matter of this pill mischief was dealt with and until they could be sure she would be safe in her own home. When he saw who was really at his gate, he hesitated.

"Is something the matter?"

His voice echoed across the still night air.

"Mr Coppleburg, we need to talk," Park-Coombs declared. "If we can get to you without breaking our necks, that is."

Sigmund hurried to the gate and opened it for them. The latch had frozen up and he had to wriggle it several times before it popped free.

"I put salt down on the garden path," he said to reassure them as they entered. "I did not think about the lane. Where is Rose?"

He looked deeply worried and once again Clara found herself unable to believe he was responsible for all this.

"We shall explain inside," Park-Coombs insisted. "I cannot abide this cold any longer."

Leaving the constable with the car, they headed into the cottage and were welcomed into the compact parlour. A hearty fire was burning briskly and warming the small room, so stepping from the outdoors into it was like walking into a snug oven. Park-Coombs gave a sigh of relief and stepped to the fire to warm his legs.

"Please, what is going on?" Sigmund asked desperately, the delay tormenting him.

Tommy showed him the empty bottle of pills.

"Miss Pink took all the pills you gave her," he said. "Unfortunately, this bottle was laced with arsenic."

Sigmund blinked. The colour visibly drained from his face and then he made a gurgling sound.

"Excuse me," he gasped and fled to the kitchen.

Park-Coombs went to follow him, thinking he was making a dash for freedom. Clara placed a hand on his arm to stop him. A moment later, the sound of retching informed them exactly why Sigmund had bolted. After a while, they heard taps being turned and Sigmund returned to them, looking pale and drawn.

"Is she at the hospital?" he asked.

"Yes," Clara replied. "She realised at once what was the matter and made herself sick. That might just have saved her."

Sigmund nodded weakly, then edged his way to an armchair and flopped down.

"You think I did this on purpose," he said, demonstrating he was not as oblivious to the situation as might have been supposed.

"I was considering it, yes," Park-Coombs told him. "You made a fresh batch of pills for Miss Pink before tonight?"

"I made them yesterday," Sigmund nodded. "Before you ask, I also installed a lock on my workshop door. No one but me could have touched those pills."

"You are incriminating yourself," Tommy told him gently.

"There is no point lying," Sigmund replied. "I cannot fathom how this occurred and I did not do it, but clearly something has happened in my workshop that I cannot explain."

Clara was frowning thoughtfully.

"Sigmund, the pills were not poisoned, it was the bottles they were put in. Where do you keep those bottles?"

"In the workshop," Sigmund answered. "In a box. Miss Pink bought a large quantity of them at a good price. She hoped she would run through them quickly."

"Can we see the bottles?" Clara asked.

Sigmund shrugged his shoulders, then rose and showed them the way to his workshop. As he had stated, there was now a shiny new latch on the workshop door and a brand-new padlock. He opened it with a key and allowed them inside.

The workshop looked undisturbed. It was cold and quiet, a stillness about the air. Sigmund lit an oil lamp that hung from the ceiling and illuminated the musty space.

"The bottles are all here," he headed to a corner where there was a stack of three boxes. He lifted the top one and it rattled as he brought it over. "I believe there are something like three hundred bottles here."

He placed the box on his workbench. Clara opened the box flaps and took out the first bottle that came to hand. She held it up to the light of the lamp.

"What are you doing, Clara?" Park-Coombs asked.

"The bottles were poisoned, not the pills," Clara explained. "And only some of the bottles at that. We assumed the only bottles tampered with were those that had already been filled, but what if our saboteur was a little more thorough than that?"

"You mean they might have tampered with some of the unused bottles, just in case Miss Pink managed to salvage the first situation?" Tommy elaborated.

"It would be cunning," Clara concurred. "Think about it, if tonight had gone smoothly, Miss Pink might have been able to begin selling her pills again. The first incident might have been forgotten or considered an accident, which was obviously not what the saboteur wanted."

In her mind, Clara was replacing the word saboteur with Abigail Sommers. She was doing it unconsciously, even when she reminded herself not to jump to conclusions.

"If other bottles from this box were tampered with, we shall know our poisoner was cleverer and far more wicked than we first imagined," she said. "I assume the bottle you put your new batch of pills in came from this box, Sigmund."

Sigmund indicated that was the case, then he drew out a bottle himself and held it to the light. It seemed fine. Tommy and Park-Coombs dug in now and there were a few minutes of silence as they each worked through the process of collecting a bottle, examining it for any sort of powder and then placing it on the table. For a while, no one found anything, then Tommy noticed something about the bottle he had just picked up.

"This bottle has liquid in it," he said.

"Some of the bottles had water in them from where they had been washed out," Sigmund explained. "I took those ones indoors and dried them in the oven. It was only a handful."

Tommy moved the bottle from side to side.

"You washed them out?"

"No," Sigmund said. "The place Rose ordered them from had done that. I was going to mention to her about the water left in some. However, once dried in my oven they would have been sterilised, so it was hardly an issue."

Tommy put down the bottle and they carried on their search; however, no bottles were discovered to contain powder. All they had for their efforts were three bottles with a tiny amount of water in them.

Clara was staring at these bottles curiously.

"Is it not odd only a handful of bottles retained water? Surely, if they had all been through the same process, there ought to be a lot more with leftover water in them," she said.

Sigmund shrugged. The thought had not crossed his mind.

"Arsenic doesn't completely dissolve in water," Park-Coombs said thoughtfully. "It leaves a gritty residue. It is not easy to spot unless you are looking for it, but I have been on a few poisoning cases and seen the signs. It is a heavy metal, after all."

Park-Coombs picked up one of the bottles with water in it and held it close to the lamp. He moved it around with care, screwing up his eyes to try to see everything perfectly.

"I might be seeing what I want to see," he said after a moment, "but this water looks to me to contain small particles of something."

"The saboteur did not use arsenic powder on its own to lace the bottles. They used arsenic in water," Clara understood. "It would be easier to get it into the bottles without a spillage and less likely than powder on its own to be noticed."

"Exactly," Park-Coombs nodded. "Drying them out in the oven would only have removed the water, leaving the arsenic particles in the bottle, and it does not require much arsenic to make a person unwell."

"It can build up in the body," Sigmund said, the horror of the discovery sinking in. "That is how people can be slowly poisoned as if they were suffering from a natural stomach complaint."

"The bottle you put the new pills in, did it have to be dried first?" Tommy asked him.

Sigmund had to stop and think. So much had happened in the last few days and certain small actions had become lost in his memory. He took a while to visualise his work yesterday. Had he dried some bottles in the oven?

"I might have," he said, then he became firm. "No, I am sure I did. Yes, I put a bottle in the oven because it had a bit of water in it and I wanted to be sure everything was perfect for the new pills.

He looked aghast as this sunk in. Clara nodded at him. "Yes, that is exactly how they did it."

Chapter Seventeen

"You still think Abigail is responsible for all this?" Tommy asked as they walked the last few steps towards their front door.

They had been solemn and silent on their return trip from the cottage. Sigmund was in a state of shock, deeply shaken by what had occurred. Park-Coombs had confiscated all the bottles in his workshop to analyse them and determine how many had been tampered with. Clara was just quiet, wondering if a friend had committed this terrible crime and trying to determine how to prove it.

"I do," she said with a sigh as she opened the front door of the house.

They could hear voices from within, an argument was taking place in the kitchen.

"Annie!" Tommy hissed, thinking that his wife was not aware of Abigail's proclivities for lacing things with arsenic.

"She said she would not let her leave before we returned," Clara said anxiously. "I had utterly forgotten!"

They raced through to the kitchen where they found a strange scene. Abigail was stood in her stockinged feet on the kitchen tiles. Annie was stood before her, arms crossed across her chest and looking fearsome with a wooden spoon clasped in one hand. It was not clear if this was coincidental or whether she had armed herself.

Abigail turned to Clara as she arrived in the kitchen and gave her an exasperated look.

"She has hidden all my shoes and refuses to tell me where they are!"

Clara took in this information and nearly laughed. Of all the things she had anticipated, even feared, as she had dashed to the kitchen, Annie having hidden Abigail's shoes was not one of them.

"I came home from that ridiculous display," Abigail went on, boiling over with outrage, "and I took off my wet shoes while I hurried upstairs to pack my suitcase. I then discovered someone had been in my room and removed all my shoes, every pair. Even my slippers! I came back down to ask where they were, not supposing in that moment it was malicious, which is when I noticed my last pair of shoes, the ones I had walked into the house wearing, had disappeared as well!"

Annie had her lips pressed into a thin line, determined to reveal nothing.

"I almost thought the dogs had taken them, but that seemed preposterous," Abigail flapped her hands in consternation. "I even checked the downstairs rooms before I allowed myself to suspect Annie of doing this thing. She denies knowing anything about it, but I know it must have been her!"

Annie had squeezed her mouth up even tighter in her determination not to say anything. She looked like she was about to pop.

Clara pulled out a chair from the kitchen table and sat down.

"Annie is a little put out by your erratic behaviour, as are we all. You turned up on my doorstep asking for a place to stay with some story of a sudden holiday and not caring for hotels. The next thing we know you are disappearing all day, returning late at night and refusing to say where you have been. Your shoes are covered in mud and leaves, which is remarkable in itself, because, Abigail, you are always pristinely dressed. Then there is the way you happen to keep turning up in my investigation of Pink's Pills. Like tonight."

"I was curious, that is all," Abigail shrugged. "It could be argued Pink's Pills are a beauty product and so it is of interest to someone in the beauty industry."

"It could also be argued that you have been sent here by Albion to spy on Miss Pink, discover the formula for her pills and steal that information for your employers."

Clara had been blunt, perhaps even rude, but she was tired of these games. Abigail was determined to lie to her, and her deceit was troubling when other events were taken into account. Abigail gaped at her, made speechless by the accusation. She made a sort of aghast laugh at the back of her throat, as if she were choking on it.

"Don't mince your words, will you Clara!"

"Abigail, I have been trying to give you the benefit of the doubt through this case, but your actions keep casting you back into the spotlight of my suspicions. If you would just be honest with me…"

"You stole my shoes so I could not leave this house and avoid Clara," Abigail turned to Annie accusingly. "I see it now. You are all in on this ploy. I am hurt, deeply hurt. I thought we were all friends."

"Stop trying to act as if you are the victim here," Tommy snapped, fed up with Abigail's attempts to avoid their questions. "Your actions have made people terribly sick. One person is dead and now Miss Pink is in the hospital suffering from arsenic poisoning."

"Miss Pink has been poisoned?" Abigail said, appearing shocked. "Wait, my actions? What are you talking about?"

"Abigail, this is tiresome," Clara sighed.

"Do you not think it is tiresome for me to stand here hearing these accusations and not knowing what you are talking about?" Abigail snapped. She looked around them, at their stern faces. "You do not believe me. You do not believe that I am ignorant of all this."

"It is rather hard to believe, under the circumstances," Clara replied. "You have been acting in a very peculiar fashion, Abigail. Don't try to deny that."

Abigail was trembling with emotion, defiant to the last, but certain things she had just heard were cracking through her determination to keep her secrets.

"Was Miss Pink poisoned by her own pills?" she asked when the silence had dragged out a while.

"You know she was," Tommy snapped at her.

"Whatever you think you know about me, Tommy Fitzgerald, you are quite mistaken. Until this moment I was not aware that arsenic had contaminated those pills," Abigail said sternly.

"And turning up at Miss Pink's demonstration tonight was just a coincidence?" Clara asked, her tone implying she would not believe a denial.

"A coincidence with her being poisoned, yes," Abigail said stiffly. "I do not wish that woman ill."

"Then why have you been hanging around Sigmund Coppleburg's cottage at all hours?" Clara threw in the remark to see the response she got. She did not have proof Abigail was the one who had been lurking near the cottage, but she had a good hunch it was her.

Abigail, for the first time, faltered in her denials. They saw it then; Clara was completely correct.

"That was how you ruined your shoes!" Annie, who had been desperate to speak for some minutes, but had not known what to say, blurted out those words. "I took a look at them after they had dried overnight by the range. You must have walked somewhere that was thick with mud, it was caked all over them. They are quite ruined."

Abigail was silent, unsure what to say.

"This is becoming ridiculous. Why don't we just tell Park-Coombs all we know? He will have enough to question Abigail, at the very least," Tommy interrupted.

"No!" Abigail said sharply. She had spent time at the police station once before and did not care to go through the ordeal of being suspected of a crime by them again. "Please, do not do that."

"You are starting to leave us with no option," Clara replied. "It is difficult to trust someone who lies and misleads you."

Abigail's expression of hurt had changed, now she looked sad.

"I know I have been a dreadful friend to you, Clara," she said meekly. "I have abused your hospitality, treating your home as just a place to lay my head. All I can offer in my defence is that I have had nothing to do with the misfortune that has befallen Miss Pink."

Clara looked at her for a long time, their eyes locked as she considered what she had heard.

"I do not believe you," she said at last. "How can I when you offer me nothing to explain why you have been sneaking around and spying on Miss Pink."

Abigail dropped her head, silent.

"That's it, I am ringing Park-Coombs and telling him all this," Tommy said, catching his sister's eye as he spoke.

It was a ploy, he would not ring Park-Coombs without Clara's agreement, but Abigail did not know that. He made a move towards the door.

"Please, Tommy, don't!" Abigail cried out. "I shall explain, I really will."

He turned back. Abigail looked strained, a trembling hand going to her mouth as if she felt a little sick.

"I have done things this last week I should never have been asked to do," she said. "I am not even sure I want to work for Albion after all this."

"Then you did sabotage the pill bottles," Clara said despondently.

"No!" Abigail was indignant. "I have been nowhere near those bottles. The closest I came to them was standing before the window display, on the outside of the window, before you ask. I am not responsible for any poisoning. Do you really think I would do something like that?"

Abigail's hurt look returned as she gazed at Clara.

"I do not want to believe it," Clara told her. "I just cannot see an alternative reason."

The mood of the room had become sombre. The heightened emotion of the last few minutes had burned out, leaving everyone drained and ready to speak more honestly. Abigail slowly loosened her stance, dropped the tension from her shoulders, and lost some of her defensiveness. She took a chair at the kitchen table opposite Clara.

"All right, you have worn me out with all this," she admitted. "I am done with all these lies. They seem pointless now with all this poisoning business going on."

Abigail frowned.

"You think someone has deliberately sabotaged Miss Pink's pills?" she was slowly catching up with what Clara and Tommy had been saying.

"We know someone has," Clara answered. "Some of the pill bottles had arsenic laced water added to them. It would have been easier to squeeze in a few drops of the poisonous liquid then to try to add powder. Safer for the poisoner too as they would be less likely to get any arsenic on their hands."

Abigail took this all in.

"That is a very serious business," she said. "I understand now why you thought I might be responsible, considering my strange behaviour."

She paused for a moment.

"You are right that I have been lurking about Coppleburg's cottage. I followed Miss Pink there the day I arrived in Brighton. I realised at once that Coppleburg must be her pharmacist. He answered his door wearing a calico apron and showed her to the back of the cottage to an outbuilding. I slipped as close as I dared and listened at the door. For the most part, they talked about the pills and their future plans."

"For the most part?" Tommy asked.

Abigail reddened a fraction.

"I became aware they were lovers as well as business

partners," she said.

"You have been back to the cottage more than once," Clara pointed out.

Abigail nodded her head stiffly. She was not going to distract Clara from learning the whole story.

"I was just observing at first. I will not lie, Clara. I had instructions to steal a bottle of Pink's Pills and I spent a good deal of time on the public footpath behind the cottage waiting for an opportunity. But it turned out I had arrived too late, and the pills had already been delivered to Mr Dyer. I was hoping with it being quite the sell-out Mr Coppleburg would make a new batch, so I kept watching and waiting. It was a horrible business. I was cold and wet, and I felt a fool. I asked myself why I was doing something so awful, and I found I had no real answer."

"Then Albion Industries are interested in the diet pills," Clara said, pleased to discover she had been correct.

"Not in the way you imagine," Abigail told her, dimming her enthusiasm. "Albion Industries have no interest in marketing a diet pill. They believe it is too complex and difficult a market. Diet pills promise the sorts of results that are difficult to fake. If you get the recipe wrong, you either fail to live up to your promises or suffer in the manner Miss Pink is now doing. She sent them details of her pills, you know, asked if they would be interested in developing them with her, but they turned her down. Too many risks in that market."

"If Albion does not want the recipe to make their own, why would they have you stealing the pills?" Tommy picked up on the obvious.

Abigail drew a hand over her eyes, weary of all this business, exhausted by her antics and wondering when she had stopped being a sales representative and had become a spy.

"They wanted the pills because they fancied they were their last hope, as ridiculous as that sounds," Abigail groaned. "Sometimes, things go wrong in the most peculiar of ways. Do you know how many meetings I have sat in where people have ranted about how Miss Pink should have won that beauty pageant? How much better it would have been if she had. Hindsight is all very well when judging our past decisions, but it is not very helpful."

"This is to do with the beauty pageant from the summer?" Clara asked. "Last hope? Last hope of what?"

Abigail gave her a wry smile.

"Last hope of salvaging what is fast becoming a publicity disaster," she said. "You know about the pageant then?"

"Miss Pink came runner-up," Tommy interjected. "She has used her winnings and the publicity to start her business, which now looks to be in ruins."

"That is a crying shame," Abigail sighed. "Albion have been watching her progress and are impressed. Well, until now. I think they are considering offering her a position at the company, perhaps a partnership where they become the exclusive supplier of her products. Except, this mess with the arsenic will put them off. I am sorry for Miss Pink. I like to see a woman making her way."

"Go back to the publicity disaster," Clara said hastily. "That does not involve Miss Pink."

"No," Abigail concurred. "It involves Alice Minsk, the girl who won the overall pageant, beating thousands of other girls to demonstrate she not only had looks, but intelligence, and reliability."

"What happened to Alice?" Clara asked, fearing some terrible tragedy that might suggest a motive for all this mess with the pills. "Has she been harmed?"

Abigail gave her a tight little grin.

"Worse," she groaned. "She has become fat."

Chapter Eighteen

The revelation released the tight bindings Abigail had been controlling herself with and suddenly she wondered why she had been so hesitant to explain. Hearing the words aloud, the scandal Albion Industries had been terrified of, and which they had impressed upon her must not be mentioned, now seemed ridiculous. It helped that this poisoning escapade had rather placed things into context. A fat beauty queen was simply not as dreadful as people being poisoned by supposed diet pills. It certainly was not as dreadful as Abigail being accused of that poisoning and facing the wrath of the Brighton police.

She let out a long exhale, as if she were physically releasing everything that she had been holding tight inside.

"I do not understand all this fuss about Miss Minsk putting on a little weight," Annie said, at last allowing her own mouth to open. "She probably looks better for it. I have seen how skinny some of these girls try to be, it is unhealthy and unnatural. I think I should make a cup of tea."

She said all this in such a rush, because she had felt so deprived of speaking for the last hour or so, that it took everyone a moment to understand what she had said. She was already getting the big copper kettle filled with water before Abigail responded.

"She has not just put on a little weight," Abigail said, careful not to stir the ire of Annie once more. "She has become fat. I cannot make it any plainer. She must be four times the size she was when she won the pageant."

"That is quite impressive, considering the short time there has been since that event," Tommy pointed out. "She must be one of those girls who has to starve herself constantly to obtain the figure they think they need to have."

Abigail nodded her head, agreeing with him sadly.

"Miss Minsk was beautiful," she said with a sigh. "She was perfect to be the face of Albion. She was not only stunning, but well-mannered and with this sparkle to her. It was a close thing between her and Miss Pink, but ultimately, we agreed there was something too hard about the latter. She was not terribly approachable."

Having met Miss Pink, Clara could see Abigail's point. In photographs she could mask her stern cynicism, but in person her demeanour was obvious. She was cold-hearted, calculating, not someone to appeal to the public.

"After her victory, Miss Minsk was feted by many of our subsidiary businesses. She was invited to dinner after dinner, encouraged to celebrate. It began, I suppose, as a reward of indulgence for having succeeded. The problem was, Miss Minsk never stopped," Abigail sighed. "It was first noted she had expanded by two dress sizes when she came to the offices in London for her first photo shoot. There was a ripple of shock through the senior managers when they noticed. Quiet words were had, which resulted in Miss Minsk bursting into floods of tears. No more was said at that juncture, it was too awkward."

"And you all hoped Miss Minsk had heeded the warning," Tommy said, not convinced the words spoken would have be so quiet or so subtle.

"It was not a warning, due to the fact she had signed a

contract for five years and there was nothing in it that stated she could be dismissed for gaining weight. It was an oversight that the company shall not make again, but where it comes to Miss Minsk our hands are truly tied. The legal department has made that plain," Abigail groaned at the difficulty of it all. "Miss Minsk appears to be incapable of stopping eating now she has begun, and her weight increases each month. We have cancelled all our publicity involving her, it would just be unseemly. We have considered taking on another girl, a doppelganger, if you will, but again the legal department says this would be awkward with our contract. Miss Minsk would have to agree and, besides, this whole time we have been paying her for doing nothing!"

"I think Albion are being fools," Annie said in her usual practical manner. "There are plenty of girls of generous dimensions buying their products, why not celebrate them by having Miss Minsk as the face of Albion? Better to have a healthy, robust lass as your symbol than those weeds you normally see."

Abigail winced at Annie's suggestion, the mere thought making her shudder.

"I am afraid the beauty industry does not work that way, Annie," Clara spoke for her. "More is the pity."

"We cannot persuade Miss Minsk to diet. Or, rather, she claims she is, but it is not working. She was on quite a savage regime to keep the weight off before her success in the pageant. Now she has triumphed, I suppose she does not fancy going back to those levels of deprivation," Abigail sighed.

"Would anyone?" Annie remarked. "If a person has to starve themselves to achieve a certain figure, then clearly nature did not intend them to look that way. I feel for Miss Minsk."

"Albion was hoping they could find a magic cure for all this," Clara said. "They hoped they could give Miss Minsk a pill and all their problems would melt away."

Abigail gave a groan.

"Exactly. Someone in the senior management team recalled a letter he had received about a diet pill. Perfectly safe, all natural and highly effective. He had dismissed it because that was not a direction Albion was planning to go in, but when someone mentioned the Miss Minsk situation he remembered. It was thought, if we could discreetly obtain some, then our problems may be solved."

"Then, why did you not just write to Miss Pink?" Tommy asked. "Would that have not been the logical thing to do?"

Abigail chuckled at his innocence.

"You don't understand the complexities of all this. Miss Pink was our runner-up, do not forget, and if she gained the information about Miss Minsk's fall from grace, we could not be sure what she would do with it. Runners-up can hold grudges."

Abigail pulled a face. Clara raised an eyebrow.

"Not to mention you had cut her off when the competition was over, making it plain you wanted nothing to do with her," she said. "Her pills were dismissed without even a response, her letter approaching you for assistance discarded. Miss Pink might just bargain hard over her diet pills for that."

"I told you, we saw how cold and calculating she was," Abigail answered sinisterly. "We could never prove a thing, and, honestly, the company did not care, but we had heard rumours she scuppered some of her competition. The rivalry between her and Miss Minsk was something to behold. They hated one another. After Miss Minsk won, Miss Pink was not precisely gracious about it. She refused to shake hands with her, even for a photograph.

"We feared that were she to learn of our situation, Miss Pink would use it to her advantage, perhaps demand the pills become an Albion product or do something more drastic, such as telling the papers of our sordid story."

"It is not sordid to be fat," Annie huffed. "That is what's wrong with the thinking of this world."

Abigail thought it prudent to ignore her.

"We were considering our options," she carried on. "Trying to think of a way around the situation that would not be quite as devious as our previous exploits."

She was referring to the business with Mr Mokano and the stolen formula for his new shade of lipstick. That had caused Albion's legal department some headaches when it all came out.

"We would have come up with an idea too, but then we read about the launch of the pills and my superiors panicked. They thought, if the pills were a success, then they would have no leverage left and so I was sent in haste down to Brighton to... steal some."

Abigail dipped her head at the indignity of it all. She knew how petty and nefarious it seemed, how disgraceful for a company such as Albion, how disgraceful that she was placed in such a position.

"Once you had the pills, Albion's research laboratories could discover their ingredients and make their own," Clara concluded. "No one would need to know about it. Miss Minsk would be given the pills, she would lose the weight and become the face of Albion as she was meant to. No one would be the wiser."

Abigail nodded her head again, words failing her. She felt dreadful about the whole sorry affair. It had been bad enough trying to steal the pills, lurking outside the cottage, hoping to spot a moment when they were untended. Cold, wet, fed up and wondering why she was doing this. It was even worse now Clara knew her secret.

"Abigail, I am not sure what to say," Clara answered after a while. "It is just so... underhand."

"Have some tea, it will make everything clearer," Annie said with her usual kitchen wisdom.

She placed teacups on the table, along with the milk jug and teapot. She pointedly nudged a dish full of sugar in Abigail's direction.

"You need the sweetness for the shock," she said.

"I don't think I am in shock," Abigail replied. "I just feel ashamed."

"Albion should never have asked you to do this," Tommy said sternly.

"I should not have agreed to it," Abigail sighed. "Of course, with all this new scandal about poison in the pills I am somewhat glad I never succeeded in obtaining a bottle."

"You never entered Sigmund's workshop?" Clara asked her, a fierce look in her eyes.

"Never," Abigail swore. "I never worked up the courage. Besides, he had taken all the filled bottles to Mr Dyer by the time I was hanging around. I needed him to make some more, but by the time that happened he had started to lock his workshop."

"You knew the pills were poisoned," Tommy pointed out. "Why keep after them?"

"At first I was not going to," Abigail admitted. "I was going to go back to London and report that the pills were a disastrous fraud, but then I heard rumours that the pills had been tampered with, that someone had sabotaged Miss Pink's products. That renewed my hope that if I could get a fresh bottle, I would have the genuine, unharmful, diet pills."

"Such fuss over a few extra pounds," Annie tutted to herself. "If people just embraced themselves for who they were, this situation would never have happened. I really do not understand."

She drained her tea and poured out a second cup, adding two spoons of sugar to make a point.

"Why were you at the demonstration tonight?" Clara asked her.

"I was thinking it might be my last chance to secure a bottle. I had been watching the cottage and saw that Sigmund had been in his workshop nearly all day. When I read the notice about the demonstration I knew why. I told myself that if I could just get hold of the pills Miss Pink would have with her at the demonstration, I would be able to take them to Albion and this whole sorry mess would be over."

Abigail looked morosely at her cup of tea.

"I was foiled when Miss Pink consumed all the pills before the audience. And you were there, of course, Clara, and I did not want to tangle with you. I knew you were aware I was up to something. I thought it best I slip away as soon as I could."

Abigail was utterly defeated, the result of not just her failure to secure the pills, but a combination of the cold and damp she had suffered the last few days, and which had led to her being exhausted. Suddenly her resolve slipped and with a look of grim determination, she heaped a spoonful of sugar into her tea and stirred vigorously.

"I have ruined my favourite shoes over this nonsense," she cried, before downing her tea in one long swallow.

"Well, I fancy Miss Minsk has had a narrow escape from being poisoned too," Tommy said. "Supposing she had just been given the pills straight off without the laboratory examining them first?"

Abigail did not reply. Though it was peevish, she rather blamed Miss Minsk for her current misfortune.

"While you were lurking about the cottage, did you see anyone else who should not have been there?" Clara asked her.

"No one," Abigail answered. "No one came down that footpath. They had more sense. When it was not muddy, it was icy."

"Then we still have no clue as to who tampered with the pill bottles," Clara said thoughtfully.

"You believe me?" Abigail asked her.

"The story you have just spoken is too convoluted to be anything but the truth," Clara answered. "Besides, I could swiftly enough confirm it with Albion if I wished to."

Abigail nodded solemnly.

"I am shocked myself at what has happened with these pills. It is dreadful to think someone would put people in harm's way to get revenge."

"Perhaps we should consider Miss Minsk a suspect," Tommy said lightly. "As she hated Miss Pink."

"From what Abigail has told us, it would seem more

prudent to look towards the local girls who were up against Miss Pink. If she is as savage as you say, Abigail, then she is bound to have caused someone to feel vengeful," Clara countered. "Could you get us a list of all the local girls who competed in the contest?"

"That is easy enough," Abigail agreed. "I would just need to make a phone call."

"Maybe we shall find our saboteur upon that list," Clara finished her tea and yawned. "I think it is time for an early night. I assume, now we have aired all this out, you will not be leaving us?"

Clara was speaking direct to Abigail.

"If you are willing to allow me to stay, I would certainly prefer that," Abigail replied sheepishly.

"You are welcome to continue here," Clara said. "Isn't that right, Annie?"

"She is very welcome," Annie said, rather like she was the king bequeathing an honour upon someone. "As long as she promises to be around for meals."

"I promise," Abigail smiled. "In fact, I rather think I shall not even go out tomorrow, but actually take the time to relax."

"Then I shall return your shoes," Annie announced graciously.

"You are not quite done with the pills, are you?" Tommy asked Abigail insightfully.

Abigail had the decency to hesitate just before she answered.

"You are correct. If you can resolve this business with the arsenic, well, the pills may still be of value to Albion."

She paused for a just a moment.

"I promise I won't be stealing them, however."

Chapter Nineteen

Despite the dramas of the night before, Clara slept surprisingly well – deep exhaustion taking her straight to sleep. She awoke with renewed energy for the trials ahead. When she came downstairs for breakfast it was a relief to see Abigail sitting in the morning room, watching smoke rising from a distant bonfire. The air smelt autumnal; damp, leafy and tinged by the aroma of many fires burning in neighbouring hearths. Clara smiled at her, for the first time feeling that her school friend was present rather than the unhappy imposter who had taken her place the last few days.

Abigail returned the smile.

"I have something for you."

She retrieved a sheet of notepaper from a side table and presented it to Clara.

"The Albion offices open at eight o'clock, so I rang up first thing and asked for a list of all the girls who competed in the local pageant. I also asked that those that placed be listed at the top. The local pageant awarded prizes to fifth place."

Abigail pointed to the top of the page where five girls were listed, at the head of this list was Miss Rose Pink.

A Diet of Death

"I would say if you wanted to find a vengeful rival, someone angry enough to stalk Miss Pink and poison her pills, you should begin with the girls who placed just after her in the contest."

Clara thought that was a fair point. She examined the full list which contained the names of thirty girls. She groaned at the extent of the names. Any of these girls might have felt resentful enough towards Miss Pink to decide to sabotage her products. Working out which had the means, opportunity and sheer savagery to do such a thing would take ages.

"I know, it is a lot of names," Abigail nodded. "But I would concentrate on the top ten. The other girls did not get past the initial rounds and probably had little contact with Miss Pink."

"It still beggars' belief that someone would be so hateful of Miss Pink they would poison innocent people."

"Look what that mad woman did at the Albion trade fair because she thought her husband was having an affair," Miss Pink pointed out.

"I know. I should not be shocked after all this time. I think, the truth of it is, I am disappointed. Thank you for this."

Clara folded the list and slipped it into a pocket in the long cardigan she was wearing.

"I am glad you are still here," she smiled.

Abigail reddened and turned her head away a fraction.

"After the aggravation I put you all through, I owe you an apology. I behaved unspeakably. When I think about it now, I shudder at the thought. I am sorry."

"Apology accepted," Clara replied. "I am just glad to have the real Abigail back, not this stranger who was acting like some sort of spy."

Abigail cringed at the description and laughed at herself.

"I have to ask, Clara, do you believe I am innocent in this poisoning?" her face had fallen, she was desperate to have Clara say she believed in her innocence.

154

"I believe you," Clara told her. "If I doubted you, I would have rung up Albion Industries and asked them about why you were here. I think, given a choice between saying they had sent you to steal pills or to poison them, they would choose the former."

"They might deny all knowledge of my presence here," Abigail pointed out.

"Then, they do not deserve the loyalty you show them," Clara told her seriously. "Honestly, their actions are not becoming of a professional company with a reputation that is already tarnished. Maybe you need to consider transferring to somewhere else?"

Abigail did not take the suggestion to heart; they both knew she would never leave Albion.

"Maybe the House of Jasmine would take me on?" she jested, which told Clara all she needed to know about whether Abigail would ever consider leaving her employers.

Tommy arrived in the morning room and Clara showed him the list. They agreed they would hold off interviewing anyone until they had spoken to Miss Pink, who would hopefully be well enough to tell them which of the named women was most likely to hold a grudge.

The next step was to contact Inspector Park-Coombs and see if he could arrange for them to visit Miss Pink outside of regular visiting hours. That was when they received a surprise.

"Miss Pink is not at the hospital," he told them. "I rang this morning. She discharged herself first thing and has gone to Mr Coppleburg's cottage."

"She surely was not well enough?"

"She was able to walk and talk for herself so the hospital could not stop her. I am somewhat surprised she has gone to recuperate with Mr Coppleburg. It is scandalous for a single lady to be staying alone with a bachelor, but what do I know? You young people these days do all sorts of things I would never have even considered in my youth."

Clara was smiling at his talk.

"You are not so old, Inspector."

"I feel old," Park-Coombs grumbled. "On dull days like this, after a long night."

"I would suggest you take things a bit easy for a while, but I fancy that is impossible."

Park-Coombs huffed and then hung up. He wasn't one for farewells.

"Miss Pink has discharged herself and gone to stay with Sigmund," Clara told her brother the second she was off the telephone. "I imagine his cottage is the one place she feels safe."

"Does she not have family around Brighton?" Tommy asked, surprised like Park-Coombs that Miss Pink would opt to stay with a single man rather than with family, considering what people would say if they knew of the arrangement.

"She has never mentioned any," Clara shrugged. "And when we told her she needed to go somewhere other than home, she decided she would go to Coppleburg. Miss Pink struck me as someone who is very isolated and who prefers things that way."

"Well, I guess I know where we are going this morning. Better bring an umbrella, looks like rain and I don't fancy getting wet waiting for the bus."

Tommy was right about the rain. By the time they had travelled by bus to the countryside and left it behind at the stop near the lane that ran to Coppleburg's home, the heavens had burst open and were thundering down on them.

"Lucky for Abigail we got the truth out of her last night, so she does not have to lurk on that footpath anymore," Clara said, feeling a pang of conscience that the thought amused her somewhat.

Abigail had hurt her more than she realised with her antics and the thought of her getting soaked playing spy over these ridiculous diet pills had a certain appeal. She shook off the thought the second it entered her head, feeling guilty it had ever cropped up.

The lane leading to Coppleburg's cottage had turned into a quagmire of mud that reminded them of their holiday to Ireland and the muddy bog where archaeologists had found a body. They did their best not to slip over as they navigated the treacherous footing.

"This is ridiculous!" Tommy snapped as he nearly fell over, saving himself by snatching hold of the nearby hedge. "He has to do something about his lane!"

"I rather fancy Sigmund does not leave his home very often," Clara replied. "And therefore, can ignore the diabolical nature of the lane leading to it."

They survived the ordeal and reached the cottage with no more than muddy shoes and a few splatters on their clothes to show for their bother. Clara was trying not to think about the return trip they would have to face after further rain had fallen.

Sigmund opened the door and did not seem surprised to see them.

"Rose said you would probably come to see her," he said. "Don't hang around in the rain."

He took them through to his cramped little parlour, where Miss Pink was sitting in an armchair next to the fire, wrapped up in blankets.

"I knew you would come," her voice was raspy, after the ordeal of the stomach pump. She was sipping from a glass that appeared to contain black mud.

"Dissolved charcoal," Sigmund explained when he caught the look in Clara's eye. "It helps neutralise toxins."

"It is disgusting," Miss Pink winced. "But right now, I do not much care."

"How are you feeling?" Clara asked her. "I was not expecting you to leave the hospital so soon."

"I cannot abide hospitals," Miss Pink pulled a face. "I could not remain in the place longer than necessary. As soon as I could get myself out of bed, I insisted on leaving. They cannot do anything more for me than Sigmund can, anyway."

"She is right about that," Sigmund nodded. "There is no

medicine that can remove arsenic from the body. Pumping the stomach to empty as much of the poison as possible is all that can be done, and then it is really all about the patient's constitution and how much has been absorbed by their system before the intervention of the doctors."

"I made myself sick swiftly and that, I am informed, made the difference," Miss Pink explained. "Otherwise, considering the amount of arsenic I must have consumed, I should be dead."

"That is an unpleasant thought," Tommy frowned. "Why on earth did you take all those pills once you realised they were poisoned?"

Miss Pink stared at him as if he were a fool.

"I told you already. I had to prove my pills were safe."

Clara had no words for that sort of stupidity, it was not ground she wanted to go over again.

"I have a list of the girls you competed against in the local beauty pageant," she said. "I wondered if you would take a look and note any of the girls you might have had an issue with, or who were staunch rivals."

"You think someone who resents Miss Pink for winning the local pageant did this?" Sigmund asked, as astounded and appalled by the idea as any right-thinking person would be.

"It has crossed my mind," Clara replied.

Miss Pink was not stunned by the idea, she took the paper Clara had removed from her pocket and glanced over it.

"Sigmund, could you bring me a pencil?" she rasped.

Sigmund disappeared for a moment, then returned with a pencil for her. Miss Pink started to put marks next to names.

"I shall organise the names based on how severe a dislike I think the girl may have for me," she said without irony for what she had just said. "One shall mean they hated my guts, two shall indicate a moderate dislike for me, and three shall indicate a more general disregard."

Clara gave Tommy a look at this information. He

responded by raising his eyebrows. Sigmund was quite distressed to hear his lover talk this way about how others felt towards her.

"There," Miss Pink said, handing back the list. "I suggest you concentrate on the ones."

She had marked three names with a one beside them, including the girl who had come second to her in the local pageant.

"Ethel Mayhew?" Clara said.

"Never forgave me for beating her. It was a close-run thing, you see, and she had been dispensing her favours quite freely with some of the judges. Unlucky for her that someone mentioned this to Albion Industries and several of the judges were replaced at the last minute."

"Did you tell Albion?" Tommy asked.

"No," Miss Pink said plainly. "However, I might have encouraged other girls to do just that. Ones who thought they might gain an advantage that way."

"Specifically?" Clara asked.

"Specifically, June Beatty, who came fifth. She was quite a nervous little thing who would have spent her time better in pursuing some sort of political agenda, such as campaigning for more women's toilets in the town. It did not take much to have her jotting off a stern letter. It also happens her father is involved with the council, which is why her accusation was taken seriously."

"Taken more seriously than a complaint by you might have been," Tommy said, grasping her meaning.

Miss Pink shrugged.

"June Beatty is already marked with a one," Clara pointed out.

"I rather fancy she thought the letter would put her in the top spot, she was set for third place before it was sent. Afterwards, the change of judges did not go in her favour, and they pushed her down to fifth. Honestly, I think she would have not been in the placings at all if it was not for the knowledge her father had a bit of clout," Miss Pink was unrepentant that she had used June in this manner.

"And both Ethel and June are the sort of girls to consider sabotaging your pills?" Clara asked.

"Ethel, certainly. She spiked some of the girls' drinks during the event, laced them with gin so they would become drunk. You know that one of the rules was that the girls must not drink during the event?"

"Have you seen either of these girls hanging around you?" Tommy asked. "They would have had to follow you here to learn about the pills."

"I have been thinking about that," Miss Pink said. "It is all I can think about. Who would have known about the pills? It occurred to me there was one strange incident a few weeks ago at my house. I had popped out to do some shopping and when I returned, I discovered that the French window in my dining room was slightly open. It was summer, so I assumed I had been careless. I did open the French windows often to let air into the room. Now I am reconsidering. I use the dining room as a sort of study and my paperwork for Pink's Pills as well as the draft for my next diet book were all on the table. Some of the papers had fluttered to the floor in the breeze from the open door."

"In hindsight, you wonder if someone broke in to look at your papers and learned of your pills?" Tommy interpreted.

"It was just a thought," Miss Pink said. "One of those things that come back to you in the dead of night."

"What about this third name, Audrey Cole?" Clara asked.

Miss Pink had a wistful smile on her face at the name.

"Really, perhaps I should have made her a one all on her own and added a fourth category for the others," she said. "Audrey detested me long before the pageant. Our rivalry extends over many years."

"Why is that?" Tommy asked.

Miss Pink chuckled.

"I rather fancy it came about because she is my half-sister."

Chapter Twenty

Miss Pink did not care to elaborate further on her relationship with Audrey Cole. She was exhausted and needed to rest. She gave them an address for her half-sister, though she admitted she had no idea if they would find her there, and then they left her in peace.

Sigmund saw them to the door.

"I knew nothing about a sister," he said to them in a whisper. "I am beginning to think I know very little about Rose at all."

"Miss Pink is used to keeping secrets as a means of protecting herself," Tommy told him. "Do not take it personally, rather, understand she needs to learn what trust is before she can open up. You have to ask yourself if you are the man to warrant that trust and whether you have the patience and willingness to give her the time she will need."

Clara was impressed by his words of wisdom. Sigmund glanced in the direction of his parlour, unable to see beyond the doorway to Miss Pink.

"Maybe," he said at last.

It was not a convincing response and Clara sensed he was not sure himself if this was the path forward he desired.

Miss Pink was not easy to love, after all.

They said their goodbyes and headed out into a grim day with a dark grey sky overhead promising plenty of rain. They slipped and slid along the lane and made their way back to the bus stop.

"I am thinking of getting a car," Tommy grumbled.

It was not the first time they had had this conversation. Tommy envied Captain O'Harris' car collection and had a desperate desire to own such a piece of technology. Clara had no issue with hopping on buses or walking. The former gave her time to mull over a case, the latter gave her the exercise she needed to burn off all the good meals Annie plied her with.

They had timed their arrival at the bus stop with lucky precision and it was not long before the vehicle hove into view. It would not normally stop at this point, but they waved it down and clambered on board just before the skies opened and dropped an ocean of rain upon them.

There was nothing more satisfying than just avoiding a deluge and they sat at the back of the bus and watched the rain falling all the way to Brighton.

Audrey Cole lived at a residence down one of the narrower back streets of Brighton. The road was lined with small terraces that had been built around the 1850s and not with the greatest of care. There were noticeable signs of crumbling around the corners and the brickwork looked particularly shoddy in places. It was a semi-respectable district, people were in the main trying their best, but a few of the residents had occupations decidedly on the illegal side of things.

They found Audrey's house and knocked on the door. A dog started to bark furiously and then a woman was heard hushing it. The next moment the door swung open.

Had they not been told that Rose Pink and Audrey Cole were half-sisters, they would have surely considered that a likelihood the second Audrey stood before them. There was the same line to the nose, the same stern stare. Audrey, however, did not disguise her face with make-up. She faced the world as she was and asked it to make its choice whether to embrace her or not. In that regard, she had one up on her half-sister.

"Audrey Cole?" Clara asked her.

"I don't need anything," Audrey said. "Especially not my soul saving."

She was about to shut the door on them, assuming they were the sort of visitors trying to sell God, charity or insurance to her. Clara spoke in haste.

"We are not here to sell you anything. We hoped to have a word about your sister, Rose Pink."

Audrey narrowed her eyes. It was not plain whether this news made her more or less willing to let them into her home.

"I don't have anything to do with my sister," she said.

"You did both enter the beauty pageant, however," Clara pointed out. "We really must talk. Are you aware your sister has been unwell?"

"I don't keep up with what she is doing," Audrey shrugged. "I am far too busy."

She had folded her arms across her chest and was no longer holding the door, which indicated to Clara she was willing to talk a bit and was not going to slam the door in their face.

"Could we come in and have a chat?" Clara asked. "No one needs their business spread up and down the street."

Audrey's frown grew and then she sighed.

"I suppose I ought to listen."

She stepped back from the door and allowed them into a tiny front room. She was unwilling to allow them further into her home, giving them just enough room to come inside and shut the door.

"If Rose needs me to act as a go-between her and our mother, I will consider it just because we are family. But that is all."

"We were not aware Miss Pink's parents were still living in Brighton," Clara remarked

"Our mother is," Audrey explained. "She lives here, with

me. Except she is out at the moment. She works at the hospital doing all the laundry. Rose has not spoken to her in… well, it must be six months if not more."

"You have all fallen out?" Tommy asked.

"It is difficult to know with Rose," Audrey said. "She will not speak to you for ages then just turn up out of the blue and act as if nothing has happened. I am not sure if she just gets so wrapped up in her life, she forgets about everyone else, or whether she really has taken against us."

"She is a complicated person," Clara said.

"Not complicated," Audrey raised the side of her mouth in a smile. "Awkward."

"Have you heard about her new venture?" Clara added.

"Pink's Pills," Audrey shrugged. "I heard. Based on an old family recipe, my mother's recipe given to her by her mother and by her mother's mother. I suppose it would be too much to ask for a little share in the profits."

"There won't be any profits from these pills," Tommy remarked darkly.

That caught Audrey's attention.

"Why?"

She seemed to genuinely not know.

"You have not heard about the pills?" Clara frowned, thinking Audrey was doing a remarkably good appearance of ignorance if she was lying.

"I choose not to know about them," Audrey replied. "I knew about the launch because I had reason to pass by Mr Dyer's shop and there was my sister grinning from the window. I confess, I was rather annoyed to learn she was making a profit from a family recipe but I long ago learned it was best not to get involved in Rose's business."

"The pills have been sabotaged," Clara said, expecting perhaps a flicker of recognition if Audrey was guilty of the sabotage.

She made no such sign.

"How can you sabotage a pill?" she said, looking baffled and beginning to wonder who these people were she had allowed into her home.

"They were laced with arsenic," Tommy answered. "A person has died from taking them."

Audrey's eyebrows raised up, then, somewhat inexplicably, she started to laugh.

"Oh! I am sorry! I am not amused someone has died, but it suddenly struck me how it served Rose right to have her scheme tampered with in such a way!"

"You do not like to see her succeeding," Clara suggested.

"Not at the expense of her family!" Audrey remarked back. "She took that recipe from under our noses. My mother deserves a share in those pills, but now I am rather glad Rose decided to do things alone as it means we are out of this whole, sorry mess!"

She was gleeful in her spite and triumph, for a moment, that was all she could think of, then slowly her more rational side reminded her of what had been said and she became sombre.

"She has killed someone?"

"Not on purpose," Clara said hastily. "Someone slipped into where the pills where being stored and poisoned the bottles. Only a handful, so that it was very unfortunate that certain people ended up with the tampered pills."

"Rose was always good at making enemies rather than friends," Audrey shrugged.

"Rose has been poisoned too," Clara pressed on. "She took some of the pills herself to demonstrate they were harmless. Unfortunately, the pill bottle contained arsenic."

"Well, I am sorry about that," Audrey answered, still oblivious to why they were really there. "Does she want me or mother to rush over to her aid? We shall not. We may be family, but she has treated us with such disregard that we refuse to have anything to do with her. She never visits when mother has a flare-up of her rheumatics. Nor when I broke my finger falling down the stairs and could do hardly anything for myself. She had better things to do than tend to us."

"We have not been sent for that reason," Clara

explained. "We are trying to determine who might have had enough of a grudge against your sister to wish to harm her."

Audrey shot a look at her.

"What has she said?"

Clara had hedged around long enough. She laid her cards on the table.

"She says you hate her and if anyone who was involved in the beauty pageant might hold a grudge against her, it would be you."

There it was, laid out bare.

Audrey gaped for a moment, then let out a croaky laugh.

"She said that?"

"We are working on the theory that someone who was against her in the beauty pageant felt badly enough towards her they would go to any lengths to cause her harm. She mentioned you were a staunch rival."

Audrey laughed in astonishment.

"Well, I never! This is priceless!" she turned away and paced across the small room, coming to a narrow fireplace, and resting her hands on the mantelpiece. "I thought I was used to all the games my sister pulled, but this is another matter."

"This is not a game," Clara said quietly. "Whoever put poison in those pill bottles is responsible for the murder of one person and attempted murder on a number of others, including Miss Pink."

Audrey turned back to her, fire in her eyes.

"And she thinks to blame me? She really does despise me. I had hoped I was mistaken, but I should have known."

"You deny it?" Clara pressed.

"Of course, I deny it!" Audrey snorted. "I have no interest in those pills. I have no interest in Rose. I would rather she stay far away from me and mother. She only brings us heartache."

"What about the pageant?" Tommy asked.

"What about it?" Audrey responded.

"You and your sister both entered."

Audrey just stared at him for a long time. He was not sure quite what he had said to cause her stony silence or the look of detestation on her face. Very slowly, she breathed out and regained her composure.

"I did not enter because she had entered, if that is what you mean. I entered of my own volition and only learned she was also a contestant when the pageant began. We kept our distance during the whole thing. We never shared a word."

"That does not mean you did not hate one another," Clara pointed out. "Silence can be as angry and hurtful as sharp words."

"It was better we did not speak," Audrey answered. "Rose could only speak hurtful things and I always seemed to provoke them from her. No, we were better in silence."

"And then Rose placed higher than you did," Tommy observed. "That would have stung."

"Rose placed higher than all the girls," Audrey replied. "It was a contest, that is how it works. I am not one to hold grudges, not even against my half-sister. I have better things to do."

"Sometimes it is not as simple as all that. We hold a grudge even when we don't mean to," Tommy suggested.

Audrey gave him a smile that implied he did not know her at all.

"You might not believe me. I know Rose will not believe me because she thinks everyone is like her. Now, she holds a grudge. She wanted to win that contest more than any other girl there, and I guess that is why she did win. The moment she turned up in all that make-up and with new clothes I realised she had decided that prize was hers and no one was going to stop her. I also knew I did not stand a chance," Audrey laughed at herself. "You cannot have failed to notice that I look like my sister and we both share a rather plain appearance. Nature was not favourable to us in that regard. We have good figures, but above the shoulders and neck we are rather lacking. No one would call us beauties. However, Rose had made very impressive efforts with her make-up to transform her limitations. I was impressed by her determination if nothing else."

"I take it not all the girls wore make-up?" Clara said, wondering of there was anything to that, whether someone might have considered it cheating on Miss Pink's part.

"There was nothing against it in the rules," Audrey answered. "But a lot of girls never considered it. Others used it, of course. You could rather tell the rustic girls from those who knew how to paint their faces. I am not going to pretend I was anything but rustic."

Audrey was honest and blunt; in many regards she had a similar nature to her sister and called a spade a spade. She was more honest about herself than her sister was, however.

"She really thinks I would sabotage her pills?" Audrey went on. "She really has taken leave of her senses. You can tell her, when you see her, she best not show her face around here again. I will have no time for her. I am finished with her."

"You realise the seriousness of these accusations?" Tommy asked her.

Audrey snorted.

"I am not stupid, but I know there is no proof against me because I am innocent. It is a sad state of affairs when your sister accuses you of something like this, but that is how it is. Go back and tell her I want nothing to do with her or those pills."

Audrey marched to the door and opened it for them.

"I have better things to do with my life than hold grudges over a beauty contest."

Chapter Twenty-One

"I don't know about you, but I am stumped," Tommy said to Clara as they stood back on the road and contemplated their next move. "Every suspect we talk to denies everything."

"You are surprised by that?" Clara smirked at him. "Audrey told us a lot of things about why she might not have done this crime, but she remains a potential suspect. She gave us no reason to suppose she did not do it, after all."

"We have no proof of anything, do we?" Tommy sighed to his sister. "No clue as to who might want to commit such a hideous crime."

Clara had to admit they were facing a brick wall for the time being. But in her experience, brick walls did not last, you just had to be patient and work out a way over them. She suggested they return home to contemplate everything, rather than stand around waiting to be drenched.

It was good to be back indoors on a bleak day. There was something reassuring about the lights and warmth of a cosy home when the sky was grey as lead and rain was constantly descending. Annie was toasting muffins by the fire, looking quite content. She was a little surprised to see them back so soon.

"I wasn't expecting you," she jumped up. "I have not made tea."

"Carry on with what you are doing," Clara told her firmly. "It is nice to see you relaxing for a change."

Annie considered ignoring this suggestion for a moment, then relented and settled back to her muffin.

"How is it going?" she asked.

"Badly," Tommy groaned.

Clara gave him a stern look.

"We have yet to find the key to this puzzle," Clara told Annie, correcting her brother. "Where is Abigail?"

"She went to buy some pears and sugar so she could show me how to make this dessert her mother cooks. It is a sort of tart. It sounded a little Continental for my liking, but I sensed she was attempting to make a peace offering, so I did not argue."

This was truly gracious from Annie, who was prone to being territorial around her kitchen. Clara wondered just what had occurred between her and Abigail while they were out, and would have asked more, except the telephone began to ring.

"I hate the noise that thing makes," Annie grumbled. "It is such a savage sound."

Clara went to answer it, leaving Annie to enjoy her afternoon pause from her self-imposed busy schedule.

"Hello, Clara Fitzgerald speaking."

"Clara! It's Park-Coombs!"

The inspector sounded anxious and spoke swiftly.

"I am glad I caught you at home. We have another poisoning."

"Don't tell me someone failed to see the notices about Pink's Pills," Clara said despondently.

She had feared something like this might happen, since, despite all the police's efforts, several of the bottles of Pink's Pills were not accounted for.

"That is just the thing. The person was not taking

170

Pink's Pills," Park-Coombs said hastily. "Can you come at once, Clara? This is starting to look like a far bigger issue than we first suspected!"

"Where do I need to come?" Clara asked.

"Old Steine," Park-Coombs replied. "You will spot the house at once, as I have a constable outside."

With that he hung up.

"I really must teach him telephone etiquette and how to say goodbye," Clara grumbled to herself, putting down the receiver and going to fetch Tommy.

"That brick wall I mentioned? It looks like we might have a glimpse over it," she said to him. "Grab your coat."

Tommy was following her fast.

"You never mentioned a brick wall to me."

Clara hesitated, scrolling back through her memory.

"Oh, no, I just thought it to myself. Never mind, the outcome is the same."

She was out the door before Tommy could say anything else.

Old Steine was one of the smartest areas in Brighton. It was where the old-monied families lived. The houses were enormous and had a battery of servants to keep them running. Some of the homes were only used during the season, their owners having at least one other house they chose to spend time at. Others were in use all year and housed some of Brighton's most elite residents.

It was a long time since Clara had been down this road on a case. She wondered what she was about to discover.

As Park-Coombs had specified, there was a police constable stood outside a grand door, watching the world go by in that dull way anyone serving such duty develops. He nodded at Clara and Tommy, before opening the door for them.

"The inspector is in the drawing room on the first floor," he told them. "You can't miss him. He has holed up the entire household in there until he works out what has occurred."

Clara wondered just what the inspector was up to.

Confining the entire household seemed somewhat dramatic, unless he now suspected the Pink's Pills poisoner was among them.

"We best hurry," she said to her brother.

The drawing room was, indeed, easy to find. There was another constable stood outside it and from its confines they could hear the strained voice of the inspector as he talked to whoever he had trapped in there. He was going on and on about having the truth before the day was done and would not stop until he knew what had happened.

"He has lost the plot," Tommy said, as he heard the ranting.

"He gets nervous around the wealthy," Clara corrected. "Especially when one of them is involved in a crime."

She knocked on the door, but the inspector was too absorbed to hear her, so she barged straight in instead.

Park-Coombs was thrown from his stride by her arrival and his words faltered. Clara found herself looking at a room full of people. There were five people dressed smartly and obviously part of the family, while another half dozen were servants, including a butler who looked as though he used too much starch on his collar. All their gazes fell on Clara, and she was sure more than a few were pleading with her to assist them to get away from this mad policeman.

"I came as swiftly as I could," Clara told the inspector. "What has occurred?"

Park-Coombs had stopped with his mouth open mid-word. He now closed it and walked towards Clara.

"We need to speak privately," he said in a hushed tone that was not quite as quiet as it ought to have been.

He showed her to another room a couple of doors down from the last. It was a library and upon a table sat several items that appeared part of Park-Coombs' investigation.

"Don't look in the bowl," Park-Coombs motioned to a white basin that had been discreetly covered with a cloth. "That is a sample for the laboratory boys. I am waiting for Dr Deáth to come along and collect it, but we are currently having trouble locating him. It's his bridge evening and he has gone out to buy chocolates and Scotch, according to his wife, and apparently this process can take him some time as he gets distracted."

Park-Coombs was rambling, and he realised it. He ran a hand over his face.

"Sorry Clara, this has rather taken me by surprise."

"You best explain what has occurred," Clara suggested.

Park-Coombs nodded, then helped himself to a chair at the table. He looked done in.

"This is the home of Sir Joseph Medlar," he explained. "We received a telephone message at the station about an hour ago from his personal doctor. The man was very agitated as he had been summoned to see Medlar and had discovered he was suffering the consequences of arsenic poisoning. Sir Medlar is dangerously ill but refuses to be taken to hospital. His doctor is with him as we speak and will likely remain with him through the night. Doctors don't mess around when it comes to rich patients.

"When I arrived, I started to determine how Medlar could have ingested the poison. He had not consumed anything since breakfast this morning. Medlar is the sort of fellow who believes abstinence is the key to long existence. He has three cups of tea in the morning with his breakfast and then consumes nothing until afternoon tea, which ought to have been served around about now."

Park-Coombs took note of the time on the grandfather clock in the room.

"At first, it seemed impossible he was poisoned. If he had consumed arsenic at breakfast, he would have shown signs much earlier. Medlar, fortunately, has been able to speak, and after we probed him for a bit, he did reluctantly confess to consuming one item that afternoon. He had not wanted to mention it in front of his doctor. He had consumed a pill that had not been prescribed by the man, and my understanding is that the doctor is rather fierce on such matters."

"You said he had not taken Pink's Pills," Clara reminded him.

"No, he had not. Sir Medlar is not the sort to diet. He is as thin as a rake and monitors his weight by the methods of abstinence I just explained. No, the pills he took were for something quite different," a slight smile crept onto the inspector's lips, finding dark humour in the situation. Sometimes, if you did not find something to smile about, a case could cripple you. "Vanity has been Medlar's weakness. This afternoon he took a dose of medicine from this bottle."

Inspector Park-Coombs indicated a bottle on the table.

"Dr Patterson's Restorative Hair Tonic. It allegedly encourages hair growth. Sir Medlar is somewhat on the bald side. His doctor was not impressed he was taking an over-the-counter quack medicine, and he told him so."

Clara moved forward and picked up the bottle that was sitting on the table. It still contained a considerable amount of liquid and appeared to have been recently opened.

"He bought it yesterday," Park-Coombs answered the question she had not asked. "He took his first dose today. The bottle has yet to be tested, obviously, but it seems the tonic is the likely source."

"Where did he buy it from?" Clara asked.

"A pharmacy run by Watling and Sons," Park-Coombs explained. "No connection to Mr Dyer."

Clara was studying the bottle very carefully.

"I might be mistaken Inspector, but this bottle looks remarkably similar to those that Pink's Pills were sold in," she turned the bottle over and noticed there was a maker's name on the bottom. "Grindle, 1921."

"Probably the maker of the bottle and the date it was made," Tommy added. "Which means that bottle is a couple of years old."

"I don't know of a glassmaker around here, and certainly not one with the name Grindle," Clara continued. "But it would be very odd if both this bottle and the bottle that contained Pink's Pills were made by the same maker. A strange coincidence."

Park-Coombs was watching her face closely.

"What are you thinking, Clara?"

"I am not sure yet," Clara said. "It is just this niggle at the back of my mind. Have your men had a chance to look at the bottles we retrieved from Coppleburg's workshop?"

"They are still working through them. There are a lot of bottles, and each takes time to test. What I can say is that out of the twenty or so they have tested, none have contained arsenic."

"Instead of testing all the bottles at once, what if they picked out the ones that appeared to contain a little water?" Tommy said. "It was those ones we thought had been contaminated."

Park-Coombs had overlooked this fact in his haste. He saw now that by narrowing the search to locating first the bottles with a trace of liquid in them the process would go quicker, and the bottles that held no liquid could be used as controls.

"Ah," he said, not wanting to admit that neither he nor his boys in the lab had considered such a thing.

"Have you confiscated all these bottles of tonic?" Clara asked the inspector.

Park-Coombs brightened because in that regard he had acted at once.

"Yes, I sent constables out as soon as I knew to get all the bottles from Watling and Sons, as well as a list of customers who have bought some. My guess is we will see a similar pattern, with some bottles laced and some not."

Park-Coombs became sombre.

"It is troubling that someone appears to have been going around randomly poisoning bottles of medicines. When we thought it was only Pink's Pills affected, we had something we could focus on, as it seemed plain it was a deliberate attack on Miss Pink. Now it looks as though we may be dealing with someone who just wants to poison people anonymously. How am I supposed to catch someone like that?"

Clara was not listening, staring instead at the bottle of

tonic, and thinking her own thoughts.

"We must not become despondent, Inspector," Tommy spoke. "I assume as you have rounded up the household, you are considering other possibilities?"

"The bottle would have been easy to tamper with," Park-Coombs agreed. "And it is always possible someone among Sir Medlar's family decided to do away with the old man. He has a vast fortune and sometimes people are a little too eager for their inheritance. He keeps a tight hold on the purse strings from what I have heard so far."

"Let us postulate another theory, then," Tommy said, suddenly being inspired by an idea. "Supposing one of the family had read the papers about the drama with Pink's Pills and it gave them the notion of trying something similar? They thought that maybe by poisoning another medicine bottle it would shift the blame from the family to this mysterious and anonymous poisoner?"

"I have had a similar thought," Park-Coombs nodded. "I like that idea a lot. People do things like that and surely there must be motive aplenty among Sir Medlar's family?"

"Just because a man is wealthy does not mean all his relatives want him dead," Clara spoke up, proving she had been listening after all. "And just because a bottle has been poisoned does not mean we have a wanton poisoner on the loose."

"What are you saying Clara?" Park-Coombs muttered.

"I am thinking aloud," Clara responded. "Where did Sir Medlar keep this bottle and was anyone else in the house aware of it?"

"He was trying to keep it a secret, I believe," Park-Coombs replied. "He was rather uneasy about others knowing he was uncomfortable about his hair loss and prepared to try such a thing. It was in his medicine cabinet, he tells me."

"Then anyone could have come along and spotted it," Tommy piped up. "And to be sure they only poisoned something that Sir Medlar would take, they chose to tamper with the bottle."

"That's good Tommy!" Park-Coombs said enthusiastically. "I like that idea."

Clara sensed they were getting carried away with themselves.

"One step at a time," she reminded them. "Let's talk to the family first."

Chapter Twenty-Two

The Medlar family were not impressed they had been crowded into the upstairs drawing room and told they could not leave until the police said so. They were the sort of people who did not take kindly to being told what to do, especially by civil servants they saw as a long way beneath them.

The family consisted of Sir Medlar's younger brother, his three daughters and his nephew. Park-Coombs eyed the family up, thinking that here were prime candidates for wanting an old man out of the way so they could inherit early.

Clara was less inclined to make such a sweeping analysis. She saw the family in her own way. They were uptight and self-righteous as is the remit for families of grave wealth and social standing, but she also saw they were anxious and upset. One of the daughters had been weeping and was wringing a handkerchief through her hands. Another was putting on a brave face but was close to tears herself. Medlar's brother looked strained and worried, each time the door opened he looked up at the new arrival with anticipation. He was not looking at the inspector at all, rather he was keeping alert for the appearance of the family doctor with either good or bad news.

Clara saw a family who was not wishing away a relative for the sake of his wealth, but who were deeply upset about the suffering of a loved one and scared for his wellbeing. Park-Coombs was going to blunder in and set them on edge now he had his new theory. Clara liked the inspector, but she knew all too well how he was like a dog with a bone when he had an idea and could be belligerent in his determination to prove himself correct. She felt it was best if she stepped in first.

"Miss Clara Fitzgerald," she introduced herself formally to the family. "I have been summoned because this incident bears the hallmarks of something that has occurred among several families within the town. I am a private detective. Also, a dear friend of mine was one of the victims of this poisoning trouble."

She had spoken fast to get everything out before the family had a chance to argue with her. They looked a bit dazed by all the information she gave them. It was Sir Medlar's brother who was the first to comprehend what was occurring and speak.

"Rupert Medlar," he introduced himself. "I had not heard of poisonings in the town."

"They have occurred over the last few days and, until today, were associated with a product called Pink's Pills, which was on sale in Mr Dyer's pharmacy. Have any of you been to the shop or heard of the pills?"

There were no signs of recognition among the family. Clara had imagined as much. She did not see the Medlars as the sort of people who bought their own medicines but would rather sent a servant to fetch them.

"What was the nature of the poison in these pills?" Rupert Medlar asked.

"Arsenic," Clara told him bluntly.

He went pale with horror at the news.

"Arsenic?" he hissed the word. "That is a terrible, terrible poison. Will my brother survive?"

"That depends on a lot of things," Park-Coombs spoke up, mildly aggrieved Clara had talked to the family first. "Including how much he consumed and the strength of his constitution."

"My father is as strong as an ox!" one of the girls blurted out, taking Park-Coombs words as a personal affront against her father's physical strength.

Clara hastened to speak before people became more agitated.

"Can you tell me when you first learned Sir Medlar was unwell?" she asked the group.

"It was just around three," Rupert Medlar answered. "I had been assisting my brother in the library. We are working on a complete history of the family, and it consumes many hours of our time. We had been working since half two and then he began to complain that his stomach hurt. I suggested he ought to have had some tea when I did. He refuses to touch food and drink during the day, convinced it is the reason he keeps so well. He rapidly became worse and asked for help to reach his bedroom. We had barely arrived when he said he needed to purge, and I only just managed to secure a bowl for him to be sick into. I was concerned at his sudden indisposition and sent the butler to fetch our doctor at once."

"Being sick will have helped to remove some of the arsenic from his stomach and that is a good thing," Tommy said, trying to supply the worried family with hope.

Rupert Medlar was not going to allow hope to comfort him just at that moment, not when he had seen how sick his brother was.

"The doctor had not been here long before he declared my brother had been poisoned and he insisted he must call the police at once. I could hardly argue with him, but I never thought the family would be accused of this!"

Rupert's temper had suddenly flared, and he glowered at Park-Coombs.

"My brother is beloved to his family. We all cherish him and to suppose we would harm him is utterly preposterous!"

Park-Coombs was unmoved by his words. He had spent the better part of his life as a policeman, being harangued by people who were angry at being accused of something. Sometimes those people were innocent and sometimes they were guilty.

"Do you take the Brighton Gazette?" Clara asked.

This sudden change in direction distracted Rupert.

"Sorry?"

"The local newspaper, do you take it?"

"No," Rupert replied. "We have The Times from London and Horse and Hound. Local news is very boring."

Clara thanked him and then moved away, motioning subtly for the inspector and Tommy to follow her.

"What was all that about?" Park-Coombs grumbled.

"Your theory that the family committed this crime is reliant on them having heard about the Pink's Pills fiasco and deciding to copy it to drawn attention away from them as poisoners. But, if they had not heard of Pink's Pills and not read about the poisoning in the paper, then that theory is hard to persist with," she explained gently.

Park-Coombs was annoyed by this news.

"I shall have the house searched for a copy of the Brighton Gazette," he said, determined not to be wrong. "They are probably lying."

"You do that," Clara said, confident that she was correct.

Her self-assurance put Park-Coombs in an even worse mood.

"We need to speak to the servants," he snapped. "Maybe one among them read about Pink's Pills and got the idea."

"For what reason?" Clara asked.

"We don't know until we question them," Park-Coombs hissed fiercely.

Clara allowed him that.

"I believe it would be best to question the servants away from the family," she suggested, and for once the inspector did not disagree.

The group of half dozen servants were ushered into another room, this one a sort of private sitting room, and lined themselves up like a row of convicts along one wall. The butler began the row and the other servants followed him, placing themselves automatically in the correct position relevant to their rank.

They consisted of the butler, cook, and four maids, varying from the housemaid who served the three Medlar daughters, to the lowly scullery maid. There did not seem enough servants for such a big household and Clara mentioned this.

"Most of the household staff have gone to the London townhouse to prepare it for the family's Christmas celebrations," the butler explained.

That made sense and explained the limited staff. It also narrowed down their potential suspects, though Clara was still not convinced the poisoning was an 'inside job'.

"Who knew about the bottle of tonic Sir Medlar drank from today?" Park-Coombs interjected before Clara could speak.

"I believe I alone knew about it," the butler once more spoke. "The master asked me to fetch it for him. He wished it to be a secret from the rest of the household. I went to Watling and Sons yesterday and secured the bottle. I delivered it directly to my master the same afternoon. He asked me to place it in his private medicine cabinet."

"Ah, and once in that cabinet it could be seen by any of the family who happened to look in," Park-Coombs said in triumph.

"That is unlikely," the butler continued in his politely monotone voice. He sounded almost bored by all this talk. "The cabinet is in my master's private bathroom, which adjoins directly to his bedroom. No one else uses it."

"But someone could have gone in there, looking for a bottle or something," Park-Coombs said, his theory starting to look rather fragile.

"I suppose so," the butler replied. "However, what would be the purpose? All the family have access to their own bathrooms and there is a well-stocked medicine cabinet in each."

"Did you notice anything amiss with the tonic bottle?" Clara asked him next. "Did it appear to contain particles, for instance?"

"I cannot say I examined the bottle closely," the butler answered.

The butler's calm was irritating Park-Coombs. If only he and Medlar had touched the bottle, then the prime suspect for the poisoning would have to be the butler, and the man seemed to have no concern about this, and no motive for wishing his master dead.

"This is ridiculous," Park-Coombs grumbled storming across the room and glaring out of a window.

Clara noticed the maids were watching him with ill-concealed nerves. She sympathised.

"I do not believe the poison entered the tonic in this house," she told them. "We have already determined few had access to it and no one appears to have a reason to wish Sir Medlar harm. Obviously, this is a ghastly business, but I think the culprit behind it is somewhere else, somewhere away from the drama and pain they are causing."

The maids did not look entirely comforted, but it was the best Clara could do. Park-Coombs finally turned around and said the servants could return to their usual duties. They were obviously relieved, but decorum stated they had to leave the room in a modest and proper fashion, not dash out as they wanted to.

Alone in the sitting room, Clara, Tommy, and Park-Coombs considered their situation further.

"I am deeply concerned there is a poisoner roaming about Brighton, randomly lacing medicines with arsenic," Park-Coombs flopped down onto an overly stuffed couch as he spoke. "You are probably too young to have heard about the Brighton poisoner, even I am a little too young to recall it. She was operating in the 1870s."

"It was a woman?" Tommy asked.

"Yes. Mad as a hatter," Park-Coombs shook his head.

"She was found insane and send to Broadmoor rather than hanged. She set out to poison the wife of her lover with deadly chocolates, but her lover suspected her and refused to have any more to do with her. In her warped mind she believed she could prove her innocence to him if she poisoned more chocolates and randomly distributed them about Brighton. She wanted people to think it was an industrial accident and place the blame on the chocolate manufacturers. It almost worked as well, but she was overly confident, and people recalled she was always around when poisoned chocolates appeared. Some children even accepted some directly from her and could point her out."

"What a horrid thing," Clara said, thinking of the mindless pain the woman had caused to others just to try to prove she was not a poisoner. "How was she caught?"

"I forget the exact circumstances, but I believe she tried to poison her lover's wife again and also various chemists recalled her buying poisons, even though she had used different names and tried to disguise herself. Various things tied her to the crimes and, of course, the biggest thing is the whole affair ceased once she was arrested."

"This does sound remarkably similar," Tommy nodded. "But, if you suppose someone is trying to cover up one murder, we have to ask ourselves who has died to warrant it? We thought at first this was to sabotage Miss Pink, but now we have these poisoned tonic bottles, it starts to look as though we were just being misdirected."

"Or this really is about Miss Pink and the poisoner is trying to distract us," Clara pointed out. "Spreading confusion by poisoning other products. No, wait, that does not work as then it makes the sabotage of Miss Pink's pills pointless as everyone will realise it was accidental and not blame her."

"Well, I don't know then," Tommy leaned against a wall and sighed.

The big house was suddenly quiet, just the ticking of a mantel clock marking down the drift of time. They were all lost in their thoughts for a while, then a tentative knock came at the door.

"Come in," Park-Coombs called.

A police constable appeared around the door.

"We have been to Watling and Sons, Sir," he said. "We have collected every bottle and have a list of customers who have purchased one. We are rounding those bottles up as we speak. Mr Watling says the bottles arrived in his shop last week. They are supplied by a local manufacturer who makes a range of health tonics. He has been stocking their products for years with no issue. He is very alarmed."

"I bet he is after the business of Pink's Pills," Tommy remarked to his sister. "That is the sort of thing that pharmacists talk about. One of their own being attacked for selling poisonous products."

"Mr Dyer has done nothing wrong," Clara said needlessly. "He sold products in good faith. He might be unhappy to know the pills were made by his former assistant, but that is beside the point."

A thought came to Clara.

"Constable, did Mr Watling tell you who made the tonic?"

"The company, Dr Patterson's, has a small workshop near the coast. He gave me the address," the constable obliged. "They make all sorts of things there and they supply them to a number of pharmacies as well as by catalogue."

"That is not good," Park-Coombs winced. "I need to get all those tonic bottles back at once. I'll have to make calls to other divisions to help me. Do me a favour, Clara, and go see this Dr Patterson and find out what is occurring."

"I will Inspector," Clara promised. "Never fear."

Chapter Twenty-Three

It was growing late and had the matter not been urgent, Clara would have considered leaving the visit to Dr Patterson until the following morning. Instead, she and Tommy hastened to the address supplied by Watling and Sons. It was a long journey across the town, requiring them to bus hop and when they finally arrived at the industrial area where the workshop was located, it was pitch dark. There were no obvious signs of people being around, though Tommy thought he spied lights glowing in the windows of a distant building. A pair of gates blocked entry to the yard in which numerous small industrial buildings stood, however they were not locked, and Clara pushed them open. They creaked in protest.

Almost at once a man lurched out of small wooden hut set to the side of the gates and virtually invisible in the dark. He shone a bullseye lantern in their faces and barked at them.

"Who goes there?"

"Clara and Tommy Fitzgerald," Clara answered. "We are trying to locate Dr Patterson and were told he has his workshop here."

The watchman shone his lantern between them,

blinding them in the process.

"You won't find Dr Patterson here," he said.

"Then where will we find him?" Clara asked. "This is most urgent. Someone has tampered with the medicines he makes."

She was trying to get the recalcitrant watchman on her side. He puffed out his cheeks.

"Not that simple," he said. "Is it?"

Clara was getting tired of these games.

"We need to speak to Dr Patterson about his products," she insisted. "If he is not available at his workshop, then we must visit him at home. This matter cannot wait. I would prefer not to be out on a cold night like this, but we are dealing with a situation that could result in people being made seriously ill."

"All right, hold your horses!" the watchman told her. "No need to bite my head off. I merely meant Dr Patterson is not someone you can talk to, because he is not a real person, is he."

"Oh, he is just a symbol for a company," Tommy cottoned on. "Then who does run Dr Patterson's?"

"You will need to speak to Mr Higgins," the watchman said. "I don't think he has left as yet. I normally see who comes and goes from my box. This is very urgent?"

"Very urgent," Clara repeated, though calmer this time. "It is not too farfetched to say people may die if the circumstances are not dealt with swiftly."

The watchman frowned at her.

"Can't say I understand, but if it is that important, I shall take you to him."

He turned around at once and started across the yard, not looking to see if they followed him. Clara and Tommy kept close, the only source of light the man's lamp. They followed it more than him, a swinging pool of light that bobbed back and forth across the ground.

They discovered that Dr Patterson's workshop was set at the far side of the large yard, beyond several buildings that seemed deserted for the night. It was one of the buildings where Tommy had noticed a light in a window.

The watchman came to a door and pounded his fist upon it. Another light flickered on and then a gentleman appeared at the door. He was somewhere in his forties, a whippet-like fellow, with protruding ears and a moustache that looked like a fluffy caterpillar upon his upper lip. He looked at the watchman in surprise.

"Ted?"

"These people say they need to speak with you urgently," the watchman explained, motioning a hand to Clara and Tommy. "Something about tampering with medicines."

"What?" Mr Higgins was alarmed. "You best come in at once!"

He allowed Clara and Tommy through the door, while the watchman departed back to his place beside the gate. The siblings found themselves in a workshop with several long tables and various pharmaceutical equipment dotted about. There were promotional boards propped against walls, announcing Dr Patterson's products and a large stack of labels in boxes.

"I take it you are Dr Patterson," Clara remarked to Mr Higgins. "At least, as far as this company goes."

Mr Higgins shrugged.

"People find the name of a doctor reassuring on a medicine. There is no law against it, and we do not claim that Dr Patterson is a medical doctor anywhere on our advertisements."

"It is just a subtle tactic to encourage people to buy your products," Tommy said to him, nodding. "I get it."

Mr Higgins looked anxious.

"What is this about medicines being tampered with?"

"A gentleman consumed some of your new hair restoring tonic today and nearly died from arsenic poisoning," Clara explained. "I take it that is not one of the ingredients?"

Mr Higgins nearly stumbled back in alarm at the news. He gasped.

"I would never use something like that in my remedies! They are all completely natural!"

"Technically arsenic is natural," Tommy pointed out.

"I use floral mixtures, essences of flowers to produce the desired effect. Nothing harmful," Mr Higgins spun and from the nearest table grabbed up a bottle of the hair tonic. "I swear it is harmless!"

He popped the small cork from the bottle and was about to drink it down when Clara caught his arm.

"We don't need a demonstration. We have had had one of those already and it did not go so well."

Mr Higgins stopped, and then re-corked the bottle and put it down.

"When did the tonic go on sale?" Clara asked him.

"Yesterday. It is a new formulation. We sold something similar a while back, but it was a more general restorative for the body. We had people reporting the effects it had on their hair and decided to investigate whether we had a new product on our hands," Mr Higgins waved at the table nearest them, with its array of bottles, some filled and waiting for a label, others empty. "Who has suffered because of this?"

"Sir Medlar," Clara explained.

Higgins did not know the man, but he was clever enough to know poisoning a lord was never a good thing. He shut his eyes and cringed at the notion.

"And you are sure he consumed arsenic through my tonic?"

"It was the only thing he had consumed prior to becoming unwell," Clara explained. "Sir Medlar avoids food and drink during the day, which means the tonic can be the only source of the poisoning. He became unwell within half an hour of taking it."

"Will he recover?"

"It is too early to say," Tommy answered him. "His personal doctor will remain with him all night."

Mr Higgins released a hiss of emotion through his clenched teeth.

"How secure is your workshop?" Clara asked him.

"Pretty secure," Higgins moved to the doors to show her the lock. "The windows are sent on brackets so they can only open a couple of inches for ventilation. No one can climb in through them."

"Have you found the doors unlocked at all, recently?" Tommy suggested.

Mr Higgins shook his head.

"Even if this door was forgotten, which it never is because I am in charge of this door and am always last out, the yard has gates which are locked once everyone has gone."

This building was certainly far harder to get into than Coppleburg's humble workshop. Clara wondered why it had been targeted when it was clearly difficult to get inside.

"Have you heard of Pink's Pills?" she asked next.

"I had," Mr Higgins nodded. "Some of my ladies who work here filling the bottles were discussing the pills. They were badly made, as I understood it?"

"No, they were tampered with too," Clara explained. "We just don't know why. Before your tonic was also poisoned, we assumed someone had a grudge against Miss Pink who developed the pills and was trying to ruin her. Now things begin to look as though someone has a more general distaste for the residents of Brighton."

"Perhaps we should note that all the products tampered with so far are ones that could arguably be considered vanity medicines?" Tommy suggested. "Pink's Pills were to help a person lose weight, while the tonic helps restore hair. Maybe someone had a grudge against such things and thinks people should not be so self-absorbed?"

"I need to recall my tonic," Mr Higgins said, slowly coming to terms with the situation. "Fortunately, it was not sent out to multiple pharmacies, just Watling and Sons."

"The police have already confiscated all their stock," Clara told him. "And they are tracking down any bottles already sold."

Mr Higgins sighed with relief.

"At least that is something," he groaned.

Unlike Miss Pink, he had a conscience, and his primary concern was the welfare of his customers and not trying to save face.

Tommy had wandered over to the boxes of bottles stood in one corner of the workshop. The company went through a lot of little glass bottles and always had plenty in reserve. He noted that the bottles being used for the tonic were a different shape and size to the bottles used for other Dr Patterson products.

"You are using a different type of bottle for the tonic?" he said.

"Yes, well, the company we used to buy our bottles from has increased its prices significantly and made it unprofitable to remain with them," Mr Higgins explained. "I have switched to this other company and am trialling their bottles with the tonic before deciding if I should use them for all my goods."

Tommy was pulling some of the bottles from a box. Mr Higgins watched him a moment, then stepped over.

"What are you looking for?"

"Bottles with a little bit of water in them," Tommy said. He had taken out a dozen bottles and all appeared dry, but then he picked one up that caught the light and glistened with liquid inside. "Like this."

Mr Higgins took the bottle off him and stared at it.

"This is terrible," he said. "The bottles should be perfect. Dregs of water sitting in them would go stale and potentially stagnant, which would ruin my medicines."

Mr Higgins lifted the bottle to the light and looked at the thin gleam of water in the bottle.

"Can I look at that bottle?" Clara asked.

Higgins passed it to her, while he started to help Tommy search the box for more. There could be no more than a drop or two of water in the glass bottle, the amount that might be left over when a bottle was rinsed out and then emptied. If heated in an oven, as Coppleburg had done, the water would have evaporated. However, the workers at Dr Patterson's were having to move speedily and when filling numerous bottles, one with a trace of water in it could be easily overlooked.

Clara turned the bottle over and saw the same name and date on the bottom.

"Grindle 1921," she read aloud.

Mr Higgins' head snapped up.

"Let me see that," he took the bottle from her and read the bottom, his face contorting first in disbelief and then in anger. "I was told all the bottles I ordered would be brand new, but these are clearly not."

"This one bears the date 1923," Tommy said, showing them another bottle he had taken from the box. "It does not contain water."

Mr Higgins started pulling out bottles and lining them up on a table, he was checking the date on each one as he went. Clara and Tommy helped him. They soon had a large collection of 1923 bottles and a smaller assortment of 1921 bottles. All the 1921 bottles had a trickle of water in them.

When the box was empty and they could look at their tally, they all paused to assess what they were seeing.

"It seems to me that someone muddled in some old bottles with your new ones," Tommy said at last. "Maybe they had some 1921 bottles left over?"

"They had some 1921 bottles left sitting around for two years?" Mr Higgins snorted in disbelief. "This company only sells glass bottles. Those bottles should have been shipped out long ago. I have never had two-year-old bottles from the previous company I used."

Clara was thinking more about the liquid within the 1921 bottles.

"You mentioned the previous company you used had increased their prices?" she asked.

"Yes, they said the price of raw materials had gone up and they could not keep producing bottles if they did not put up their fees. I would have had to raise my prices in turn. Significantly."

Clara mulled on this information.

"What is it, Clara?" Tommy asked.

"I was just wondering how one company would need to up its prices while another could keep them lower. How much do the Grindle bottles cost you, Mr Higgins?"

"Tuppence a piece," Higgins explained. "I used to pay thruppence for my old bottles and then they had gone up to sixpence. Doubled in price, which taken into account with the other expenses for making the medicines and paying the workers would mean I was losing money with each bottle."

"How did you find the Grindle bottles company?"

"Word of mouth," Higgins explained. "I was talking with a business associate about the problem, and he gave me their name. He had used them without a problem. I was a touch concerned about the low price of their products, which is why I only bought a small shipment to try out with the tonic and to see their quality."

Clara was thoughtful again.

"We shall need to double-check, but these bottles look identical to the ones used for Pink's Pills and that raises the possibility that they were not tampered with after they reached Miss Pink or Mr Higgins, but rather before they even left the Grindle factory."

"Why would anyone do that?" Tommy said, astonished and alarmed at the thought.

"It is a good question. There could be several possibilities, but I think at last we have the source for this mystery, and it was not where we expected it to be."

Mr Higgins was frowning at her.

"What do I do now?" he said.

"Don't use any of these bottles," Clara told him. "Get back all the hair tonic and hold tight. I think I will have news soon."

Mr Higgins sagged, looking exhausted by the whole affair.

"I hope Sir Medlar survives. This is just terrible. I have been in business fifteen years and my products have never caused harm. I am not some snake oil merchant. I take care with my products."

"I believe you," Clara reassured him. "I really do."

Chapter Twenty-Four

It was late, but Clara needed to ask the inspector a couple of questions and to tell him what she had discovered. She suspected he was working late under the circumstances and took the chance when she finally arrived home to telephone the police station and ask to speak to him.

A short while later, the inspector's voice came onto the line.

"Clara, have you news?"

"I do and it is very curious, but first I have a question. Did your boys in the lab check the dates on the bases of the glass bottles?"

"Wait a minute, I have their draft report sitting on my desk," Park-Coombs explained.

There was a rustle of paper.

"Here we go. They had two hundred and forty-nine bottles in those boxes we sent them. They separated them by the ones that had a small amount of water in them, compared to ones that were bone dry. They ended up with twenty-two glass bottles with a small residue of water in them and each tested positive for arsenic. They tested a random selection of the other bottles that did not contain water, and none had arsenic in them. Curiously, the poisoned bottles were dotted throughout the boxes, some right at the bottom which rather suggests a person did not drop water into them at Coppleburg's workshop. They would have had to empty the entire box to poison a bottle right at the bottom and then re-stack everything on top."

"But did they note any dates on the bottles?" Clara asked.

There was more flicking of paper.

"I don't see anything here about that. Why?"

"I have been to Dr Patterson's, and I discovered a few things. Firstly, that only the hair restorative tonic uses bottles supplied by the Grindle's Glassworks, secondly, that all the bottles that contained a residue of water had the date 1921 on their base, while all the others without residue were dated 1923. I wanted to know if the same occurred with the bottles we took from Coppleburg."

"Hang on," Park-Coombs said, and the line went silent, except for some distant sounds of movement in the background.

Clara waited impatiently. Had the lab boys not noticed the dates on the bottles, or had they simply not realised the significance? It was the sort of thing easily overlooked. After all, it would mean nothing to them. But it had meant something to Mr Higgins. It meant instead of brand-new bottles he had somehow been given some that were two years old, and these had contained arsenic.

But why? While a picture was tentatively emerging of how these bottles came to be filled with medicines and poisoned people, there still remained that big question of just why it was done in the first place. If she was right, then someone at Grindle's Glassworks had laced a selection of old bottles with a tiny amount of arsenic. She just had no reason to explain their motivation.

She was mulling this all over when the inspector returned to the telephone.

"I went downstairs," he said, sounding breathless. "I have looked at all the bottles and I have in my hand the one Miss Pink took her pills from last night and nearly killed herself in the process."

"Well, Inspector? Do not keep me in suspense. Are they made by Grindle, and do they bear the date of 1921?"

"You are correct on both counts," Park-Coombs said, clearing his throat to try and catch his breath better. "I have asked the lad who is in the lab to check all the bottles as we speak, but so far all the ones I have looked at that contained arsenic are labelled 'Grindle 1921' and all the others are 'Grindle 1923'."

Park-Coombs paused thoughtfully.

"Something has happened at the Grindle factory."

"That seems the likeliest solution," Clara agreed with him. "This was never about Miss Pink, or dubious medicines. But don't ask me what the poisoner really intended."

"Mr Higgins recently bought the bottles?" Park-Coombs asked, trying to get his head around the matter.

"He was trialling them, after the manufacturer who he used to purchase his bottles from increased their prices significantly. He needed a cheaper source of bottles."

"And if Grindle is very reasonable in their prices, it would explain why Miss Pink purchased from them as she would have needed to be conscious about her costs."

"We need to go to these glassworks and pursue the mystery there," Clara added. "Mr Higgins has given me the address he sent to for the bottles. They are based at Shoreham-by-Sea."

"Not too far if we go by car or train," Park-Coombs sounded relieved. "We shall go first thing. I suggest we meet at the train station in the morning."

"That sounds a reasonable plan," Clara concurred. "Did you have any luck retrieving the bottles of hair tonic?"

"We have rounded up nearly all of them. Fortunately, the hair tonic was not such a big seller as Miss Pink's diet pills and only a handful of bottles had been sold. We still have some unaccounted for. We just have to hope the persons who bought them do not have a 1921 bottle."

"Maybe we shall have a bit of luck," Clara agreed,

though she did not hold out much hope with luck. "Any news on Sir Medlar?"

"When I left his house, he was the same as before, but the doctor seemed to feel this was a good thing and better than him deteriorating."

"Then we must keep him in our thoughts tonight," Clara replied. "We need to get to the bottom of this sorry mess Inspector and bring the culprit to justice."

"We certainly do," Park-Coombs agreed. "I keep worrying we have a random poisoner on the loose. They are nearly impossible to catch because they have no obvious motive aside from their insane desire to harm others."

"We shall find them," Clara said firmly. "No matter what."

The gruff noise Park-Coombs made suggested he did not have Clara's optimism.

~~~*~~~

The following day, Park-Coombs was waiting early at the station when Clara and Tommy arrived. He was somewhat bemused to see a third person with them.

"This is Abigail Sommers, Inspector," Clara introduced them. "You have met before."

"I remember," Park-Coombs nodded. "I questioned you about the possibility you had murdered a fellow employee of Albion Industries."

"That was not a pleasant experience for me," Abigail pulled a face. "I had intended to avoid you the entire time I was in Brighton, Inspector, but I realise my actions have rather made things difficult for everyone and I want to make amends, and to prove that I had nothing to do with this Pink's Pills business. I asked to come as I thought I might be of use."

Clara exchanged a look with Park-Coombs that indicated she doubted Abigail would be of any use but had consented to the idea because her friend was trying her hardest to make peace. It was also a good idea to get Abigail out of Annie's hair. After realising how she had offended her, Abigail had attempted to make things up to Annie by offering her assistance constantly, jumping to do Annie's tasks and in general showing willing. This was irritating Annie more than when Abigail was spending all her time avoiding them. It was best Abigail be removed from the house before Annie lost her temper.

"I have our train tickets," Park-Coombs waved the bits of paper at them. "Only, I have not got a fourth one…"

"I shall pay for myself," Abigail said swiftly and darted off for the ticket booth.

"She is keen," the inspector sniffed.

"A guilty conscience will do that," Clara smirked.

Park-Coombs glanced her way, wanting that comment explained.

"She was sent by Albion Industries to steal a bottle of Pink's Pills," Clara elaborated. "That company does not improve."

"You think they would have learned," Park-Coombs sighed.

"You would think," Clara shrugged. "Fortunately for Abigail, her attempts failed."

"Albion Industries are thinking of making diet pills?" Park-Coombs mused as their train pulled in.

"If only it were that simple," Clara chuckled, receiving a look of confusion from him.

She did not elaborate as they clambered into a carriage. Abigail bolted after them and hastened into the compartment looking triumphant that she had succeeded in securing her ticket before the train had departed.

"Oh, Annie put me in charge of provisions for the journey," she added indicating a wicker basket she was lugging around. "Does anyone want a fruit scone or sandwich?"

The inspector never refused Annie's cooking and gladly accepted. He munched away happily on the short journey to Shoreham-by-Sea.

It was another overcast day, and the clouds were promising rain when they set foot in the town. Park-Coombs asked directions to the glass factory from a porter and was relieved to learn it was not very far away. The porter was very helpful, explaining how they were always transporting boxes of Grindle's glassware by train. He told them how the bottles went all around the country, and how very proud the town was of its humble glassworks that not only provided steady employment for a good chunk of the residents but created work indirectly through the transport and sale of the goods. He was the sort of fellow who could talk all day on a topic if allowed and they had to tear themselves away with excuses and thanks for his assistance.

His enthusiastic praise for the glassworks had left a bitter taste in the mouth as they walked away in the direction he had supplied.

"This scandal could ruin Grindle's Glassworks," Tommy said what they were all thinking.

Well, all but Abigail who had her mind on the heavy hamper of food she had been given by Annie to carry around with her. Annie had rather made it seem as if she should guard the basket with her life, and Abigail was not about to find out what would occur if she failed. She just was getting tired of it banging on her leg as she walked.

"I hope it does not come to that," Clara replied to her brother. "Not after our conversation with the porter. He made it seem that Grindle's Glassworks is the heartbeat of this town and without it people would be a good deal worse off."

"We are not here to plot out consequences or debate the right and wrong of things," Park-Coombs told them prosaically. "We are here to find out how old bottles filled with arsenic were muddled in with new bottles."

"Calling them 'filled' is rather dramatic," Tommy said, already feeling guilty that they might be about to destroy a vital workplace for Shoreham-by-Sea. "It was more like a dribble."

"Call it what you want, the effect was the same," Park-Coombs huffed. "We are here for the facts of the matter and no more. Someone has done this thing and killed a person, not to mention made many people unwell."

They were sombre after that, feeling that whoever was poisoning the bottles had done far more than just destroy one life. They had the potential to destroy a whole town if Grindle's Glassworks was as significant a place in Shoreham-by-Sea as the porter had made out.

"Supposing this is all about destroying Grindle's, after all?" Tommy said as they left behind the main roads and headed into an area that was looking more and more industrial.

"Maybe so," Park-Coombs replied. "It is certainly working at the moment. We are honing into the source of this business and have our eyes set on Grindle's Glassworks. When the papers get hold of this, the publicity for the company will be terrible."

"Then we must be sure of our facts," Clara turned around and had them all halt. "We have jumped in all directions in this case, and as a result have nearly cost people their reputations and their lives. Had we not driven hard at Miss Pink, thinking at first, she was responsible for some sort of negligence, and then suggesting she was being targeted by someone who hated her, she would not have done that foolish demonstration. We need to be more cautious, to know exactly what is going on before we make any bolder statements."

She was not sure who she was making this statement for, perhaps, as much as anything, it was for herself. She felt guilty that her prying into Miss Pink's affairs had led to the ridiculous demonstration that had nearly killed the woman. Would Miss Pink have been so desperate to clear her name if the newspapers had not gotten a hold of her story? Could they have not been more discreet?

Yes, Clara had placed the newspaper announcement to try to avert further harm, but in doing so she had instead caused a good deal to Miss Pink. Miss Pink was a victim as well, but for a long time Clara had not realised that.

Clara turned back and carried on. Neither Park-Coombs nor Tommy had responded to her statement. Though Abigail had given her a meaningful look which had cut her to the core. She had been rash with her friend too. When had Clara become so quick to judge? She had blundered in more than once during this case with little more than hunches and wild guesses. Well, now she was paying for that.

They walked in silence a while, the only noise the occasional huff from Abigail as the wicker basket clipped her leg. They were heading along a road that was lined with what appeared to be old warehouses, many wooden in construction.

Tommy pointed out a tall chimney that was puffing out smoke.

"Bet that is part of it," he said.

The chimney seemed a long way off, behind numerous hedgerows. They started to work their way towards it, turning down a gravel drive that led to a large sprawl of old buildings. There was still no sign to identify the place, but the chimney was growing closer. As the drive led them towards the buildings, they saw people wandering about and doing their work. There was a heat to the air as they approached, a steady warmth. At last, a sign came into view.

"Grindle's Glassworks," Clara sighed with relief. "We have found it."

Chapter Twenty-Five

Grindle's Glassworks had been founded in the eighteenth century. Back then it had been a small wooden workshop, with a larger building housing the great furnace needed for heating the glass. Skilled glass blowers were employed to create the shaped bottles and other objects the glassworks supplied. In those days they had mainly served the local community, but as the country became more industrialised the original owner of Grindle's Glassworks (Mr Abraham Grindle, no less) had a vision of selling his wares farther and farther afield. He took the factory to the next logical stage and promoted his glass all across the country. He had dreamed of selling it abroad too, but that vision had never materialised before his untimely death in 1750.

His heirs had subsequently maintained the factory but had not the vision of their forebear and over the years they had even allowed the glassworks' reach to diminish. They were slowly but surely returning it to its roots as a factory that served only the local community.

They had not moved with the times, they had not adapted, they had not modernised. They were falling far behind their competitors and probably it was already too late for the company to be salvaged without serious investment. They tried to compete by keeping prices low, which was a strategy that could only work for so long. The rising costs of raw materials was affecting them as it affected their rivals. Still they kept their heads firmly stuck in the sand and ignored the warning signs. It was a policy that had largely worked for their predecessors, and they did not suppose it would fail for them.

Clara led the small party through a pair of open gates that bore the name 'Grindle' in swirling letters. The yard beyond was busy and belied any sense of trouble at the factory. Men, women, boys, and girls were going about a variety of tasks, from transporting baskets of glass pieces to be melted and reformed, to performing the endless chore of keeping the furnaces blisteringly hot with supplies of coal. No one was stopped in their work by the thin drizzle that had started to fall.

There was something old-fashioned about the scene, as if this moment had been transported to the present day from the early nineteenth century. The women's clothes seemed dated, and they all wore heavy shawls which they tucked over their heads to protect themselves from the rain. Clara had the sense of stepping into the past.

Park-Coombs had stopped a man who was going past with a crate of completed bottles and was asking him where they could find the manager for the glassworks. The man pointed to a grey building to one side of the yard which looked like a house, and perhaps once had served as a home for a foreman who was permanently on site. Now it was arranged as offices for any who needed them, and also provided further storage space for the accumulation of detritus a two-hundred-year-old company tends to accrue.

They headed across the yard, dodging muddy puddles and ruts drawn by loaded carts, to arrive at the unmarked front door of the house. Park-Coombs knocked, seeing as he had led the way this far. The door was opened by a woman who positively glowed with modernity after the grey, old-fashioned tones of the yard. She had her hair neatly shingled and it was bleached bright blonde – no one's hair was that shade of yellow white naturally. Her face was tentatively adorned with make-up, but not so much that it over-masked her pretty natural looks. She smiled at them brightly.

"Can I help you?"

"We need to speak to whoever manages the factory," Park-Coombs rumbled.

He was in a bad mood over this whole affair and sounded moodier than normal. This did not deter the girl from continuing to smile.

"You will want to speak to Mr Grindle. He deals with customers personally."

"So, there is still a Mr Grindle?" Tommy remarked. "After all these years."

"Oh yes, he is a direct descendant of the founder of Grindle's Glassworks. The factory has been in the family since 1726. Would you care to come inside?"

She had noticed the rain was getting heavier and they were all starting to look bedraggled. They gladly entered the house and found themselves in a tight hallway with a door either side of them and a staircase leading straight up.

"We have a sitting room for visitors," the woman escorted them into the room on their left.

It was arranged as a sitting room with a couch and a pair of armchairs, but it was a rather cold place, not helped by the lack of a fire in the hearth. Clearly, they did not get many visitors and so the fire had not warranted being lit.

The girl did not wait to see if they settled themselves, instead hurrying off smartly and pounding up the stairs to find her employer.

"She was wearing Pearl Pink lipstick, did you notice?" Abigail said to Clara in a hushed tone, looking proud of the fact.

"I cannot say I did," Clara smiled at her. "I noticed she was very smartly turned out."

"I like to see a woman making something of herself," Abigail said, that touch of pride now very noticeable, as if Albion Industries' make-up had had a direct effect on the woman's position.

Clara thought that while being a secretary was a perfectly fine occupation, it was not really what she would call 'making something of oneself' unless it was a steppingstone to greater things. Many girls became secretaries just to pass the time until they were married. Some, it had to be said, became secretaries just to enable them to secure a man to marry and as soon as they did, they had no interest in working again.

Park-Coombs was taking avid interest in the room as if it would reveal to him some secret about Mr Grindle, some clue as to how bottles from his factory were poisoning people. He had spied an old photograph on the wall.

"If that is Mr Grindle, he looks a shifty sort," he declared. "The kind of man who will cut corners in business."

"I would say that picture was taken some time in the last century," Tommy remarked. "Probably a previous Mr Grindle."

"Runs in the family then, shiftlessness. I see it in the eyes."

"Ahem."

They had all been distracted by Park-Coombs' assessment of a black and white grainy photograph and collectively jumped at the polite cough. They turned to see a man in his forties stood in the doorway of the room. He looked neither shiftless nor impressed one of his ancestors had been denigrated so. Clara stepped in to try and redeem the situation.

"Mr Grindle, I presume?"

She held out a hand for him to shake and he did so without hesitation. A man who did not quail at shaking hands with a woman, or consider it distinctly modern and terrifying, always went up a notch in her estimation.

"I am Mr Grindle," he said. "The gentleman you referred to as 'shifty' in the photograph happens to be my grandfather."

Park-Coombs was looking embarrassed and cleared his

throat nervously.

"Inspector Park-Coombs of the Brighton Constabulary. This is Tommy and Clara Fitzgerald, and Abigail Sommers."

He raced through the introductions to mask his embarrassment. Mr Grindle looked at his little audience. He was not an overly tall man, and his hair had gone prematurely grey, but there was a suave charm to his features that indicated he had been a very handsome younger man. He also looked clever and astute, to Clara's way of thinking, and not someone who would recklessly endanger people.

"We apologise for interrupting your day," she said, drawing Grindle's gaze away from the inspector. "We have come from Brighton because there appears to be an issue with your bottles."

Mr Grindle's attention was fully on her, and he had lost interest in the criticism of his family.

"What sort of issue?" he asked sharply.

"Some of the bottles you recently sent out contained traces of water laced with arsenic. These bottles were used without concern and now several people are very ill. Sadly, one lady has died as a consequence," Clara explained.

"Sir Medlar took a hair tonic that was in one of your bottles and is now on death's door," Park-Coombs added dramatically, trying to regain some composure by going on the attack.

Mr Grindle looked stunned.

"I don't think I understood what you said," he glanced at Clara.

"Some of the bottles you recently sent to Miss Pink of Brighton and Mr Higgins of Dr Patterson's medicines, also in Brighton, contain traces of arsenic."

Grindle could not comprehend the news any better the second time he heard it. He stepped back so he was pressed against the wall for support.

"How can that be?" he said, aghast.

"That is what we are trying to determine," Park-

Coombs explained to him. "You appreciate how serious this situation is?"

"Inspector, I think I appreciate it better than you can imagine," Grindle said coldly to the policeman. "What you are saying could result in my business being closed. It could see people ending their contracts with us, and new customers not coming to us. It could destroy Grindle's Glassworks. Therefore, I must ask you to show me what proof you have of these accusations."

Grindle had a point, and he also had a lot to lose. Both Park-Coombs and Clara had been prepared for this. Park-Coombs produced two bottles from his pocket.

"Both of these bottles came from the workshop where Pink's Pills were being produced. The police confiscated all the bottles they had and have been testing them for arsenic. We have determined that any bottle containing a trace of water will have arsenic in it, while a bone-dry bottle will be safe. I brought one of each to show you."

Park-Coombs handed the bottles to Mr Grindle. He took them carefully and held them up to the grey light coming through the window. It was plain to see that one had a smear of water in it.

"This makes no sense," Grindle shook his head. "Why would one of our bottles have water in it?"

"We thought perhaps they were washed before being sent out," Tommy suggested.

"There is no need," Grindle replied. "They are made from scratch and as soon as they are shaped, snipped and cooled, they are packaged. Washing them would be an inconvenience and a waste of time."

"Then how do you explain the water in this one?" Clara asked him.

Mr Grindle was looking belligerent.

"It must have been put in after they left the glassworks."

"No, that cannot be," Clara told him calmly. "Firstly, two different businesses had these tainted bottles, and those businesses were not connected. Secondly, some of the tainted bottles were right at the bottom of the boxes Miss

Pink had in her workshop. No saboteur would take the time to empty an entire box and lace one bottle at the very bottom, before restacking it. What would be the point?"

"You are saying this happened here, at my factory," Mr Grindle was shaking with outrage. "That is preposterous!"

"This whole fiasco is preposterous," Park-Coombs interrupted. "It makes very little sense, but more than a dozen people have been made unwell, and need I repeat that one has died as a consequence?"

Mr Grindle blanched at the reminder; he had allowed that to slip his mind.

"I still cannot believe this occurred here. There must be a madman on the loose, poisoning random bottles."

"Perhaps that is true," Clara agreed. "But we believe that those bottles had to have been poisoned here, at your glassworks."

It was obvious Mr Grindle was going to have none of that talk. He refused to believe someone at his factory could have done such a thing. He was shaking his head, in utter denial.

"Most of the people here have family ties to the yard. Their parents, grandparents, great-grandparents worked here before them. They are as invested in this place as I am. I shall not believe one of them would do this. What would be the point? They would be destroying their own means of employment!"

"I understand that, Mr Grindle, but we are following a chain of evidence that leads directly to here," Clara continued patiently. "You have to appreciate that all your denials are meaningless until we know how that arsenic ended up in a bottle."

It was Clara's turn to earn a glare from Grindle.

"I do not know what you want from me," he snapped. "I cannot help you."

"We shall have to search this yard," Park-Coombs said and now there was an edge to his voice. There was no doubting he had taken a dislike to Grindle and was not going to make life easy for the man.

"Before we jump to conclusions," Clara interjected as speedily as she could. "I have a question you should be able to answer, Mr Grindle."

Grindle had half a mind to kick them all out of his yard, he was just not sure he could do that to a police inspector. It took him a moment to register Clara's words.

"Another question?" he asked, despondently.

"A simple one," Clara said. "One that is merely about the production of your bottles."

Grindle frowned at her but did not argue.

"I happened to notice that all the bottles that contained water and arsenic were dated 1921, while all the other bottles were dated 1923. Mr Higgins found this surprising as he was certain he was receiving brand new bottles, instead of ones that were two years old."

The frown on Grindle's face deepened. He now turned over the bottles carefully, they were capped so that the poison could not escape from the tainted one. He noted the dates himself.

"This doesn't make sense," he declared. "I can't see how we could have had any bottles left from 1921. They would have been used up in early 1922 shipments. Mr Higgins is right. We make our glassware to order. A person asks for six dozen bottles of a certain shape and size, and we make them bespoke and send them out."

"You see the puzzle we have before us then," Clara added.

Grindle met her gaze.

"All right," he said. "Perhaps there is something going on here."

Chapter Twenty-Six

Mr Grindle took them on a tour of the glassworks, still retaining a sense of pride for his family business.

"The chimney for the furnace is original to the first glassworks founded by my ancestor Abraham Grindle," he explained. "It is the only part of the yard that remains from his time. The brick workshop and surrounding buildings were constructed between 1798 and 1810 to replace the previous wooden structures after a fire had destroyed the original workshop. The house we came from was constructed in 1821 to serve the purpose of housing the site foreman and his family. That was back in the day when this area was more rural and wilder. There had been attempts to steal from the yard and having a man on site was deemed advisable."

Grindle was waving his hand around, gesturing to one building after another.

"These days, things are much more peaceful, and our foreman only works regular hours and then returns to his own home. Other buildings have been added over the decades, such as the storehouses and the coal sheds. You know, originally the furnace was wood-fuelled, and timber was cut down locally to supply its needs. Coal was found to be more convenient when it became reliably available."

Grindle had stopped outside a long, low brick building. There was an arched door set in the wall and lots of windows. Snatched glimpses through the windows, which were old and the glass a little warped, gave a view of steady activity within.

"This is the packing house, where the bottle shipments are prepared," Grindle explained. "This is the last place the bottles were before their boxes were sealed and they were sent on their way."

He opened the door and showed them into the building. It had windows down both sides to provide plenty of natural light, even on a dull day like it was just then. The shed was filled with eight or so women and girls, who were organising boxes, carefully wrapping the delicate bottles and wedging them into the packaging so they would not be damaged on-route to their destination. None of the women paid much heed to the arrivals.

"Lucy?" Grindle called out. "Lucy, have you a moment?"

An older woman appeared from the far end of the building. She was in her fifties and had a stern set to her features that suggested she stood for no trouble in her packing house. She approached Grindle with a disgruntled look, annoyed her work had been interrupted.

"We are packing up the Prescott order," she informed him in a surly manner. "I don't have time for pausing. The wagon is going to be here within the hour and needs to be gone again to get everything to the train on time."

"I understand," Grindle said in a placating tone. "I shall not bother you long. I was just curious about something that has come up with a customer."

He showed Lucy the two bottles.

"Two different shipments contained bottles that were dated as being made in 1921, which seems impossible to me."

Lucy frowned and took the bottles from him. She compared them, as if that would reveal their secret. They were identical, of course, apart from the date on the bottom.

"There shouldn't have been any 1921 bottles in recent shipments. All the bottles are new."

"All the bottles are meant to be new," Grindle corrected her.

"I don't spend my time checking the dates on bottles," Lucy huffed, sensing she might be getting the blame for this nuisance. "I just pack them after they are brought to me."

"I would like to check the contents of all these boxes," Park-Coombs said suddenly.

Lucy's gaze switched to him with a mixture of horror and fiery indignation.

"You can't unpack all these boxes! We have them all sorted, ready to go."

"Mr Grindle," Park-Coombs turned his attention to the manager, "if there are more of these suspect bottles about your factory and they have been slipped into this shipment, you realise the implication?"

Grindle pulled back his lips in a rictus of terror at the thought.

"Unpack all the boxes Lucy, look for any bottles that are labelled 1921."

Lucy looked appalled.

"We shall never get these to the train on time if we do that!"

"If we do not, and these 1921 bottles are among the rest, we may never get another shipment order from Prescott again!" Grindle replied, his tone indicating his fears.

Lucy sensed his anxiety and hesitated.

"What has happened?" she asked.

Grindle was not sure whether to explain or not. Clara decided the woman needed the truth to convince her to assist them. The information would come out sooner or later as it was.

"I think you should explain, Mr Grindle," she said, verbally nudging the manager.

He winced to hear her say this and did not speak. Lucy

glowered at them all.

"Someone needs to explain this to me before I stop my girls from packing and respond to your request," she said firmly.

Mr Grindle groaned. He saw there was no choice, but he was gritting his teeth as he spoke.

"Someone has laced the 1921 bottles with arsenic," he said, bitter to have to explain.

Lucy's eyes went wide. She turned to her girls and her words bellowed across the building.

"Stop packing and start unpacking! Look at the dates on the bottles and pick out any marked 1921!"

The packing women and girls had been listening to the conversation with Grindle, naturally, and did not hesitate to do as she said. Within moments one of the girls called out and held up a bottle.

"It ain't labelled 1921, but it has 1919 on the bottom."

She passed it to Lucy, whereupon it was nearly snatched from her hands by Mr Grindle.

"1919" he said in a voice that suggested he had never heard of such a date.

He stared hard at the bottle.

"This makes no sense at all. How could we still have a bottle from 1919 lurking about?"

"I have one too, Mr Grindle," another girl called out, holding up the suspect bottle.

This time Park-Coombs took it from her.

"At least it does not appear to contain any water," he said. "It is chipped, though."

Grindle snatched at the bottle.

"Chipped?"

Park-Coombs pointed out a small notch on the neck of the bottle where it had been damaged at some point. The chip was sharp and easily felt with a finger. Grindle was looking more horrified by the minute.

More cries went up from the girls as further bottles emerged with old dates upon them. They had begun to gather them onto a separate table.

"Golly, this one says 1912!" one declared with glee.

Grindle rushed forward again and snatched at the bottle.

"1912? How…" he was rubbing his finger against the glass, noting something marring what should have been its smooth surface. "There is a residue of glue on this bottle."

"This one has some too," a girl helpfully handed over a bottle dated 1918.

Lucy was studying the scene with a mixture of alarm and revelation.

"Those bottles have already been used," she said. "The stickiness is from a label where it has been removed. Someone has been reusing old bottles."

Grindle opened his mouth to dismiss the idea, then he let it sink in and he realised that had to be the case. The bottles bore the remains of glue from labels. Someone had cleaned them and removed the labels but could not remove all the traces of glue. They had hoped no one receiving the bottles would notice, or care – after all, new labels would be going on the bottles.

"I take it you never reuse bottles," Park-Coombs said to Grindle.

"Not like this," Grindle shook his head. "We do sometimes receive back used bottles which we store in a glass bin to melt down and turn into brand new bottles. But never would we simply reuse them. For a start the date is wrong, and the customer would realise instead of having brand new bottles we had sent them used ones. Can you imagine the outcry? Our customers would be appalled to think they were reusing someone else's bottles. They do not pay for that!"

"Where is this glass bin?" Park-Coombs asked.

Grindle was still trying to catch up with what was occurring. He managed to think straight for a moment.

"Lucy, have every box unpacked and checked for old bottles!"

The woman in charge of the packing house nodded at him and set her girls to work. Grindle showed the others outside and to a three-sided brick shelter with a wooden roof. Inside it was a pile of old bottles, dumped carelessly within. Many were broken, others were chipped or cracked from being tossed into the pile.

Tommy leaned into the glass bin and looked about for a while, before gingerly reaching in and retrieving a single bottle that was undamaged.

"Someone might have fished them out of here," he suggested.

Clara shook her head.

"They would have to dig through broken glass to try to find a handful of salvageable bottles. It doesn't seem likely."

Tommy tossed back the bottle glumly and it landed with a tinkle of glass. Clara was noting that most of the bottles still bore their labels.

"These have not been cleaned?" she said.

"No need," Grindle shrugged. "The furnace will burn off the paper when the glass is heated and melted."

"If the bottles did not come from here, then where did they come from?" Park-Coombs was mulling. "Maybe someone got hold of bottles before they reached this bin."

"Such effort to poison a handful!" Abigail gasped at the audacity of the scheme.

"I don't think this is about poisoning people anymore," Clara said, frowning as she tried to set out the thoughts that were humming at the back of her mind.

"It must be, Clara, there was arsenic in those bottles," Abigail pointed out.

"But, as far as we can tell, only in the bottles labelled 1921. All the other older bottles appear bone dry and empty. Arsenic is not invisible. We should be able to see a few grains of it if it was present."

Grindle was holding up one of the 1919 bottles and peering inside.

"There is nothing," he said. "Looks as good as new."

"Exactly," Clara said to him with a smile.

"I do not get your point," Grindle was bemused.

"Mr Grindle, how have you been able to keep your prices the same when other glassworks are having to up their prices to compensate for the rising costs of raw materials?" Clara asked him.

"Well…" said Grindle, then he flushed a little and became uneasy. "I don't really deal with that side of things. Figures are not my strong point. I deal with customers, getting new orders and so forth. Oh, and I am rather good at the catalogue design."

"In essence, Mr Grindle, you are more figurehead than businessman," Park-Coombs said bluntly.

Grindle almost argued, but he realised there was no point.

"Yes, if you want to put things that way. There has always been a Grindle in charge of the glassworks, but we Grindles have not always had the business minds necessary to run the place."

"Who is really in charge of making sure all the orders are completed and for purchasing more materials?" Clara asked.

Grindle was looking gloomy now, having to admit he was not really in charge of his own glassworks had rather dented his mood and his ego.

"You will need to speak to Mr Pond, the glassworks foreman. He deals with all that and makes sure we keep running. But why do you want to know?"

"I have a theory about the old bottles," Clara said. "But elements of my theory do not quite make sense at the moment. I need more information, which I hope your foreman can provide."

"Could we perhaps summon him to your house over there," Park-Coombs rumbled. "I am fed up with being out in this damp weather and I need a strong cup of tea to take the chill from my bones."

Grindle was flustered, trying to piece together all he was being told and running through the potential consequences of this crisis in his mind. He would need to have all the orders they were in the process of packing checked and then he would need to be in touch with anyone who had received a delivery of bottles in the last few weeks, to ensure no one else had accidentally acquired arsenic tainted goods. He was thinking of the potential impact of all this scandal, how it could destroy the reputation of the glassworks and the good name of Grindle.

He was not too proud to admit the thought horrified him, along with the notion that he might be the last Grindle to stand in a functioning glassworks. What if, on his watch, the company failed? Generations of Grindles had worked here and kept the business going, how could he be the one to destroy all that?

He was starting to feel a little faint as the enormity of the notion crept over him. Tommy shot out a hand to grab his arm when he suddenly looked perilously close to falling back into the glass bin. Mr Grindle regained his footing and came back to reality, blinking furiously and trying to draw in a deep breath to still his fluttering heart.

It was starting to rain hard now, and Park-Coombs was growing impatient.

"Mr Grindle, must we stand here all day?"

"No, no," Grindle recalled himself. "Back to the house, of course, and I shall have the fire in the parlour lit and tea made."

"And the foreman summoned," Clara reminded him, just in case.

"Yes, I shall track him down," Grindle was now ushering them towards the house as if they were wanton geese he needed to herd away. "I want this riddle solved too."

"I hope you mean that," Park-Coombs muttered. "We have had enough of this mystery and its many dead ends. I want no one else made dangerously ill by this business."

"Me neither!" Grindle said heartily. "Supposing someone is trying to destroy the glassworks? Or my family name? That could be the case and they were cunning, only poisoning 1921 bottles."

Clara was tired of the sabotage notion that had dogged

this case from the beginning. If it was not Miss Pink believing she had been sabotaged, it was Mr Grindle and it was all a means of deflecting blame and masking the real truth.

"Mr Grindle why would anyone mix old bottles in with your new ones for the purposes of sabotage and then only poison certain ones?" she sighed. "Why go to the bother when they could just have laced a few of the regular bottles with arsenic."

"But... but, what else..."

"Fetch Mr Pond," Clara said firmly. "And then, maybe we shall at last have an answer to all this."

Chapter Twenty-Seven

Mr Pond was a man who put you in mind of a squirrel, it was the way his nose was sharp and rather upright, and he had a pale ginger moustache that twitched as he talked. He was scrawny and bunched his hands together all the time. He looked like he might startle and bolt at the slightest thing, such as a loud bang from the glassworks yard. His eyes jumped from person to person anxiously, enhancing the overall squirrel-like appearance.

Mr Grindle had not explained why he had been summoned, other than to say he had a question about a recent order. Mr Pond was naturally paranoid and took the summons to mean someone's order had arrived incomplete or smashed and they would now have to deal with replacing it or refunding it. Such things were never good.

"Mr Pond, we have a situation with some of the bottles we recently sent out," Mr Grindle began, stalking over old territory because he did not really want to get to the point at hand. "We thought you might be able to help us. It is just a minor thing. I am sure it is purely an oversight…"

"For crying out loud!" Park-Coombs barked, his patience at an end even though he had been refreshed by the tea and cake Mr Grindle had managed to conjure up for them. "Some bottles in a recent consignment were laced with arsenic."

"Arsenic!" Pond said in horror. "Which bottles?"

"The ones that had the date 1921 on them instead of being brand new," Park-Coombs went on in his surly fashion. He produced the 1921 bottle from his pocket and set it on the mantelpiece in front of Pond.

"Mr Pond, what are old bottles doing among an order?" Grindle asked, suddenly remembering that someone had filtered reused bottles into the packing crates, and this could damage the glassworks' reputation if customers discovered it and realised they had not been sent new bottles.

Pond had his eyes fixed on the bottle, for the first time they were not darting about, and he stood oddly still. He let out a shaky breath.

"I hoped no one would notice," he said. "Who looks at the dates on bottles?"

"You knew of this?" Grindle said, though it had seemed obvious the foreman had known all along. "Why Pond? Why?"

"Because we were running low on supplies. The price of coal has jumped up, along with other things, but you insist we keep our prices the same as they were pre-war," Pond grumbled.

"That is how we keep our custom!" Grindle reacted. "We have gained customers, in fact, by being cheaper than our competitors."

"New customers are the problem. We can barely afford to make bottles for our regulars at the pre-war prices. With new customers we are simply overwhelmed. I cannot afford more coal, nor to pay the glassblowers to work extra hours. Not to mention the price of the coloured glass ingots we use has gone up. The glassworks are barely viable."

Grindle was appalled by this news.

"Why did you not tell me?"

"I have tried, repeatedly, but you do not want to know," Pond berated him, he was suddenly fierce towards his employer. "I said we had to put up our prices up and you told me to find another solution, which is what I did. I walked past the glass bin one day and it occurred to me how our bottles have not changed in over a decade. A bottle from 1915 once stripped of its label looks the same as one made yesterday. Why waste all the coal and time melting them down and reshaping those bottles when we could just reuse them?"

"But we promise our customers new bottles," Grindle protested.

"And how many have ever bothered to look at the date on a bottle?" Pond asked him. "They are too busy filling them. As long as they are clean and the labels gone, what does it matter?"

"It matters when some of those old bottles contain arsenic," Park-Coombs rumbled.

Pond's full attention snapped to him.

"I cannot see how that would happen. I had the bottles washed before they were reused."

"Which explains why the 1921 bottles had a trace of water in them," Clara nodded. "But why not the others? The ones from previous years were dry as a bone."

"Who washed them?" Tommy asked.

"I had some of the youngsters do it," Pond shrugged. "It did not take much. Just scrub off the old labels and rinse them out, before placing them somewhere to dry upside down."

He paused.

"Now you mention it, one of the lads did not put the batch of bottles he had cleaned upside down to dry and they still had a little water in them when we went to add them to an order. There was no time to dry them so I just hoped no one would notice. I don't understand how arsenic got into them, though!"

"Mr Pond has been deceitful, but has not broken any law," Grindle came to the defence of his foreman. "I am as much responsible for failing to appreciate his concerns and forcing him to find alternatives to making new bottles."

"The lad would not have put arsenic in them," Pond continued to insist. "He is a good boy, maybe not the brightest, but he would not have even had access to arsenic."

Clara did not suspect the lad who had been in charge of washing the bottles, her mind was working in another direction.

"Where did the old bottles come from?" she asked Mr Pond.

Pond was unsettled by the change of direction. He cleared his throat nervously.

"I contacted some of our customers and asked if they had any bottles that could be returned. I said we needed them for a charitable project we had committed to, to cover why I was not having new bottles made. I said we were helping to supply free bottles of medicine to the poor and any old bottles we could reuse would help us enormously," Pond looked duly guilty at the lie. "Most were very keen to help."

"Did you keep track of where the bottles came from?" Clara continued.

Pond looked bleak as he recalled he had not kept notes of who had sent him what.

"My only concern was making sure the old bottles were mixed up with bottles sent to new customers, so our regulars would not see what we were doing," he said.

"Then you cannot tell us where these 1921 bottles originated from?" Clara asked.

Pond frowned for a while; his gaze fallen on the suspect bottle.

"I had a lot of 1921 bottles," he murmured to himself. "More than any other year. I was pleased to have so many. They topped up two orders which I did not have enough new bottles for."

"Those shipped to Miss Pink of Pink's Pills and those sent to Dr Patterson's factory. Both new customers," Clara confirmed.

"That's right," Pond agreed, before hesitating again. "It was a really big batch of used bottles. I thought at the time it was a lot."

He was trying hard to remember who had sent him those old bottles for reuse.

"Logically it must be one of our 1921 customers," Grindle said. "Someone who takes a considerable quantity to enable them to have so many to return. I have an idea."

He hurried off and returned a short time later with a large ledger.

"Customer orders," he explained dropping the book onto a handy side table. He had to dislodge a bowl of dried flower petals that were giving the room a soft perfume in the process. "Maybe if you see the name, it will ring a bell?"

He was looking at Pond now.

"It might," Pond agreed.

He joined Grindle at the ledger and they started to go through the orders, looking for the biggest ones first.

"Smith and Sons," Grindle suggested. "They have hundreds of bottles from us every year."

Pond shook his head.

"Wasn't them. I telephoned their head office and was told they never accepted any bottles back."

Grindle ran his finger further down the page.

"Ah, Bleake's Bitters! They have a regular, sizeable order."

"Wrong shape and size of bottle," Pond said at once.

"Of course," Grindle frowned, concerned he had not realised that himself. He scanned the pages further. "Rose and Thorn Herbals? Orange's Syrups and Cordials? Mr Hathaway's Veterinary Products?"

"No, none of them," Pond shook his head, starting to look fraught. "Let me look at the book."

He moved the ledger in his direction and scanned the pages, looking for a familiar name that reminded him of where the bottles had come from. When he saw the name and his memory suddenly woke up, he sighed with relief.

"Spooner's Farm Shop," he said. "Mr Spooner has lots of bottles from us. They use them to put their own produce in. They make up things such as herbal perfumes for ladies from their own fields, and bottles of speciality oil, like lavender. When I asked if they had any bottles they could return, they said they had a number as their customers are encouraged to bring the used bottles back to be refilled and sold on again."

"Farmers like to be economical," Park-Coombs said, attempting to sound knowledgeable on the subject. "But if the 1921 bottles came from them, that does not explain why they contained arsenic."

"Did you tell Mr Spooner about your plan to supply medicines to the poor?" Clara asked Pond.

"Of course, I told everyone the same. I don't think Mr Spooner would have relinquished his bottles had I not. As the gentleman over there said, he is very careful about such things and prefers to reuse bottles. He still has to order a sizeable amount new each month, despite that."

Clara was thoughtful about this, but it was not her but Abigail who inserted the next notion into their heads.

"I have just had a terrible thought!" she said. "What if Mr Spooner laced those bottles because they were going to be used for medicine for the poor? Perhaps he is one of those terrible people who resent the poor and think they would be better off without them. Like Scrooge."

"Scrooge was a fictional character," Clara reminded her, but she had to admit there was something horribly plausible about the idea. Could Spooner have poisoned his bottles thinking he was doing the world a favour by killing off some of the poorest in society?

"That is an awful thought," Tommy declared. "No one would behave in such a fashion."

"Oh, now that is not so true," Park-Coombs corrected him. "You read things about it. Doctors or nurses in hospitals bumping off elderly or sick patients because they think they are doing everyone a favour. We thought Sir

Medlar might have been poisoned for his wealth, well, why not consider someone killing others because they are poor? How is it so different if the person behind the crime thinks they will benefit."

Grindle and Pond were listening with abject horror on their faces. The thought that they had been the catalyst for all this was troubling enough, but Pond's knowledge that he had lied to Spooner seemed to make it all the worse. Innocent people had suffered because of all the things they had done, or rather, had tried to hide.

"We need to get to Mr Spooner and find out the truth of all this," Park-Coombs said firmly. "We have chased this drama nearly to its nest, but we have one last place to journey to."

"You are going to accuse Mr Spooner of trying to murder people?" Grindle said, trembling as he realised the crisis about to befall his glassworks. "He will know we sent you to him."

"Precisely what else can we do?" Tommy asked him.

"Could we not just consider it a mistake and move on?" Grindle asked. "I shall allow our prices to be raised so that Mr Pond no longer has to use old bottles, and no one shall be the wiser of this little fiasco."

"Mrs Wood died because of this little fiasco," Clara pointed out to him. "Many were made dreadfully ill, and others have been blamed for the problem when they are wholly innocent. How can we just ignore all that?"

Grindle gaped at her, still desiring that they just forget about the whole matter. Mr Pond was not on the side of his employer. He felt deeply guilty that his efforts to serve Grindle as best he could had led to this. His conscience would not allow him to ignore what had occurred.

"They have to do this," he told Grindle. "They have to discover why Spooner sent us bottles laced with poison. This whole thing could have been much more serious."

Grindle was angered his foreman would side with Clara and the others. Pond just shook his head.

"I can't forget about this, not just like that."

It was as much an apology as a statement.

"Mr Pond, did the 1921 bottles go in any other orders you have shipped recently?" Tommy asked him.

The others had overlooked the worrying thought that more of the 1921 bottles might be lurking about, too busy thinking about catching up with the person responsible at last.

Mr Pond thought for a moment.

"I am pretty certain the bottles only went in the two orders. The one for Pink's Pills and the other for Dr Patterson's Remedies."

"Dr Patterson's came to us after their old bottle supplier had put their prices up too high for them," Grindle recalled. "It was a good contract to get. They use lots of bottles. We might have lost a highly valuable customer!"

"We have to get past all that for the moment," Clara reminded him, thinking that this was altogether too much like talking with Miss Pink. Was it the prerequisite of people in business to think of themselves and their profits first? "We need the address for Spooner's farm."

"You will be discreet, will you not?" Grindle said, his face falling in his anxiety.

"You shall see for yourself," Clara told him. "For you shall come. We need to prove all this to you as much as to those affected."

Grindle sucked in his lower lip and moped. Mr Pond was writing out the address for them.

"It is not far as the crow flies, but we have a horse and cart you can borrow," he explained. "You don't want to be getting wet, if you can help it."

Pond demonstrated he was much more practical than his employer. Grindle still looked as if the floor had disappeared beneath him, and he was trying not to tumble to his death.

"It will be all right, Mr Grindle," Clara told him.

It was no surprise he clearly did not believe her.

Chapter Twenty-Eight

It was far from the most elegant way to travel; the cart was used mainly for delivering boxes of bottles. It was covered, meaning they could keep dry in it, but it lacked anywhere to sit, so they perched as best as they could on the bed of the cart. Mr Pond was put in charge of driving the vehicle, to avoid anyone else being involved in the drama. He had the unenviable position on the driver's bench, which was exposed to the elements and so he was slowly becoming sodden to his core.

"It isn't far," Grindle said, not the for the first time as the cart bumped along the rapidly flooding roads. "Spooner is a very good customer. Reliable. Always pays on time and he makes regular orders."

"He also fills old bottles with arsenic," Park-Coombs muttered.

Grindle flinched.

"He won't have done this on purpose. I am sure he does not detest the poor."

Grindle huddled into himself, wondering why things had fallen apart so suddenly for him and what his father and grandfather would say about this mishap. He had thought he was doing alright at the factory helm, keeping everything running smoothly. It seemed he had been wrong.

The journey, as Grindle had said, did not take long and they swung through the gates of a rather smart farm. Spooner had invested in modernisation, and this had paid off. He had dairy cattle and poultry, along with arable fields, some devoted to herbs such as lavender which he made up into scents and oils or sold on in bulk to other manufacturers.

Mr Pond brought the wagon to a halt before a large building with a sign over the door that indicated it was the farm shop. Their arrival had attracted attention, and a gentleman in relatively clean farm clothes was wandering over to see what was going on.

"Ah, Mr Spooner!" Grindle jumped out of the cart and greeted the man keenly. "Are you well?"

"Never better," Spooner said.

He was a man in his fifties, with a slightly ruddy complexion and a confidence to his bearing that made Grindle seem fawning and sycophantic.

"We just have come about bottles. Nothing serious, ah…" Grindle kept saying.

Pond launched himself off the driver's bench and landed before Spooner.

"Those bottles you returned to me were full of arsenic!" he yelled at Spooner, his words ringing around the farmyard.

Spooner stared at him, confused, but not alarmed by his words.

"What are you talking about?"

Park-Coombs produced the 1921 bottle he had been carrying around.

"These bottles were laced with water and arsenic. When they were refilled with other products, they contaminated them and have made several people ill. One person has died as a consequence."

Grindle was pulling faces, horrified at how blatant everyone was being. He wanted to go home and climb into bed and pretend this day had never occurred.

Mr Spooner carefully took the bottle from Park-Coombs.

"This certainly looks like one of the bottles I returned to the glassworks, but I cannot say how they came to have arsenic inside them," he handed it back. "You best come into the shop, and we shall talk further."

He was taking everything in his stride. Clara was not sure if that bothered her or not. Shouldn't he be as agitated as the rest of them over this?

Spooner showed them into the shop which was relatively quiet at that point in the day. A young woman was stood behind a counter bagging up onions to put on sale. She did not pay much attention to their arrival other than glancing up.

"I sent those bottles in good faith," Spooner explained now they were out of the yard. "I asked Molly to fetch them from our storeroom. Some of our customers return bottles to us rather than throw them away. We always have a small amount we keep to one side and reuse if necessary."

Molly had looked up again at her name.

"What is this about?" she asked, looking worried.

"Molly, you fetched these bottles, didn't you?" Spooner showed her the 1921 bottle.

"I suppose," Molly said. "You told me to fetch any old empty bottles from the storeroom and put them in a box to be sent to Grindle's Glassworks and that is what I did."

"They have arsenic in them," Spooner said bluntly, putting the bottle on the counter before her.

Molly's reaction was more what Clara had expected. Her eyes flew wide open, and she gaped in astonishment.

"Arsenic?" she hissed the word.

"You did not know?" Park-Coombs asked her, his stern gaze enough to break most ordinary suspects.

"No!" Molly insisted. "How could I know that? The bottles were just on the back shelf in the storeroom. I barely looked at them as I packed them up!"

"Well somehow this poison got into these bottles and

has made people sick," Park-Coombs repeated his dire news. "Someone put it there and we need to discover who did it and why."

Molly was looking appalled.

"You don't think I did it?" she glanced between them all, panic on her face. "Why would I do something like that?"

From a doorway behind her an elderly woman appeared. She had a mortar and pestle in her hands and appeared to be in the process of crushing up fragrant herbs.

"What is the matter Molly?" she asked.

"Mother, this does not concern you," Spooner muttered at the old woman. "Go back to whatever it is you are making."

"Don't you talk to me that way!" Mrs Spooner came further forward. "Just because I am old doesn't mean I can't be useful. You treat me as if I am a child."

"How am I supposed to treat you when you are always messing around with your witchcraft potions," Spooner snapped at her.

"Witchcraft!" Mrs Spooner growled. "These are tried and tested herbal remedies, passed down through the female line of the family. Oh, you always were too big for your boots and since you became all 'modern' you have no time for the old ways. I should tell you…"

"My apologies, madam, but we are here on an urgent matter," Park-Coombs interrupted as he sensed a family dispute about to arise. "We must find out how these bottles came to contain poison."

Mrs Spooner shut her mouth, though she still had one finger pointing at her son. She glanced at the bottle on the counter.

"Where did that come from?" she asked.

"The storeroom," Molly said, close to tears now at the thought she was being accused of poisoning people. "There is a shelf full of them."

"Yes, there is," Mrs Spooner declared. "I put them there myself. Why is it here?"

"I was asked by Mr Pond if I had any old bottles I could return to him," Spooner explained to his mother as it was now plain she was not going to leave. "I asked Molly to fetch them."

"And she took the ones from the back shelf?" Mrs Spooner asked. "Not the ones already boxed up and ready to be reused, but the ones I had put to one side especially."

They were all looking at her with sharp interest.

"Yes," Molly said quietly.

"Well, then I am not surprised you found poison in them," Mrs Spooner said calmly. "Those bottles on the back shelf are the ones I use for my homemade rat, mouse and wasp poison. Main ingredients are arsenic, treacle and a touch of gin."

Everyone fell absolutely silent, even Spooner was shaken from his normal calm. After a moment, Clara managed to find her voice.

"These bottles all contained pest poison?" she clarified.

"They did," Mrs Spooner nodded. "I believe there were twenty-three bottles. I made up the poison back in the spring, when the pests were starting to become troublesome, and I emptied the last bottle in this batch about a month ago. I was planning on making more and then my special bottles vanished and until I had more it was not worth making up my recipe. Now I know where they disappeared to."

"You could have poisoned us all!" Spooner declared. "We use those bottles for our own products when we run out of new ones."

"That is why I put the bottles on a back shelf, tucked away," Mrs Spooner shrugged. "And I marked all the labels with a big black X. I thought someone would notice that if nothing else. If you talked to me more about what was going on here, rather than ignoring me, then I could have told you about those bottles."

She threw this last statement at her son, who was still trying to comprehend what was occurring. Mr Pond had a strange look on his face as he comprehended what he was being told. He had been sent bottles that had recently contained rat poison. Despite them being washed out, they retained enough traces of arsenic to make people sick. It was all a dreadful case of miscommunication, an accident.

Mrs Spooner was glaring at them, waiting for a response. It was Molly who gave it to her, when she clasped a hand over her mouth, tears in her eyes.

"I did not know about the poison. I just saw empty bottles and packed them up. I am so sorry."

"You have nothing to fret over," Mr Spooner told her. "My mother ought to be more careful about where she stores her 'traditional potions'."

"Have we had issues with rats this past summer? Or wasps?" Mrs Spooner retorted. "That recipe was written up by my great grandmother and it has been used generation after generation. I remember my mother used to store hers in old beer bottles."

Mrs Spooner paused suddenly.

"Come to think of it, there was that year the farmhands all became sick, and no one could say how, but mother never used old beer bottles again."

Park-Coombs rubbed a hand over his face and groaned.

"All this rushing around the countryside to discover it was all an accident," he sighed. "No one deliberately set out to poison anyone."

"I deliberately set out to poison rats and wasps," Mrs Spooner said defiantly.

"Be quiet, Mother," Spooner snapped at her.

He turned to Park-Coombs.

"Is my mother in trouble?"

"For what?" squeaked Mrs Spooner. "I am allowed to poison rats!"

Inspector Park-Coombs considered for a moment.

"No law was broken," he said. "We might suggest it was negligence on Mrs Spooner's part to leave bottles that had once contained poisoned sitting on a shelf. But she could not have known they were to be sent back to the glassworks, or that they would be used for anything people would consume."

"Exactly," Mrs Spooner piped up. "I fill and label all the bottles we use, so if those bottles had been handed to me, I would have known at once they must not be filled. I had no way to know they would suddenly be sent back to the glassworks."

"I think we have our answer and can leave this matter alone now," Park-Coombs continued. "If I arrested Mrs Spooner for storing rat poison in old bottles, I would have most of the old women in the county in fear of me doing the same to them. I doubt there is a single woman over fifty in Brighton who does not store such poisons in any handy container they have. It is not exactly sensible…"

"It is sensible if your son does not go about interfering," Mrs Spooner interjected fiercely.

"It is the way things are," Park-Coombs concluded.

"I am very sorry about this," Spooner said to Mr Grindle. "I feel dreadful about it."

"No matter," Grindle said. "I am just relieved it was not done deliberately."

He had cheered up immensely now he knew the matter had all been a terrible misunderstanding, an accident that could easily have befallen anyone.

There was nothing more to be done at the farm. There was nothing more to be done with the matter of the poisoned bottles, except to ensure they had all been retrieved. No one had done anything wrong. No one had deliberately set out to poison people. In many regards, it was a huge relief.

They ended up back in the cart travelling once more to the glassworks. Abigail was looking quite invigorated by their trip. Before leaving Spooner's shop she had purchased several bottles of fragranced oil and homemade lavender soap which Mrs Spooner had proudly declared she made herself. Abigail was contemplating how such products could be incorporated into Albion Industries' ranges, perhaps as a 'cottage' range. Something old-fashioned and niche for the discerning woman about town. The wealthy

London lady who wants a bit of countryside in her townhouse.

Mr Grindle was thoughtful as he sat on the bed of the cart and considered all he had just witnessed. He looked at Park-Coombs after a moment.

"It is my fault, when you get to the nuts and bolts of it all," he said.

Park-Coombs glanced his way.

"How do you work that out?" he asked.

"If I had not put pressure on Mr Pond to find a solution to our bottle crisis that did not involve raising prices, he never would have asked Spooner for old bottles."

"I think that counts as being indirectly responsible," Tommy overheard and told him. "You did not tell him to go fetch old bottles, after all."

"No," Grindle nodded, "But I placed him in that position. I really have been a fool. I could have destroyed the glassworks. I need to take a better look at everything. I need to think of the future, not merely mark time until someone else takes over."

"Now, that is very wise," Clara said. "Businesses are rather like beautiful gardens. They need constant tending and improving to ensure they stay that way."

Mr Grindle smiled, a little happier.

"Yes, all this has rather alerted me to things. I feel I can make amends for my neglect now."

They were arriving back at the glassworks. Everything seemed to be carrying on as normal as they drove through the gates.

"I shall need to apologise to Miss Pink, of course, and Dr Patterson's," Grindle was muttering to himself. "Perhaps there is some way I can make things up to them?"

"I would say a public statement published in the newspaper saying how the mistake occurred would not go amiss," Clara told him.

"Ah, well…" Mr Grindle wasn't keen on that idea.

"Better you explain what occurred than it come from a second-hand source," Clara remarked to him. "You cannot allow either Pink's Pills or Dr Patterson's reputations to be tarnished by something that was your fault."

Grindle grimaced.

"I suppose you are right," he sighed.

His good mood had evaporated.

Chapter Twenty-Nine

The following day Clara made the trip out to see Miss Pink and Sigmund Coppleburg to explain that after all her efforts, it turned out there was no real culprit behind this strange crime. There was no poisoner with warped notions of killing random people, there was just human error, misunderstanding and bad luck. A series of seemingly innocuous individual events had come together to create this disaster. The only slight consolation was that the death toll had been so low. Mrs Wood had been an unfortunate victim of the pills and in many regards that was tragedy enough, but Clara could not help but think that things could have been far, far worse. What if the bottles had been used for tonics and remedies aimed at children and infants? Then there could have been many, many more fatalities.

Inspector Park-Coombs had delivered the news to her that morning that Sir Medlar was firmly on the mend and his doctor was confident in him making a full recovery. The household were no longer under suspicion, now they knew how the arsenic had reached the lord. No doubt he would never complain about his thinning hair again after the consequences he had endured in his efforts to fix it. It would be a relief for Mr Grindle as well to know he had not fatally poisoned a member of the nobility.

The sun was softly shining as Clara made her way down the muddy lane towards the cottage. She had left Tommy in charge of explaining to Mr Higgins about the bottles he had been sent and how they had come to nearly ruin the reputation of Dr Patterson's Remedies. He would no doubt be deeply relieved to learn the police had managed to get hold of all the remaining bottles of hair tonic that had been sold and no one else had been made unwell by them.

Clara reached the cottage without slipping in the mud that still caked the lane. She knocked on the front door and was greeted by Sigmund, looking a little bleary-eyed as if he had not been awake long.

"How is Miss Pink?" Clara asked.

"She was in pain last night and couldn't sleep. We stayed up and talked. She seems better this morning," Sigmund yawned. "Do you want to come in? I was just making some toast to see if she could eat a little."

Sigmund moved back from the doorway without waiting for a response, acting rather dazed due to lack of sleep. He stumbled away to the tiny kitchen. Clara headed for the front parlour where she found Miss Pink wrapped up in blankets, sitting in a chair. The room smelt stuffy and with that hint of sickness that lingers around a space where someone has been unwell for a time.

"Clara," Miss Pink said, her voice still husky from her recent mishap. "You have news?"

"I do, but firstly I would like to summon the doctor again and make sure you are recovering as should be…"

Miss Pink was shaking her head before Clara could finish.

"I am much better," she said in a tone that belied argument. "Tell me your news."

Clara sighed but could see she would not win this argument. In any case, there was very little doctors could do in cases of poisoning other than monitor the victims. However, she had felt the need to try.

"Very well," she said, settling into an armchair. "I have discovered how the bottles came to be poisoned. Really Mr Coppleburg should be present to hear what I have to say."

As she spoke, Sigmund had appeared from the kitchen with a plate of burnt toast. He offered this to Miss Pink who looked appalled at the sight, but for once had the good grace not to complain and simply took it.

"What should I be present for?" Sigmund asked.

"Clara knows how my pills were poisoned," Miss Pink said, her throat sounding as gritty as sandpaper.

"It will take a little while to explain," Clara elaborated. "The important thing to bear in mind is that none of this was intentional. No one was targeting either of you."

Clara began the lengthy explanation of how the bottles reused for rat and wasp poison had made their way from Spooner's farm to Grindle's Glassworks and then to Miss Pink. As the story unwound it sounded incredible, and yet also alarmingly plausible. Once she had finished, Clara waited for the questions that were bound to follow. Sigmund spoke first.

"Then, no one broke into my workshop?"

"No one," Clara promised him, though at the back of her mind she was thinking that Abigail had certainly intended to. Bad timing had eliminated that possibility for her, thank goodness for Alice Minsk.

"There was no one watching me?" Sigmund carried on. "I was certain I saw someone on the footpath once or twice and they tried to hide from me."

Clara cleared her throat, for once not finding a lie swift to hand. She had promised Abigail she would not reveal what she had been up to. What would be the point, after all?

"There was no poisoner lurking on the footpath," Clara clung to the truth as best she could and avoided truly answering his question.

Sigmund looked relieved. The thought that someone had been standing in the dusk watching his cottage and workshop had unsettled him more than he would care to admit to himself.

"I shall start a lawsuit against Grindle's!" Miss Pink declared fiercely. "They may have cost me my entire business!"

"I doubt you will achieve much," Clara replied to her. "You may have a complaint that they did not supply you with brand new bottles if that is specified in the contract you agreed with them. But I doubt any court will find them guilty when it comes to the arsenic. They took the bottles in good faith. In any case, Grindle had no knowledge of them, the arrangement was made by his foreman, and that man does not have the money to afford to pay you anything. You would be wasting your time and money."

Miss Pink looked furious at being told this, Clara quickly hastened to further explain.

"Mr Grindle has agreed to be interviewed by the Gazette and to tell them the full story. The article will be published in the next edition, and you will be vindicated, along with Mr Dyer. I suggest you have copies of the article reproduced and stuck in Mr Dyer's window so everyone can see them."

Miss Pink did not look satisfied with this, she was going to argue, she wanted to have someone's scalp for what she had been through, especially with how she had endured being personally poisoned. It was Sigmund who proved the voice of reason.

"Mr Grindle is a victim in this too," he said. "Ruining him will achieve nothing. The cost of the lawsuit will outweigh any compensation he might pay you. Why put yourself through all that stress? Especially as a judge may not even rule in your favour?"

Miss Pink glared at him, for a moment it seemed she would refuse to listen to reason. Then her face softened.

"I am so exhausted by all this," she groaned. "I just want it to be over and to get on with my business."

"Then I suggest forgetting about lawsuits and concentrating on the relaunch of Pink's Pills," Clara said, though with reluctance because she did not really like the pills.

Miss Pink studied her burnt toast, now somewhat cold. She had not taken a single bite. Slowly she nodded her head.

"You are right. I have too much to do to worry about Grindle."

Sigmund smiled. The matter was resolved, and he seemed pleased life could return to a sort of normality. Clara wondered how long his association with Miss Pink would last, but she decided such speculation was unproductive. People were rarely predictable and the most unlikely of partnerships could end up working well. Clara preferred to hope for the best in all things.

She headed home and arrived just as Tommy was returning.

"How did things go with Mr Higgins?" Clara asked.

"He was very understanding," Tommy said. "Though he will not be renewing his order with Grindle's Glassworks."

"Did you explain it was not their fault. They could not have known the bottles had contained arsenic."

"I did, but he is an experienced businessman, and he sees things this way – if they lied about supplying him with brand new bottles, what else might they lie about?"

"I get his point," Clara nodded. "It is just a shame. Grindle's Glassworks is an important local business."

"They are not owed anything by Mr Higgins," Tommy reminded her. "At the end of the day, you cannot choose the businesses you support simply by who you feel the sorriest for."

"You are right, of course, I am just a tad soft hearted in these matters."

They headed into the house and were engulfed in the comforting warmth of indoors, after the frigid temperatures outside. It was cold enough as it was, Clara considered, without contemplating the possibilities of it getting even colder.

Abigail Sommers was sitting up the dining room table

busily writing upon sheet after sheet of paper. Clara wandered over to see what she was doing.

"Miss Pink has agreed to leave things alone," she told her as a means of getting her attention. "She is going to carry on promoting Pink's Pills."

Abigail nodded at her briefly, then went back to her work.

"You seem to have lost interest in the pills?" Clara observed.

Abigail was a touch frustrated to be drawn from her writing but made the effort for the sake of her friend.

"I have come to the conclusion diet pills are a dead end," she said. "I have also come up with a new idea for Miss Minsk. These oils and homemade soaps I picked up yesterday from Mr Spooner would be the perfect start of a range of products for the country girl. Albion Industries knows that its main market for make-up and beauty products are urban girls, living in towns and having the time and inclination to use those products. But what of the many girls living in rural and semi-rural areas who want to smell and look good, but find make-up and hair tongs impractical for their lifestyle? What about the 'Countryside Range' for them? Products that are easy to use, practical and make a girl smell and look divine without being time consuming. All the products will be handmade, rather than mass produced in factories, and will have that touch of luxury as well as being based on old recipes. A mixture of the earthy and the modern altogether."

"That sounds quite a proposal," Clara said, thinking that it was not just rural girls who had limited time or desire for fussing with elaborate make-up or hair products. "Where does Miss Minsk fit in?"

"Miss Minsk does not represent the urban girl as Albion Industries currently perceives her," Abigail said. "At least not anymore, but her hearty appearance would suit the Countryside Range, which is about promoting healthy and robust women and their needs and desires."

Clara frowned, thinking that what Abigail was saying

was that country girls tended to be fat and town girls thin. That a country girl could never aspire to look like a town girl, and that no town girl would ever dream of looking like a country lass.

"We will still need to edit the photographs a fraction and avoid public engagements, but we have a fellow who is good with a paintbrush, and it is amazing what can be done with the right lighting," Abigail continued. "I think this could be quite the success for us, promoting beauty products with a certain innocence and rustic charm. I am writing a proposal."

Abigail motioned to the papers before her, and Clara sensed she was done with the conversation.

"I shall leave you to it," she said. "I am glad you have found a solution to Albion's problems that does not involved stealing pills."

Abigail had the decency to blush, then she cleared her throat.

"Right, yes. Look, I shall be leaving tomorrow, and I won't bother you further."

"You were no bother, once you remembered we are your friends," Clara said gently.

Abigail's blush deepened.

"I really made a pig's ear of things at the start."

"We have already forgotten about that," Clara told her. "Just, next time you choose to visit, make it a real holiday."

Abigail smiled.

"That sounds good."

Clara left her alone and went to the kitchen where Tommy and Annie were consuming tea.

"Who are we charging for this case?" Tommy asked her with a frown. "Did Miss Pink actually hire us, or did we take this on because Oliver was sick."

"A touch of both," Clara replied. "But I will invoice Miss Pink, all the same, she has put us through quite a lot."

She joined them at the kitchen table.

"I am just glad it is all over," Annie said. "All this talk of poisoned bottles was making me twitchy. I went through my supply cupboards and checked everything for arsenic. You would not believe the products I found that contained it, including some old fly papers. I was rather appalled."

"People are too casual about arsenic," Clara shrugged. "But that is not something I can do much about. I am just glad Oliver is well again, and we know how this all happened."

"Talking of Oliver, I was thinking of asking him over for Sunday dinner. He needs some meat on his bones," Annie said.

"I think the meat on his bones was the start of this problem," Tommy chuckled at her.

"Nonsense!" Annie retorted sternly. "A man ought not to be skinny, it is unnatural. I shall tell Oliver that."

"Poor Oliver," Clara grinned. "He shall never forget this."

"I am just glad he is alive to never forget it," Tommy said solemnly.

That thought made them pause and consider Mrs Wood, the sole victim of the drama.

"On the whole, we have been very lucky," Clara said, referring to Brighton and those who had consumed the pills.

"Maybe people will think twice about going on diets in the future," Annie huffed. "God makes us the size we are meant to be."

"Of course, he does," Tommy smiled at her. "And you are quite his angel, helping us to keep that size."

Annie narrowed her eyes at him.

"Sometimes, Thomas Fitzgerald. Sometimes…"

Printed in Great Britain
by Amazon